If her suspicions were true, they were both in grave danger...

After a few moments of rummaging around, Morgan exclaimed loudly, banging on the desktop in frustration. "Shit, Alex, it's not here. I left it in my calendar, folded up at the relevant date, here—the day I overheard the conversation—but it's gone. Someone must have taken it. Shit, shit, shit!"

"Are you sure, Morgan? It's got to be there. Look again. Search all over. Maybe it fell out. Things don't just disappear."

Alex got out of bed and came over to where she was kneeling by the desk, still naked.

"I have looked everywhere. It's not here, Alex."

"Well, who the hell could have taken it? Claire? Or Rashid?" He reached around from behind, cupping her breasts in his hands.

"No, they've been away for some time. Besides, Claire and I never go into each other's rooms."

"Who then?" He kissed her on the back of the neck. "The cleaning woman?"

"Oh, fuck!" Morgan said, disentangling herself from Alex. She hardly ever used that word. "Fuck, fuck, fuck!"

"Whew! What now?"

"Could it have been Luc who found it? When he stayed in the apartment with Sandrine? When he gave his place up to Anne and Serge that night they were here?"

"Hmm. Would he come in here?"

"Alex, it must have been—Oh, no, no, no!" Morgan was on the verge of tears. "That means he knows that I may suspect—"

"What?"

"—what Les Nouveaux Girondins are up to."

Morgan Kenworthy—a Berkeley student studying abroad and a guest of the de Carduzacs, family friends who have a château in St. Émilion in France—uncovers a coup against the government of France. Soon after she arrives, a bombing at the Brassault Aviation plant kills several ministers. The investigation, led by General Tolbert, the head of French intelligence and friend of Joseph de Carduzac, points to jihadists. However, clues Morgan unearths about Joseph's past suggest that the two blew up the Greenpeace ship *Rainbow Warrior* in 1985 and committed other nefarious acts while serving President Mitterand. After another explosion, killing most of the cabinet, Tolbert announces that he is in charge. As General Tolbert suspects she knows about the plots, Morgan's life and the life of her lover, Alex, Joseph's stepson, are in danger. Morgan tries to leave Europe for the US but is thwarted, and Alex is captured by the general's thugs. Now the two must rely on their wits, and their friends, for survival until they can convince the French Government who the real criminals are…

KUDOS for *Rainbow Vintner*

In *Rainbow Vintner* by Geza Tatrallyay, Morgan Kenworthy is visiting friends in France while studying as an exchange student. While at her friends' chateau, Morgan overhears a strange conversation regarding a bombing that has just taken place in France. As other clues emerge, she begins to suspect that her friends' stepfather and his general friend are responsible for the bombing that is being blamed on Jihadists. But when they find out she knows her own life is in danger and even her friends in the American CIA cannot help her escape their clutches. Like Tatrallyay's other books, this one is a page turner that will keep you glued to the edge of your seat all the way through. Thriller fans will love it. ~ *Taylor Jones, The Review Team of Taylor Jones & Regan Murphy*

Rainbow Vintner by Geza Tatrallyay is the story of a young American college exchange student in France. Morgan Kenworthy is visiting her friend Claire at the family chateau just after a bombing has rocked Paris. While at the chateau, Morgan overhears Claire's stepfather talking about the bombing and begins to suspect that he had something to do with it and that it was not the Jihadists as the government is claiming. Morgan confides in her lover, Alex, who is Claire's brother, and he tries to get Morgan to safety. But his life is also threatened, and the two of them have to use all the resources at their command to stay one step ahead of the thugs. Combing mystery, suspense, espionage, and a hint of romance, *Rainbow Vintner* will keep you enthralled from the very first page. I couldn't put it down. ~ *Regan Murphy, The Review Team of Taylor Jones & Regan Murphy*

RAINBOW VINTNER

GEZA TATRALLYAY

A Black Opal Books Publication

GENRE: THRILLER/SUSPENSE/WOMEN SLEUTHS/NEW ADULT

This is a work of fiction. Names, places, characters and incidents are either the product of the author's imagination or are used fictitiously, and any resemblance to any actual persons, living or dead, businesses, organizations, events or locales is entirely coincidental. All trademarks, service marks, registered trademarks, and registered service marks are the property of their respective owners and are used herein for identification purposes only. The publisher does not have any control over or assume any responsibility for author or third-party websites or their contents.

RAINBOW VINTNER
Copyright © 2019 by Geza Tatrallyay
Cover Design by Jackson Cover Designs
All cover art copyright © 2019
All Rights Reserved
Print ISBN: 9781644370834

First Publication: FEBRUARY 2019

All rights reserved under the International and Pan-American Copyright Conventions. No part of this book may be reproduced or transmitted in any form or by any means, electronic or mechanical, including photocopying, recording, or by any information storage and retrieval system, without permission in writing from the publisher.

WARNING: The unauthorized reproduction or distribution of this copyrighted work is illegal. Criminal copyright infringement, including infringement without monetary gain, is investigated by the FBI and is punishable by up to 5 years in federal prison and a fine of $250,000. Anyone pirating our ebooks will be prosecuted to the fullest extent of the law and may be liable for each individual download resulting therefrom.

ABOUT THE PRINT VERSION: If you purchased a print version of this book without a cover, you should be aware that the book is stolen property. It was reported as "unsold and destroyed" to the publisher, and neither the author nor the publisher has received any payment for this "stripped book."

IF YOU FIND AN EBOOK OR PRINT VERSION OF THIS BOOK BEING SOLD OR SHARED ILLEGALLY, PLEASE REPORT IT TO: lpn@blackopalbooks.com

Published by Black Opal Books **http://www.blackopalbooks.com**

DEDICATION

I would like to dedicate this book to all the victims of terrorism in France and elsewhere in the world.

When man has destroyed the world through his greed, the Warriors of the Rainbow will arise to save it again.
~ an ancient Cree legend

CHAPTER 1

Morgan sighed contentedly as she looked along the sweeping curve of the Garonne, the serene, crescent moon shaped embankment that had earned Bordeaux the moniker of the Port de la Lune. The vista was magnificent: the Pont de Pierre gracefully traversing the murky river and the spire of St. Michel slicing the clear blue sky in the distance. It all reminded her of Canaletto's London views of the Thames and Westminster Bridge.

The decision to spend her Berkeley junior year here, at L'Université de Bordeaux, had been a good one, even though it had cost her the relationship with Michael, her boyfriend of two years. *Fabulous to be free and in France though*, she thought, as she turned to smile at Claire, who was just finishing a conversation on her cell phone. The two girls were lounging in the comfortable armchairs at La Voile Blanche Restaurant on the Quai des Marques, having enjoyed a croissant and a couple of *noisettes*—as Claire had corrected her when she ordered a macchiato.

"*Maman*. Inviting you to come down to the chateau with me this weekend," Claire said, returning her mobile to her purse. "You'll love it."

"Thanks. That sounds awesome," Morgan responded in English, even though she knew she should be practicing her French. Enough time for that though during the coming months.

Claire had picked Morgan up at the airport that beautiful early September morning and brought her back to the apartment on the top floor of the grand, late eighteenth-century townhouse her parents owned near the Jardin Public. Claire had invited her to share, since her current flat mate, Sandrine, was moving out. Then they had gone out for a long walk to give Morgan her first experience of the town.

The de Carduzacs were acquaintances of the Kenworthys through the wine business. Morgan's parents owned a choice vineyard overlooking the sea near Santa Barbara, while the de Carduzacs had a first growth property just outside the charming little town of Saint Émilion. Morgan's parents had met Claire's mother and stepfather at Vinexpo, the biennial international wine and spirits festival in Bordeaux many years earlier, and had become friends over numerous tastings and dinners, ending with an invitation from Joseph and Chantal for Bill and Linda and their two daughters to come to the chateau. There, Morgan had met Claire, the youngest, as well as the other four children of the de Carduzac couple.

Morgan's older sister, Carrie, thirteen at the time, came away with a huge crush on Luc, Joseph's eldest child from his first marriage, who was already close to twenty then—although it was Chantal's son, Alex, who had shown more interest in the older Kenworthy daughter. Morgan had hit it off with Claire, Alex's younger sister, and they corresponded for a while as pen pals. The families had not seen each other since that June almost twelve years ago, although the parents still exchanged newsy letters every Christmas.

"Let's go," Claire said, glancing at her watch. "My mom asked me to pick up a dress she was having altered near the Marché des Grands Hommes. And some cheese, from Jean d'Alos, which is right there. Then we have to head out. My parents have made dinner plans for tonight, but they would like to have drinks with us first."

The girls walked along the quay, dodging joggers, bikers and skateboarders out for some exercise and Vitamin D. Their path took them across the Quinconces, a large square—which, as Claire explained—was the site of the former Chateau de Trompette, a fort built by Charles VII in the fifteenth century to make sure the city he captured remained loyal to him after three centuries of domination by the English. They passed the Monument aux Girondins, a column that rose more than fifty meters above two baroque-looking fountains, topped by winged Liberté breaking free from her chains. It had been raised at the end of the nineteenth century in memory of the twenty-two deputies to the Assemblée Nationale in Paris from the faction known as the Girondins, guillotined during the French Revolution for counter-revolutionary activities. Claire had done a paper on them for her French history class the previous year. Largely from Aquitaine, these were the "good guys" of the Revolution, first campaigning for the end of the ineffective and insensitive monarchy, but then speaking out against the spiraling excesses of the Reign of Terror.

On the way back from the central Marché—which had long since been converted from a market of farmers' and individual tradesmen's stalls into a mini-mall that housed a number of posh boutiques as well as a supermarket, with a parking garage in the basement—they passed through the Jardin Public. This was a jewel of a park, full of students sunbathing on the grass with book in hand and small groups of soccer-playing boys wearing blue jerseys sporting the numbers and names of stars Ribéry or Benzema in huge white letters, a playground with its very own Guignol puppet theater at one end, so loved by countless generations of French children, and a Natural History Museum for all ages at the other.

The townhouse was just two blocks from one of the side entrances to the park, on the tiny Rue Ernest Godard. Morgan was struck by the beauty of the eighteenth-century architecture, the wrought-iron work of the terraces and the massive double-leafed door which was up a few marble steps, and in particular, the oversized handle and knocker. As they went inside, Claire explained that Joseph and Chantal rarely used the spacious apartment occupying the entire main floor—only here and there to entertain, or on the occasions when they had an evening event and stayed in town. Lucas lived one floor up and also ran Carnot & Cie., the family catering business, from the basement that had been turned into a spacious office. Claire had the entire top floor, but she liked to share since she did not relish being in the big house by herself with her stepbrother on the road a lot. Indeed, it was fortuitous that Morgan was coming for the academic year just when Sandrine had decided she would accept Luc's invitation to move in with him. The two, having been brought together by Claire, were spending virtually all their time together now, and it no longer made sense for Sandrine to spread her life across two apartments.

CHAPTER 2

It was an easy ride of just under an hour to St. Émilion in Claire's tiny Twingo, and Morgan enjoyed it thoroughly. Along the way, Claire informed her that Luc had called to say that he would be at Chateau de Carduzac, but would arrive separately as he was on his way back from Paris. And, much to her joy, he would be bringing her brother Alex, two years Claire's senior, who had just returned from a year-long trip traveling throughout the South Pacific.

Luc's sisters would not come, though, since both Hélène and Martine were married with children and living in the capital.

Claire had also explained a bit of the family dynamics to Morgan: her mother, when she married Joseph de Carduzac, had taken his name, but she and Alex had—as French law stipulates—kept their father's. De Lavallée. From Claire's rather strained account, Morgan also got the sense that neither she nor Alex was fond of their stepfather and that some things may have transpired in the past that her friend did not feel comfortable talking about.

So she did not press with any more personal questions.

"Wow! This is awesome," Morgan blurted out, as Claire swung a hard left in between two rectangular limestone columns and came to a halt in front of a massive, ornate wrought-iron gate. "I didn't remember it to be so beautiful. You've fixed things up quite a bit…"

The vista ahead, of the early seventeenth-century chateau built from the ochre limestone of the region, magnificently restored and spreading its wings on either side of a courtyard into the luscious green vineyards, was truly a sight to behold. Claire opened her window and pressed three buttons on a white console on the driver's side, and with an even, low hum the two leaves of the gate swung open.

An immaculately dressed woman with graying hair coiffed in a bouffant style came down the steps leading up to the grand front entrance as Claire and Morgan clambered out of the car.

"Hello, Maman!" Claire rushed ahead to kiss her mother.

"Hi, dear. And you must be Morgan. My, how beautiful you have become!" Chantal had scrutinized her as she was greeting her daughter.

"Thank you, Madame de Carduzac. You are too kind."

A tall, thin, tanned, and fit-looking man wearing a gray cotton cardigan over a crisp blue shirt and cuffed chinos came out the door and down the stairs.

"My husband, Joseph. But you will not remember him, I am sure. You were so young! Joseph, this is Morgan. Is she not a darling?"

"*Bonjour, Monsieur!*"

"Hello, Morgan—yes, yes, my dear. Just like her mother."

"Come, let's go inside. Claire, you can take Morgan to her room. You know, *chérie*, Hélène's. And then, if you want, show her around the chateau and the grounds. Joseph and I have a dinner to go to at eight, but we will all have drinks on the terrace at seven. Luc should be here by then, with Alex. It's so exciting that finally, we will all get to see him. It's well over a year since he left."

"Yes, Maman," Claire said, rolling her eyes at Morgan as they carried their bags up the stone steps.

"No need to dress up, girls," Chantal instructed, raising her voice a notch to make sure they heard as they disappeared into the chateau, dwarfed by the front doors.

೧⁄౩೧⁄౩

Morgan did change, though, into a blue cotton dress with string straps, low-cut and above the knee, to show off her California sun-bronzed shoulders and long, shapely legs.

The pearl necklace her parents had given her for her twenty-first birthday added the perfect touch. She looked fabulous, Morgan ascertained contentedly, as she took a last glance in the mirror hanging above the marble mantelpiece, before making her way along the corridor past the staring portraits of de Carduzac family ancestors, and down the stairway that led to the front hall opening onto the terrace with the vineyard encircled gardens in the back of the chateau.

While she was upstairs changing, it had rained, one of those late summer evening showers, during which it pelts down hard enough so that all the vintners hope and pray that it will not damage the nearly mature grapes. But by the time Morgan came out on the terrace looking for the de Carduzac clan, the heavens had cleared, and she was greeted by a kaleidoscope of colors arching across the sky in a double rainbow.

The family was already assembled, taking in the breathtaking tableau: Claire and her mother, sitting by a little wrought iron table with a champagne bucket and six Baccarat *flûtes*, *tartines* with *foie gras*, and a bowl of olives, while Joseph and two handsome, much younger men Morgan assumed must be the sons were talking in low tones over by the balustrade.

"Ah, the lovely Morgan!" Joseph said, beckoning. "Come, come over here. You may not remember the boys. This is Luc—" He placed his hand on the shoulder of the taller, better-dressed young man. "—my eldest, who lives in the apartment below you. And this, Alex, freshly back from the South Pacific and God knows where else. Guys, this beautiful young lady is Morgan, whom you may remember from twelve years ago when the Kenworthys—our dear friends from California—visited us."

"Hi," Morgan said, stretching her hand out first to Luc, who shook it.

"Hello, Morgan," Luc said with a smile. "You've certainly changed!"

Then she turned to Alex, who took her hand between both palms, not uttering a word, drowning in the deep blue sea of her eyes, and then leaned forward to kiss her on both cheeks—the French way—pulling her toward him with his muscular arms. Dressed in jeans torn above the knee, a T-shirt, and sandals, he was stockier and more tanned than Luc and had clearly not shaved for several days.

Morgan found him wildly attractive. And, as she ascertained, it was quite clear from their looks that Luc was Joseph's son and Alex was Chantal's son with her previous husband.

"She has changed a lot since the Kenworthys visited so many years ago, has she not?" Chantal came over and put her arm around Morgan's waist. "But see what we have arranged for you, Morgan, a double rainbow to welcome you. It will bring you good luck."

"Thank you, I love it!"

"Very pleased to see you again, Morgan." Alex finally

came back up for air. The attraction was evidently mutual.

"Indeed," Luc agreed.

"Your sister, Carrie. How is she?" Alex asked.

"Oh, she's great. She is in Los Angeles trying to get into the movie business."

"Well, if she is as lovely as you are, she won't have any problems," Joseph said, taking the Dom Perignon 1990 out of the ice bucket. "Champagne?" Just then, from Joseph's cardigan pocket, the tune of Ravel's "La Valse" started to play. He took the cell phone out and looked at it, saying, "Sorry, but I do have to take this. Here, Luc, you pour," as he handed the bottle to his firstborn. Joseph went down the stairs into the garden, but those assembled could still hear snippets of his end of the conversation. "Yes, André, I was waiting for your call. Thank you." And as Luc poured the champagne, "Well, that's great news. I am sure he will be delighted."

"Come, Morgan, have some foie gras. It comes from my sister's estate in the Dordogne. Alex, you too. You must have really missed this delicacy in the Far East. It's the *mi-cuit* that you used to love so much." Chantal played the hostess and loving mother, while at the same time, she threw the odd glance in Joseph's direction.

"Yes, yes, I will be at the meeting. Of course, André, you can count on me. See you then." Joseph slipped his mobile in his pocket and came back up the stairs.

"The general?" Luc asked.

"Yes. And he has tremendous news, my son. He has made the necessary arrangements for Carnot to win the contract to cater the reception and the dinner before the meeting of the African Heads of State the president has planned here in Bordeaux in a few months' time. The lunch, too, the next day. We will certainly have our hands full."

"Tolbert? So he's still around?" Alex asked.

Luc ignored his stepbrother's question. "That's terrific. Did he talk about other things?"

"Yes. A meeting—you know about security arrangements. But I'll tell you later."

"Here, Morgan, have a tartine. And Luc, pour our guest some more champagne, for heaven's sake," Claire's mother said, passing the platter. Morgan had the impression that she was trying to divert attention from the call.

They drank the Dom Perignon on the terrace, peppering Morgan with questions about her family and herself, until the bottle was empty, the canapés all eaten, and the late summer air starting to cool.

"We need to leave for dinner, unfortunately," Chantal said. "Alex, you said you want to go see some of your friends in St. Émilion, and, Luc, you also have plans you said, so it will be just the two of you, my dears, here tonight. But I have made sure Gaston will put out something for you to eat."

When the parents left, the four lingered on the terrace, finishing their glasses.

"Too bad Joseph and Chantal had to rush off," Alex said. "I would have liked to hear what they have to say about what's happening here in France. Especially Joseph. His views have always been rather unique. It would have been interesting for you, Morgan."

"Well, Alex, if you had not been gone so long and had to live through the trauma of all these terrorist attacks and the tightening security, the terrible unemployment and the ridiculously high taxes that have been imposed by this government, you might share some of those views," Luc said in defense of his father.

"I don't want to get into it now, but I am sure we will expose you, Morgan, to the usual family argument in due course." Alex stood up, sucking the last drops out of his flûte. "Anyway, I have to run off now. Enjoy Gaston's cooking."

"I've got to go too. I'm late already," Luc said. "But I am sure we will see each other soon back in town."

The boys left, and the girls soon went inside to enjoy the delicious *magret de canard* and potatoes sautéed in duck fat that was a staple of Gaston's *cuisine bordelaise*. And to accompany the duck, Claire had the butler open a bottle of the 2004 vintage of the de Carduzac wine.

CHAPTER 3

Morgan slept late, deliciously cozy between the cotton sheets in Claire's stepsister's four-poster bed, with the open window letting the sweet summer air of rural Aquitaine stroke her gently awake. Seeing the sun already high up in the sky, she jumped out of bed in her pink *"J'aime Bordeaux"* T-shirt and skipped over to the window. The view was stunning: stately rows of vines stretching toward the spire that marked the town of St. Émilion, and where the vineyards started closer to the chateau, the aquamarine water of a swimming pool and a stone patio with six recliners, on one of which Claire had stretched out her lithe body, clothed only in the scantest of bikini bottoms, breasts bare.

Morgan quickly performed her morning ablutions in the bright, white-tiled bathroom, put on her scarlet bikini—equally risqué, but with a tiny top—tied a wrap around her midriff for modesty's sake, and hurried down poolside.

"Bonjour, Claire," Morgan said, greeting her friend. "What a gorgeous day! How long have you been out here?"

"Hi! Oh, maybe twenty minutes. How did you sleep?" Claire asked, turning onto her side and elbow.

"Just great, thanks. I had so many dreams…"

"Hope they were good ones. Come, why don't you join me? Pull that recliner over, here beside me. I'll have Gaston bring us some breakfast. *Café crème*, fruit, and yogurt? And a croissant? Will that be okay?" She pushed a button on a portable console.

"Fabulous!"

"My mother has gone to St. Émilion to shop. Joseph, too, to meet up with his friend. The general. Ugh. The boys are probably still in bed, the lazy bones. I heard them: they stayed up with the cognac after they got home. They have been so close, and they haven't seen each other for a while. A great deal of catching up, no doubt…"

"Yeah, the air is so wonderful here. And we also had a lot to drink last night. That was really delicious, the magret de canard Gaston served us."

"That's a great bathing suit, Morgan. But do take your top off," Claire turned over on her stomach, spicing her instruction with a little laugh. "When in France, do as the French."

"Well…" Morgan looked around hesitantly.

"For heaven's sake, drop your prudish American ways while you're here," Claire continued, reaching over to undo Morgan's top. "No one cares. Besides, you have a fabulous body."

"What about Gaston?"

"Oh, don't worry about the old geezer. He has seen a lot of boob around here in his day. Get with it, Morgan." She peeled the bikini top off, revealing Morgan's shapely breasts. "You need to tan those a little, my dear. But you don't want to burn. Here, let me put some cream on you."

Morgan lay back, closed her eyes, and let her friend smear sunscreen on her body, enjoying Claire's creamy touch.

She could get to like the life of a chatelaine.

❦❧❦

"Well, well, what a feast for the eyes!" Morgan heard Luc's chortle from behind her closed eyes. She sat bolt upright, folding her arms across her chest.

"Oh, you are a dirty old pervert, Luc. You should know better than to surprise our American guest like this. And besides—"

"Mesdames, Monsieur, where would you like me to put the breakfast?" Gaston, too, had sneaked up, in full butler's attire, keeping his eyes modestly lowered to the large tray he was balancing in his white-gloved hands, carrying a silver coffeepot, china plates and cups, linen napkins and the ordered delicacies.

"Right here, Gaston, thank you. Here…" Claire jumped up to pull the glass-topped table over, breasts undulating immodestly with her movements.

"Should I bring out some armchairs from the pool house?" Gaston asked after he set the tray down, still averting his look from the girls, and glancing in the direction of the little hut.

"No, this is perfect, isn't it, Morgan?"

"Of course."

"An extra coffee cup and plate for monsieur? And perhaps a croissant?"

"No. No, thank you, Gaston. I can't stay," Luc said, not taking his eyes off Morgan, who involuntarily thrust her chest forward as she tried to clasp her recovered bikini top behind. "Much as I'd like to. I've got to get back to Bordeaux for a meeting. Someone has to work around here so that we can pay those hefty taxes."

"Come on, Luc, don't spoil the morning by starting on that *merde* again," Claire said, pouring two glasses of freshly squeezed orange juice.

"Sorry, Morgan. I hope I didn't put you off France with my comments."

"No, no. Of course not."

"Well, in any case, I hope now that you will be my upstairs neighbor, I will get to see you regularly." Luc bent down to kiss Morgan's cheeks, brushing his hands against her breasts. "And in such full splendor—"

"Oh, Luc, stop being such a pig," Claire said, putting some Mirabelle jam on her croissant. "Or else I will tell Sandrine on you."

ං෬෬

After lunch and an afternoon walk through the vineyards, they went to the pool again for a swim and a nap. Dozing off for a while with her book, Morgan woke up all of a sudden in the comfortable lounge chair, sensing she was getting too much sun. Stretching, and then slowly sitting up, she looked around and saw an inviting shady spot beneath a huge oak tree over where the grass ended and the vineyards started. Remembering that Gaston had mentioned armchairs in the pool house, she found her novel, *Twisted Reasons*, beneath the recliner, and moved quietly around Claire so as not to wake her. The hinges of the rusty door squeaked as she pushed it open, and her friend stirred and changed positions. Looking around inside the hut, she saw the chairs piled up in the back, stacked there neatly by Gaston.

As she fought her way through the accumulated clutter toward the stack, Morgan was surprised to see two divers' suits hanging on the wall just behind the chairs. Curious, she felt one of the wetsuits with her fingers, ascertaining that the material was old and had lost all its flexibility. And leaning in the corner beside the suits were two rusting oxygen tanks. Morgan had earned her diving C-card from the Scripps Institute of Oceanography two summers earlier, so she was quickly able to ascertain that these were re-breathers that did not leave any bubbles, even though they were by now somewhat dated. Probably, at least twenty-five or thirty years old, she reckoned. Real antiques.

As she struggled to lift the top armchair down from the pile, Morgan heard a noise behind her. Turning around, she was surprised to see the muscular body of Alex in a colorful bathing suit, framed in the sunlight by the doorway.

"Well, well, well. What are you doing in here, Morgan?"

"Oh! Hi, Alex. I thought I was getting too much sun. I was just going to take a chair over to that shady oak tree down by the vineyards."

"Here, let me help." Alex took obvious delight in rubbing against Morgan as he squeezed past her to lift two chairs off the stack.

"By the way, Alex, what's with all the diving gear over there?"

"Oh, God, that! They still have that ancient stuff around? It used to be Joseph's. You can ask him. It's quite a story—"

"What are you guys doing in here?" The ruckus had woken Claire, and she had come to check. "Oh. Alex, aren't you being a little forward? Just having met Morgan again last night after such a long time, for God's sake?" She saw Alex standing right next to Morgan. "Getting reacquainted, huh?"

"No, no, it's all right, Claire. He was just helping me get a chair."

Morgan reflected briefly that the story of the diving gear would have to wait for another occasion.

CHAPTER 4

The girls drove back to Bordeaux on Sunday, and Morgan spent the rest of the day settling into her room and discovering more of the city with Claire. Then on Monday morning, after the frantic rush to get ready, they set off for school, stopping at Café Bonnet on Place Paul Daumer to have a quick café crême and croissant before boarding the tram at Quinconces. The Institut d'Études Politiques—the "Fac des Sciences Po" was in Talence, and the sleek-looking, modern streetcar was filled with students, some loudly greeting each other with high fives or mesmerized by the messages on their mobiles, still others sinking low in their seats, trying to get an extra few minutes of shuteye before the first big day of university.

Morgan had pre-registered during the "ILP" or Intensive Language Program in Paris earlier in the summer, before going back to California to see her parents and sister, but still had to go around with Claire to sign up for all her courses.

"Morgan, you must take this seminar at the Centre Les Afriques dans le Monde given by Professor Konaté." The girls were in the cafeteria for a mid-morning coffee and were flipping through the course book. "Jérome, he calls himself here in France, but his real given name is Boubacar. I think his father was from Mali, but he has a French mother and a French wife. He is brilliant. Sandrine took his course last year and said he is the smartest prof she's ever had. It's an elective, and the best by far. I am definitely signing up."

"Sure. I guess I do need to understand what is going on between France and those African countries and the Middle East with all this bombing that's in the news. All this terrorism, horrible."

"Of course. Besides, Jérome speaks English fluently and is very good looking. And loves to mix with the students. Unlike most of the other old geezer professors. He has a lovely wife, too. Marie. Sandrine and I invited them over several times toward the end of last year. You'll really like the couple."

"You've convinced me."

"Hi, Claire," said a voice from behind Morgan, greeting her friend.

"Rashid! How lovely to see you," Claire said, jumping up from the bench to hug a handsome, slender young man with olive colored skin and jet black hair, and grace both of his cheeks with a kiss.

Middle Eastern, Morgan guessed. Maybe North African. But seemingly very westernized.

"Morgan, this is Rashid. Rashid, Morgan. Rashid is my best friend here at school, Morgan, so watch out! And you, Rashid, you better stay away from this beautiful California girl, or I will—"

"Okay, okay." Rashid practiced his American with a broad smile that lit up his entire face, before continuing in French. "Claire, I just overheard that you were suggesting your friend take Konaté's seminar."

"Yes, it had great reviews."

"Indeed. You are right. Several of my Muslim friends, who have taken the course, say it is excellent."

"Well, that's certainly a plus."

"Morgan, is it? It will help you understand better the views of us Africans toward our former colonial oppressors. You must take it. I am going to as well."

"Well, with such strong endorsements, I certainly will." Morgan flashed Claire's friend a smile.

"Then let's go sign up!" Claire said, gathering up her things. "Rashid, are you coming?"

"Of course. I need to enroll too. And it would be fun to talk to Professor Konaté again. I haven't seen him since that dinner at your place last spring. I wonder how his summer went."

"Wasn't he off to Chad or Mali or somewhere?"

"Not sure. But somewhere in Africa, I think. We will find out."

⁂

The sign-up sheet was pinned on a bulletin board outside Professor Konaté's office, and there were already a few names on the list. Morgan counted down as she printed her name on an empty line—number thirteen—behind Claire and Rashid. The class was limited to twenty.

"Come, we'll knock," Claire said when Morgan was done signing up. "And I will introduce you." But Rashid was already pushing down the handle on the door.

"Rashid! Claire! How nice to see you." The professor—dark-skinned and tall, and dressed in black jeans and an open-collared striped shirt—stood up from behind a desk cluttered with piles of papers and books hiding a laptop, and came toward them. "Are you here to sign up for my seminar?"

"And you!" Claire said, jumping into his arms. "Yes, we just did. How was your summer?"

"Very interesting—"

"Oh, Jérome," Claire interrupted as she disengaged from the professor. "Let me introduce my friend, Morgan. She's American, here from Berkeley on an exchange program."

Even though she was proud to be from California, Morgan was not used to such informality between teacher and student and reached out her hand, which the professor grasped between his two palms.

"Very glad to meet you, Morgan," Professor Konaté said, looking deep into her eyes.

"She has just signed up for your course, Jérome," Rashid said, smiling. "You should be pleased. Your fame has traveled all the way to America. Or certainly will now."

"Yes. I'm really looking forward to the seminar," Morgan added.

"What will the focus be?" Claire wondered. "Same as what you and Sandrine told us you concentrated on last year?"

"Well, it will be a little different this time. I intend to look at the relationship between France and its former colonies at the time of Mitterand's presidency and today under Aragon. How things have changed. If they have. I will incorporate some of what I learned talking to people in Niger and the Central African Republic and other parts of former French West Africa this past summer," Jérome answered coyly. "And how it all might impact us now, here in France."

"Hmm. That could be quite interesting," Rashid observed.

"Yes. The current situation, as you know, is not pretty. There is a lot of pent up anger there against the *métropole*. Especially in the Sahel. After so many years as the colonial oppressor, now made worse again by all this interventionism. Against local movements, such as the Seleka in the CAR or Ansar Dine and al Qaeda in the Maghreb in Mali, and others elsewhere. Most recently, Boko Haram. And of course Daesh in Syria."

"But they're all terrorists!" Claire interjected.

"You'd be surprised. Some people there view us as the terrorists. Or as still the oppressors. Definitely the bad guys, alongside the Americans, who are providing us with intelligence and other assistance. Our cooperation with them is making things worse."

"Interesting perspective."

"Yes, I intend to be provocative. We will have good discussions in class. And, Morgan, I am very pleased that you will be joining the seminar. An American point of view will certainly add to the mix." Professor Konaté glanced at his watch. "Now, if you will excuse me, I do have a meeting with the head of the institute—"

"Before you rush off," Claire interrupted, "will you and Marie come have dinner with us tomorrow? For old times' sake. I will ask Sandrine and Luc as well. My brother, Alex, too, who's back from the South Pacific—you haven't met him yet, Jérome, but I know you will really like him. And you can get better acquainted with Morgan, your new American student."

"I'd love to come, Claire. Thank you. I think I am free. But Marie is still not back from Niger. She needed another couple of weeks to finish her research there. You know, the work on tribal linguistics." Jérome ushered them out the door. "I'll call to confirm."

"Excellent. Our place, at eight."

"See you then." And he was halfway down the corridor.

"Of course, you must come too, Rashid." Claire turned to her friend, putting her right hand on his left shoulder.

"Morgan and I will cook something *halaal* for you and the professor, don't worry."

"What's that?" Morgan was not quite sure what the term meant.

"It's food that Muslims can eat. According to the Koran."

Rashid was the first follower of Islam Morgan thought she had ever met in her life.

CHAPTER 5

Morgan was exhausted when they finally got back to the apartment on Rue Ernest Godard. She quickly undressed and jumped into the shower, relishing the caress of the warm water as it washed away the tiredness and rejuvenated her. *Yes, this is going to be great*, her stay in Bordeaux, she thought. There was so much to look forward to, so many new friendships, new experiences, and so much to learn!

As she came back out into the combined living room-dining room-kitchen, hair still wet but dressed in jeans and red tank top, she saw that Claire was already preparing the *salade composée* they had agreed to have for dinner that night.

"Claire, what can I do to help?"

"Pour yourself a glass of wine. Me too, please. The bottle's over there. And here is the corkscrew." Morgan went over to the end of the counter where Claire had put out a bottle of Coeur de Zeus, the de Carduzac's second wine. "And why don't you put the cheese on, if you don't mind—"

An urgent knocking on the door.

"Oh, no, it must be Luc," Claire said, since the outside bell had not sounded, and Alex had stayed on at the chateau. "Sandrine must still be away. I was hoping, though, he would leave us alone tonight. I'm really tired." Despite her reluctance, Claire still went to undo the latch.

In burst a very agitated Luc. "Claire, Morgan, did you see the news? For God's sake, turn on the TV." He rushed straight to the salon and stood there looking around frantically. "Where is the bloody remote?"

"Hello, Luc. What is it? What happened?" Morgan asked, bottle still in hand.

"Mérignac. The prime minister. At the Brassault factory. Assassinated. Blown to smithereens. Incredible—"

Just then, Luc managed to click to France 24, the all-day news network.

"…an explosion devastated the Brassault site at Mérignac. We have no idea yet of the casualties, but we estimate that there were between eight and twelve hundred people working on site at the time. We know for a fact that Prime Minister Rostrand was at the facility along with two other ministers, to support the workers in a demonstration against the recently announced layoffs at Brassault. It seems the attack was directed against him and the government, but this has not been confirmed. We are told they were among the casualties. It is unlikely that this was an accident. An act of terrorism then? A suicide bomber? At this time, it is still too early to know details. But we will keep you informed here at France Twenty-Four." The reporter could scarcely contain his emotions.

"Horrible—President Kennedy—Not as bad as the Twin Towers, but still…" Morgan, in a state of shock, mumbled to herself as she sat cross-legged on the couch, staring mesmerized at the screen.

"Yes, who would do such a thing?" Claire echoed the reporter's question.

"It must be Daesh or al Qaeda. Or some offshoot. Paying us back for Aragon's bombing in the Middle East. Or his stupid and ineffective adventures in Africa," Luc opined.

"Shh. Just listen. You always jump to conclusions, Luc. They are not even sure it was terrorism. It could have just been an accident. As the reporter said—"

"...the President of the Republic is due to make a statement in a few minutes. Please standby." The screen changed to show pictures of the Brassault Mérignac site: it was a mess of flames, smoke, rubble, twisted metal and broken glass. The picture switched to several of the wounded, wandering in a daze, crying out for help.

No one was hungry anymore, but Claire refilled her glass and Morgan's, poured one for Luc.

The camera suddenly panned to the Élysée office of President Aragon, who was sitting solemnly behind his ornate Louis XV desk.

"Ugh. I loathe the man!" Luc could not hold back.

"My fellow *Françaises, Français.* After the terrible events in Paris some time ago, once again, a tragedy has befallen our beloved country. Today, at seventeen fifty-three, there was a massive explosion at the Brassault plant in Mérignac, just outside Bordeaux. We do not yet have a count of casualties. As you may be aware, my very dear friend and colleague, Prime Minister Rostrand, was at the plant, along with Jean-Luc Peyreire, the Minister for Economy, Industry, and Employment, and Anne-Lise Valdez, the Minister of Labor, Social Relations, and Solidarity. I have not been able to reach any of them, and survivors on site tell me that my colleagues were unfortunately at the epicenter of the blast. We are considering this as a likely act of terrorism. If so, this was an attack at the heart of France, and we will respond in kind. We will find and bring to justice those responsible, no matter where they are. I have ordered all airports and ports in France to be closed until further notice. Our borders have been sealed and I have put the armed forces and France's entire security apparatus on red alert. Units of the army are being rushed to Mérignac. A police hotline has been set up, as have emergency numbers for affected families. Right after this statement, I myself will be on the way to Bordeaux and will keep you informed personally. My fellow Frenchmen, France has survived adversity in the past. We will do so again. We will be the stronger for it. *Vive La France!*"

"Boy, what a wimpy statement. He said nothing concrete!" Luc criticized. "And what a farce—there is no way they can close the borders."

"Well, they don't seem to know anything yet."

"Come on, let's eat. Luc, you're in luck today. We'll share our salad and cheese with you, provided you go and get us another bottle of wine from your huge stock. We need a de Carduzac first wine, not this cheap Coeur de Zeus stuff we have been drinking. By the way, when is Sandrine getting back?"

CHAPTER 6

Claire picked up a copy of *Métro*, the free daily Bordeaux rag, as she and Morgan boarded the tram at Place Paul Daumer the next morning. The headline under a graphic picture of destruction read *Mérignac Brassault Site Attacked* with the subtitles *Prime Minister Rostrand and two other ministers feared dead in the blast, along with twenty-eight others. Fifty-three wounded treated in local hospitals.* Horrible, but, as Morgan read the article over Claire's shoulder, it seemed that the authorities still did not know anything for sure about how and why the explosion happened, and who the perpetrators were.

When they got to Talence, they found that classes had been canceled, and the doors of all the classrooms were locked. Heavily armed police and members of the military patrolled the campus, telling students to go back home until further notice.

❧❧❧

As soon as they arrived at the apartment, Claire clicked on the TV remote and found France 24. Coverage was exclusively about the explosion and its implications. The screen continuously showed pictures of the still-smoldering site, as talking heads excitedly spun out the little they knew, and discussed the renewed clamp down in security imposed at Mérignac and across the nation.

"President Aragon has charged Edmond Béart, the Minister of Defense, and Claude Rémolé, the Minister of Interior, to create a task force under the auspices of the National Defense General Secretariat comprising the armed forces, the several intelligence services, including the General Directorate for External Security, the Central Directorate of Interior Intelligence, the Directorate of Military Intelligence as well as the relevant law enforcement agencies such as the Judicial Police, the Police Nationale and the Gendarmerie Nationale to investigate this heinous crime."

"Great. More bureaucracy. Just what we need," Claire muttered to herself, as the camera moved from the announcer to the Brassault facility and showed Aragon and a large group of followers inspecting the ruins.

"This morning, the president toured the site with Béart and Rémolé and Pierre LeBrun, the CEO of Brassault, as well as other government and company officials, and made the following statement: 'I am appalled at the senseless destruction and loss of life…'" The camera was now on Aragon, who had one foot firmly planted on a piece of twisted and broken concrete. "'…we have the best investigators from France and all over the world working together to try to determine what took place here. We are still not sure whether this was an accident or an act of terrorism, but we are working on the assumption that it was the latter. Finding the cause and the perpetrators are my government's highest priority right now. My heart goes out to the families of the victims.'" The camera switched to show the analyst in the studio, who continued his report. "Based on the president's comments, it seems that it is still too early for the investigations to have borne any fruit, so we will have to wait until—"

Just then, over on the counter, Claire's mobile buzzed, and Morgan sprang to pick it up, since Claire had gone to the bathroom.

"Hello, Claire?" Morgan heard a voice she thought she recognized as Professor Konaté's at the other end.

"Hello. It's Morgan."

"Oh, Morgan, hi. Have you been watching the news? Isn't it horrible?"

"Awful—So many dead—"

"Yes, it keeps happening again and again. In any case, Morgan, I just wanted to confirm that I am delighted to come tonight."

"Great!"

"The only thing is that a very good friend of mine has just arrived in town. American, like you. John Stanley. He is involved in this investigation—you know, of the Brassault incident. Really interesting and fun guy, though. I thought you and the others might enjoy meeting him. He will no doubt have a lot to say. I was wondering whether I could bring him along if he can get away. In Marie's place."

"Of course. I'm sure that will be fine. We'll just add another place setting. See you later."

"Bye, and thanks."

༄༅༄

"Oh, John and I know each other from Harvard. The Kennedy School," Jérome explained over drinks and canapés. "He was recruited by the CIA before finishing his PhD and went on to do great things. He is such a star, that he is now their number two in Paris—what is it, John, Deputy Chief of Bureau or Section Head or whatever—

and tells me he was sent down here to work on this investigation."

"What have you guys found so far?" Luc asked.

"Not a hell of a lot," the tall, boyish-looking man with a tinge of red in his fair hair and a hint of freckles on his pale face answered. "We have no real clues yet. But we are quite sure it was not an accident. The facility is over seventy hectares, with twenty buildings. One of these, in front of which the ministers were making speeches, was completely obliterated. Sort of a hangar where planes are assembled, I am told. And two other buildings as well, partially destroyed. So far, almost thirty people dead and sixty or so badly wounded and burned. Terrible. The airplanes, the work in progress in the hangars, all gone. Blown up. Luckily, the employees were outside, listening to the speeches out front and not working inside the buildings."

"The site. It's near the airport, no?" Alex asked.

"Yeah, much of it is literally on the other side of the runways. It was fortuitous that the devastation did not spread to the terminals. Things would have been a lot worse then, for sure."

"It seems from the news reports that the attack—if that is indeed what we are talking about—specifically targeted the prime minister and the other two ministers," Rashid observed, picking up an olive.

"And maybe the Brassault site itself," Claire added. "Don't you think?"

"But who would do such a thing?" Morgan asked, caressing her glass.

"That is the sixty-four thousand dollar question," John said, taking a sip of the de Carduzac wine. "Umm. This is delicious. Jérome tells me it's the family brew. Luc, Alex, Claire, *félicitations!*"

"Thanks. We have an excellent winemaker in our

caves. Monsieur Martin." Luc picked up his glass, turning it slightly sideways as he inspected the contents. "He has been with us for over twenty years and really knows the trade.

"Anyway, the likelihood is that this was an act of outright terrorism," John continued. "Not just a disgruntled employee. Nor a political activist's strike against Brassault's planned job cuts. Someone—or some group—who could get his—or their—hands on enough explosives to create this much devastation. And smuggle them in there, onto the site, in spite of all the security."

"Hmm. Not too easy these days," Luc mused. "Al Qaeda, you think? Or ISIS?"

"Possible. An offshoot, maybe. Or some allied group. It could be in response to the interventions in Mali and the Central African Republic. The efforts to free those hostages. Some of the jihadists, you may remember, did promise retaliation. Or perhaps, as you say, ordered by ISIS, as retaliation for the bombings. They vowed to carry out such terrorist activities on French and American soil. And they have the money and the organization."

"In fact, this could be a double whammy. It is also an attack on France's military-industrial infrastructure, I reckon," Alex observed. "Claire, is there another bottle of wine?"

"Yes, several, over there on the counter. Can you please get one and open it?"

"Hmm. Good point, Alex. As a matter of fact, didn't the armed forces deploy some Brassault *Tempête* fighters against the rebels in Mali? And isn't it the same planes we have been using against ISIS?" Jérome asked.

"Well, there you go…"

"Interesting," Luc mused. "I hadn't focused on that."

"Somehow, it must be connected to the prime minister's visit though, don't you think?" Sandrine asked from over at the table where she was lighting the candles.

"Certainly, there is a likely connection. And the other two ministers. A clear attack on the government. For its policies—"

"Yes, all that ineffective posturing," Luc interrupted. "I mean, why the hell would Aragon send his prime minister and two other members of his cabinet to march in solidarity with demonstrators against Brassault's planned layoffs? That's not a very effective way to promote job creation. Or anything else, for that matter."

"Especially when they end up getting killed," Jérome added.

"Dinner is served," Claire announced, basket of bread and pitcher of water in hand. "Everyone, please come to table. Luc, will you pour the wine?"

"Let me be the devil's advocate. Could it have been one of the French far right groups?" Rashid asked as he pulled a chair out for Sandrine. "The various factions have been getting increasingly outspoken in their attacks on the government. Just as Luc said—"

"That's not what I meant—"

"—And the frequent clashes in the streets have often turned violent," Rashid continued, ignoring Luc's protestations. "The Oeuvre Française and the Jeunesse Nationaliste—weren't both those groups of fascist thugs outlawed a few years back? Could they—or whatever they have morphed themselves into—have done it, to try and alter the direction the country is going in?"

"Hmm. Interesting thought, Rashid. But it would not be very good politics to kill three ministers and thirty other Frenchmen. In terms of vote getting that is," Jérome countered, pulling out a chair for Morgan.

"Quite unlikely, in my view," John opined, placing himself on the American girl's other side. "I can't see how they would benefit. Also, the use of explosives would be a first for them. Unless a faction of the military were behind it. Or in cahoots with them. But it doesn't make sense that the armed forces would be complicit in destroying some of the country's military-industrial infrastructure. Anyway, you guys tell me—you are all a lot closer to what's happening in France."

"Out of the question, Rashid." Luc weighed in as well. "It just wouldn't happen in France. It was al Qaeda or some other jihadist group. Maybe ISIS—"

"Well, this will give us great material for discussion in class tomorrow, won't it Morgan?" Jérome observed. "Sandrine, too bad you are not taking the class this year. But you could come if you wanted. You too, John. And Luc and Alex, you, as well, of course. You're all welcome to listen in."

"Thanks, but no thanks. I have a full day tomorrow. In the morning, I am planning to talk to the forensic guys who were combing the site for clues today. But Claire, this looks absolutely delicious. And thank you, by the way, for including me in this fabulous dinner."

"I can't either, Jérome, but thanks." Luc declined as well. "Yes, great dinner, sis. And Morgan."

"That goes for me too," Alex was last to respond. "Do we need another bottle of wine down at that end of the table?"

CHAPTER 7

Discussion in Professor Konaté's seminar the next afternoon—as in many other much less directly relevant classes at schools and universities all around the country—focused on the still very raw attack at the Brassault facility, not even forty-eight hours in the past, and less than eight kilometers away from the Talence campus. Given the circumstances, Professor Konaté allowed the conversation to flow freely, with only gentle guidance here and there.

"We were warned," Nadège, one of the more outspoken students Morgan had not yet met, said. "Loud and clear, and several times, that there would be retaliation. Already way back when, for Mali and the Central African Republic. Then for freeing all those hostages, and more recently, for joining the bombing party in the Middle East. It was bound to come sooner or later. And there will be more for sure. How naïve can our leaders be?"

"Yes, we were warned," Bernard, a nerdy looking boy with glasses who sat beside Morgan, agreed. "Nadège is right. And the jihadists did kill that French hiker in Algeria some time ago. That Hervé Gourdel. And then they brought the battle to France *metropole*—Charlie Hébdo and that Kosher supermarket. And the killing at the Bataclan and all the other sites in Paris. But we should have known that was just the start. And that it would only escalate from there."

"So what should we have done? What could France have done differently?" Jérome asked the class.

"Whoa! Let's step back a moment. Aren't we jumping to conclusions here?" Rashid was not happy with the direction the conversation was taking. "How can we be so certain that it was Muslims—my people, and yours too, Professor Konaté, if I may remind you—which is clearly what you are all saying—who did this, and not someone else? Sure, there was Charlie Hébdo and all that—that was terrible enough. But that was done by radicalized jihadists connected to Daesh. And this is much bigger."

"Just look at Nine/Eleven, Rashid." Morgan could not help but side with the others. "And the Bataclan—"

"Well, what I mean is there has been so much going on with Brassault—their planned layoffs, contracts lost or gone wrong, competitive jealousies, probably some bribery and corruption—any of those things could have been the source of hatred or intense anger directed at the company. Plus, it could also be motivated by internal French politics—a lot of people are fed up with Aragon. Especially the far right here. It is always we Muslims who are blanketed with the blame."

"Sure. That's a valid point you make," Jérome agreed. "There is no concrete proof of anything yet. But, as you and I heard yesterday, Rashid, everything—all the circumstantial evidence—points in the direction of a jihadist response to France's intervention in the Sahel and the Levant. To its post-colonial attitudes there and elsewhere. So, if you will please bear with us for a moment, let's continue examining that line of thinking."

"Well, to answer your question, perhaps France should not have gone into Mali and the Central African Republic in the first place," Morgan said. "And not participated in the bombing of Iraq and Syria."

"Yes, in fact, wasn't Aragon's decision to intervene in Africa fairly sudden?" Claire asked, giving her friend some support. "Weren't some African Union forces with a UN mandate going to take action, when we jumped in?"

"You are right," Jérome agreed. "The problem then, though, was that the African states and the UN were taking their time about it, and the French government supposedly had intelligence that the al Qaeda-linked terrorist groups were winning in Mali. They were very close to capturing Bamako and threatening French lives and interests. And the Central African Republic was descending into total civil war, with fighting between Christians and Muslims. Mass killings, innocent women and children, tantamount to genocide. Already, those hostages had been taken in Niger, and then many more in Algeria, you will remember—at that mine. And in the Middle East, ISIS was killing off or enslaving anyone who was not a male fundamentalist Sunni—women and children, Christians, Shiites, Yazidis and other minorities—abhorrent. All in the name of strict adherence to their interpretation of the Koran. And their version of a Caliphate. And then there is Boko Haram in Nigeria, and I could go on and on. How can we morally let all this go on?"

"Maybe not. But what you bring up is part of the problem," Rashid said, sitting forward as he got angrier. "All those French and American corporate interests there, that have been exploiting local people for so many years. And that suddenly we felt we had to protect by sending troops—at the French taxpayers' expense."

"Wasn't the thinking also that once the jihadists were allowed to consolidate their position in those countries, they could then use them as a launch pad for activity against territorial France and the west?" Marie-Christine, a chic girl from Lyons sitting in the front asked.

"But as we said, they have started to do that already. Those random shootings in Paris. And last month, the suicide bomber in Marseilles. They were Muslim terrorists," Nadège said, fidgeting in her seat.

"So what could the Aragon government have done differently? If they just had to intervene, as we are saying." Jérome continued to press his line of questioning.

"Maybe they should have just wiped the terrorists out completely," Nadège opined. "Gone in with a lot more force than they did."

"Bombed the shit out of them, as the Americans say," Bernard added in English, half joking, half serious, smiling as he cast a sideways look at Morgan, hoping the good looking Californian would approve. "Nuked them."

"Do we think there would have been any support for that?"

"Well, just maybe."

"And do you think that would have solved the problem? The collateral damage—all the innocent deaths. Even if it wiped out one small group of terrorists, it would have just made the rest of the Muslim world all the more furious with us. The North African groups like al-Mourabitoun are now increasingly linking up with the powerful Middle Eastern groups like al Qaeda and ISIS. And the survivors of any bombing or their sister groups would be even more resolute to pay us back in kind. Violence always begets violence…"

"Perhaps going in more forcefully, and at the same time strengthening our defenses back home, might have been a more sane way to react," Pierre, a third-year student, mused.

"Or not intervening at all. Just spending all that money on bolstering security in France, might have been an even better option." Claire went the next step. "Let the Middle East and the Africans fend for themselves."

"Security has been tightened considerably," Jérome commented. "For sure, since Charlie Hébdo. Intelligence gathering has improved a lot, too. And even more so, post-Bataclan."

"But the problem is that if the jihadists want to commit an act of terror they will find a way, no matter how strong security is. The only solution is to root them out totally, I think." Nadège continued to advance the aggressive interventionist view.

"Well, for one, we don't know how tight security was at the Brassault site. Certainly, at Mérignac airport, it's still laughable. Just a few bored soldiers strutting about in full gear," Pierre was for strengthening security all around.

"So, what should the Aragon government do now? After this attack," Jérome asked.

"Find the guys who did it and sentence them for terrorism." Bernard, the most hawkish one, did not hold back.

"That's a must." This from Nadège.

"And beef up security at all airports, government installations, public places, important industrial complexes and buildings," Pierre added. "Put soldiers in the street, do random ID checks."

"Like they did in the US after Nine/Eleven?" Morgan asked.

"I don't know. Even more, I would say. Much more."

"But isn't that exactly what the far right wants to hear?" Claire asked. "Turn France into a military state? Take away our freedoms—"

"I think there you have a point." Rashid, who had sat silently in the back with arms folded the whole time, finally broke his sulk. "I still believe it could have been the fascists who did this—you know, not the Front National, but those Oeuvre Française type guys—making it look like it was African or Middle Eastern jihadists. To focus the country's anger against us Muslims, whom they hate. And maybe to create an excuse to put some kind of military rule in place—"

"No way, Rashid. They wouldn't kill the prime minister and another thirty plus innocent people. Not even they are that crazy." Marie-Christine countered. "And in the process wreak havoc on a well-known French manufacturer of military equipment."

"A kind of putsch? That simply would never happen in France," Nadège weighed in. "Our democratic traditions are too deep, too entrenched—"

"The right did hate Rostrand and those two leftie cabinet members with a passion." Rashid would not let go. "And they loathe Aragon even more—"

"All right, everyone. Thanks. That was a good discussion." Jérome looked at his watch and brought the increasingly heated session to a close. "So, next week, we'll talk about the jihadist movements in North Africa and the Middle East, and try to figure out which faction would be the most likely one to have done this. Of course, there is a chance that by the time we meet again, some group might have claimed responsibility—"

"Or, as Rashid would have us believe, it was the far right or another group here in France," Nadège interrupted, grinning at Claire's Algerian friend.

As she closed her books, Morgan wondered about the line Rashid kept advancing. But he was the only one, as all the French students simply could not believe that the perpetrators might have been anybody other than jihadists.

And the other day, John had been dismissive of the notion as well. He, if anybody, would know.

☙❧

"Great seminar, huh?" Claire said to Morgan as the two girls gathered their books and papers while the other students left the class.

"You liked it? Good." Jérome had overheard and came over. "Morgan, you too?"

"Yes, of course. I thought the discussion was exciting. I learned so much."

"Rashid wasn't too happy," Claire said.

"No, but that's all right. It's good to have different points of view. By the way, I am off to have a drink with my friend, John. Would you two like to come?"

"Sure," Morgan blurted out. She had rather liked the CIA officer. "I would love to. Claire, how about it?"

"I think I'm going to try and catch up to Rashid. I don't like it when he goes off sulking like that. But thank you anyway, Jérome. Morgan, I'll see you a little later. Back at the house."

"Great."

"Let's go. He's meeting us at the Café Français. At Pey Berland."

CHAPTER 8

They were surprised to find John deep in discussion with two strange men, ensconced at a table outside the café on Place Pey Berland in front of the elegant Palais Rohan, the former archbishop's palace—which now served as the *Hôtel de Ville*, the city hall—and across from St. André, the cathedral, still partly covered by scaffolding. John introduced the more distinguished looking gentleman as Charles Townsend, the Consul of the United States of America in Bordeaux, and his younger companion as a colleague from Langley, Peter Chapin.

"Jérome is a professor at the Fac here, and a specialist in African and Middle Eastern affairs," John said, continuing with the introductions. "I'm keen on picking his brains, so that's why I asked him along. Besides, he's a good friend from Harvard and I wanted to buy him a drink. And Morgan is doing her junior year abroad here at the university. From Berkeley. Thanks for coming along. It's a pleasure to see you."

"Great to see you both." Townsend welcomed them, sitting back down after pulling a chair out for Morgan. "I think I've had the pleasure of meeting you before at some function. In Paris, if I remember correctly. The Harvard Club?"

"Yes, yes, of course." Morgan racked her brains, and vaguely remembered being introduced to the consul at a cocktail in Paris when she was doing the ILP program earlier in the summer.

"Charles is here, because, as it turns out, there are at least two Americans among the dead in the Brassault explosion. So he has a definite interest in the investigation, and of course, he is the one who has to make the appropriate arrangements. Peter is an expert on explosives and has been sent over by Langley to bolster our effort to get to the bottom of all this."

"Glad you're here, Peter," Jérome said. "But that's terrible. Really bad news about American casualties. Were you able to put names to the bodies?"

"We know there were two visiting executives from Brassault's US operations who are now missing. We are still trying to identify the remains. Gruesome work. There may also have been others—employees, potential customers or whatever—we just don't know yet. We are working through the mess," the consul answered.

"Yes, that's one of the things at the top of our agenda, to find out if there were other Americans." John finally managed to catch the waiter's eye. "And to make sure the families are informed and comforted. And, of course, to help the French. Our experience after the Twin Towers bombing could be very useful."

"Have their investigators found anything at the site so far?" Jérome asked his friend after John ordered a bottle of red, along with a *citron pressé* for the professor. "Morgan, we will keep all this to ourselves, won't we?"

"Of course!" Morgan quickly agreed, knowing she could be privy to some potentially restricted information if the others were going to talk freely. She moved her chair a notch to keep the late afternoon sun out of her eyes.

"The answer to your question, Jérome, is very little. But that's what I wanted to talk to you about. Since you know so much about the different terrorist groups."

"So?"

"Well, the French have found residues of a relatively new explosive called EXPLUS. Developed by a company called EPC. They are apparently the largest manufacturer of explosives for civil uses in France. Do you know them?"

"Yes, yes. I've heard of them. I think they make explosives for the mining and construction industries. In fact, if my memory serves me correctly, there were reports earlier that another one of their products—Nitram 5, I think—was found in some stashes in Mali. Left behind by jihadists after the French forces went in. First, Operation Serval way back in 2013, you may remember. Then again on several occasions since."

"Hmm. That's very interesting." They paused for a moment while the waiter poured the wine.

"And do we have any clues as to how this EXPLUS might have been brought onto the site?" Charles asked once they were able to continue without the risk of being overheard. "It sounds like it must have been a pretty sophisticated undertaking."

"No. We are in the process of developing some ideas just now."

"Who did it, John?" Morgan asked, sipping her wine. "You think it was a jihadist group?"

"Most likely. I really believe, though, that whoever it was, they must have had a 'plant' inside the explosives manufacturer. Or at one of its customers. AREVA, for example. Someone who supplied the EXPLUS. And maybe earlier, gave them the Nitram too. But what is your view, Jérome?"

"You're probably right, John, on the 'plant' somewhere in France. Otherwise, how would they get their hands on the explosives?"

"Steal it?" Charles asked.

"Possible, but more difficult. Buy it on the black market? Maybe. Bring it in? Unlikely. Anyway, that gives us something to work with. Start with employees at EPC, then, as you say, broaden the search to AREVA and others. We have our job cut out for us."

"Yeah. That's for sure!" Peter interjected.

"And what about the jihadists? Jérome, you're the expert."

"I've been thinking a lot about this, and where I come out is that it was most likely a group with Daesh links. Although these different jihadist 'tribes' have now become blurred. But Daesh or ISIS and al Qaeda are the ones with the resources. And the celebrity name to attract the disaffected as their loyal soldiers."

"Yes, the point is well taken."

"Otherwise it could have been this North African group I have been studying that calls itself al-Mourabitoun. Or better still, the al Mourabitoun with Daesh and/or al Qaeda. At various times there have been indications that they are allied with one or the other."

"Al what?" John asked.

"Al-Mourabitoun. A-l-dash-M-o-u-r-a-b-i-t-o-u-n. The name is an echo of the fighters in the 1958 Civil War in Lebanon who remained a force right through the eighties. It's all very confusing, and you may not be aware, but after the Serval intervention we mentioned earlier, there were some interesting developments among the jihadists of North Africa. Here, let me illustrate what has happened," the professor said, taking out his pen and grabbing his unused paper napkin. "The group called Mujao—the 'Movement for Oneness and Jihad in West Africa', which sort of grew out of AQIM or al Qaeda in the

Maghreb', the ones that killed those two Agence France Presse journalists—" He wrote the letters *AQIM* with an arrow pointing to the right followed by *Mujao*. "—anyway, the Mujao and another group known as Al-Mulathameen, which means 'The Veiled Brigade'—" Jérome put a large plus sign beside *Mujao* and then wrote the first few letters of Al Mul, before continuing. "—which was the original band the jihadist leader Mokhtar Belmokhtar used to command, into which he then merged his breakaway faction, 'Those Who Sign With Blood,' who were the ones that attacked the Algerian natural gas facility and killed the thirty-eight hostages back in January 2013—" All the way on the right, he wrote TWSWB and with a left pointing arrow connected it to Al Mul, and then with an equation sign below the plus one, he wrote al-Mourabitoun," saying as he did, "—fused into al-Mourabitoun, or the 'Sentinels' as they now call themselves. These are also the guys who raided the Radisson Blu in Bamako in November 2015 right after the attacks in Paris, taking one hundred seventy hostages and leaving twenty-seven dead—"

"Wow. That is complicated," Peter interjected.

"—this then united the jihadist movements across North Africa 'from the Nile to the Atlantic,' as they themselves put it, in pursuit of the same objectives," Jérome continued, ignoring the interruption. "And they probably felt that this gave them greater strength and more capabilities. Plus, as I said, they have been forging links to both al Qaeda and ISIS in the Levant."

"So what you're telling us, Jérome, is that now we have a bigger and more united version of jihadists across North Africa and the Middle East?" John looked up from jotting some notes along the margin of the *International New York Times* that lay folded in front of him. "And could the most immediately pressing goal around which they have united be to retaliate against France for its interventions? And for all the years of colonial oppression?"

"You got it! For one, France is a lot easier to strike at than the US. Closer geographically, and perhaps less problematic to get into, or to find sympathizers in. After all, according to some reports, more than ten percent of the population of France is now Muslim. But beyond that, the aim of all these terrorist groups is to reestablish the grand Caliphate, stretching ultimately from Indonesia to West Africa. They all see themselves as doing it, or at least being a part of the effort."

"It seems that it is ISIS that has the lead on this now," John interjected. "Although many Muslims do not see them as the true carriers of the torch."

"Yes, you're right," Jérome nodded toward his CIA friend. "So, the bottom line is, I agree with you, John. It may well have been these al-Mourabitoun who were the ones carrying out the attack, perhaps with the help of the bigger al Qaeda and Daesh groups. Or maybe a Daesh cell directly."

"Well, that clarifies a few things. Gives us a possible motive, and explains how these terrorists may be becoming strong enough to strike French territory. We're also clearly very concerned that they might strike against Americans or US interests, aren't we, Charles? But let's see tomorrow where my French investigator buddies come out. You have been really helpful, Jérome. Thanks."

"Great. Glad I can be of help." Jérome finished sipping his lemonade.

"We'll keep you posted. To the extent we can. And of course, you, Charles. Feel free to call either Peter or me at any time."

"Thanks."

"In fact, Peter, why don't you exchange numbers with Charles and Jérome?"

"Sure thing."

"And Morgan, wonderful to see you again," John said, turning to the American girl. "Maybe, if the professor lets me, I can buy you dinner sometime?"

"That would be lovely. Thank you." Morgan liked the way this intelligent and interesting CIA operative took charge.

CHAPTER 9

Morgan got back to Rue Ernest Godard just after eight, and, as she climbed the stairs to the top floor apartment she shared with Claire, she heard voices. Opening the door, she was greeted by Alex.

"Fancy meeting you here, Morgan. My dear sister has decided to throw an impromptu dinner party. Yet again. Nice that you could come."

"Yeah. Since my parents are letting Alex use their place downstairs for the time being, and Sandrine is back from seeing her parents, I thought we should celebrate," Claire said, flashing a smile in Morgan's direction. "Hope it's okay and you're not too tired."

"No, of course not. That's fabulous." Morgan glanced at Alex and then down along the counter toward Rashid, and Luc, whose arm was around Sandrine's slim waist. "I'll be ready in five minutes. Just need to drop my iPad off in my room and wash my hands."

Ten minutes later Morgan had freshened up, with light make-up added and a change of clothes. She walked into the open style living area with the huge kitchen and a dining nook at the back opening onto a small terrace. Rashid was sitting on a stool at the bar, drinking what looked like cranberry juice, with Luc and Sandrine leaning against the counter on either side of him, sipping their glasses of wine. Claire and Alex were on the sink side of the island, the one preparing a green salad to go with the cheese, and the other, washing the *Mara des Bois*—the flavorful local strawberries—for dessert.

"Welcome, Morgan. Here, grab a glass," Alex said, taking one down from the rack above the central counter, "and pour yourself some wine." He nodded with his chin to the open Magnum on the counter over by the three others.

"So how was it?" Claire asked. "What did John have to say?"

"Well, the investigators have found some traces of explosives," Morgan answered as she looked at the label on the bottle and saw that it was the de Carduzac 2007 vintage. "Apparently, of a type produced in France by the same company that makes a kind of explosive that was left behind by some jihadists in Mali. Found by French troops after Serval. So John, and Jérome too, think that the terrorists must have had a plant in the company—EPC, I think it was called—or at one of its customers."

"Hmm. Couldn't it also just mean that the French far-right militants had a sympathizer at EPC who passed them the explosives?" Rashid still was not convinced that the perpetrators were Muslims.

"Rashid, I told you," Luc countered, a little testily, "that it's inconceivable that the French right would sacrifice so many of their compatriots to try and somehow implicate an unnamed Muslim group. It just would not happen."

"Maybe they did not think so many innocent people would be killed. Maybe it was just the leftist ministers they were going after—"

"But Rashid, you must admit, they did use a lot of firepower. Like they didn't care how many they killed.

John and Jérôme are sure it was jihadists. They're the experts." This from Morgan.

"Well, I still can't be absolutely sure it was Muslims." Rashid would not let it go. "Yum, Claire. That smells delicious!"

Claire had just opened the oven door, and out wafted the sumptuous aroma of three *colvert* ducks grilling on top of leeks, carrots, whole cloves of garlic and little turnips.

"In any case, the problem is that the useless, ineffectual intervention ordered in North Africa by Aragon, followed by the half-assed bombings in the Middle East, have no doubt stirred up a hornets' nest of jihadist activity against us," Luc launched on his tirade against the government. "He should have gone into North Africa with the intention of committing whatever forces and *matériel* necessary to wipe out the terrorists completely. Or else just stayed away—but then we would still have jihadists coming into France and attacking us here. The problem is much the same in the Middle East—the halfhearted intervention led by the Americans that has achieved very little."

"Stayed away totally from both would have been better in my view," Claire said, voicing her opinion.

"I would agree with that," Rashid concurred. "There is no justification today for France to continue acting like it still had a colonial empire. Those days are gone, and the North African and Middle Eastern countries should be allowed to pursue their own future. Leave them alone, and they will leave you alone."

"Well then, Aragon should have stayed out of politics, not just out of Mali, the Central African Republic, Syria, and Iraq." Luc did not let up venting venom against the president. "He's just nothing but a little bureaucrat and can't see the bigger picture on anything. He continues to bankrupt this country and create economic and social havoc. France cannot afford to wait for any longer to rid itself of this man and his cronies."

"You're probably right on that," Rashid agreed. "Before he does more damage. Either here, or in North Africa or the Middle East."

"Well, the one good thing he seems to be doing is hiring Carnot and company to do the catering for the African summit he will be hosting here in Bordeaux next month. His office just sent us the contract today."

"Is that your catering firm?" Morgan asked.

"Yes. My partner in Paris, Anne Pernot, and I, run the company for my father and a group of investors. Anne is great. You'll meet her at some point."

"Congratulations, Luc. That's quite a coup," Rashid exclaimed.

"I'm going to need some help, though. We don't have enough staff here in Bordeaux to do the job properly, so I would like to hire you guys—and maybe some other friends, Claire—to help with the serving. Part time, but excellent pay. No benefits, though, other than you can eat all the leftovers. And sneak the odd glass of champagne."

"You've got me," Sandrine jumped in, moving closer and putting her arm around Luc. "Of course, you know that."

"I'm on," Rashid said.

"I have no choice. I have to support the family business, don't I?" Claire asked.

"I may not be around here anymore." Alex did not want to commit. "But if I am, I'll help out."

"I don't think I'm allowed to work here officially." Morgan was cognizant of her status as a visiting student in France. "You would only get in trouble if you hired me. And so would I."

"Well, at least I lined three—possibly four—of you up. Send me a short bio, and I'll submit your details to be vetted by security, if that's all right with you. I am sure some of your other friends, Claire, will be happy for some extra pocket money, too, so do let me know."

"Okay then, that's settled," Claire intervened. "Everyone, come to eat."

⌘

Dinner was delicious, and after coffee, *digéstifs*, and chocolates, Luc and Sandrine begged off since he had an early start up to Paris. The food put away and the dirty dishes stacked in the sink for Mercedes, the maid, the next morning, Claire and Rashid retired to the privacy of her bedroom, leaving a still bubbly Morgan alone in the living room with Alex, who had just refreshed his snifter with a large helping of cognac.

"Morgan, it's so wonderful that you are spending this year here with us," Alex began hesitantly before continuing. "I'm really looking forward to spending time with you. And getting to know you a bit better."

"Thanks." Morgan, feeling relaxed and happy, kicked off her shoes and pulled her feet up under herself. "Your family is so kind to me. And I love the city and the region. The chateau is so beautiful, too." The warmth she was experiencing—whether it was the fine wine and the delicious meal she had just consumed, or being alone with a handsome man whom she was starting to like a lot—seemed to extend outward from her and envelope Alex, slouching next to her on the sofa, feet up on the glass table.

"I'm so glad you like it here." Alex edged a little closer, pouring Morgan a little more of the Poire Williams she was drinking. "I must say, my stepfather puts me off a bit at times. And my mother, too, now can be so annoying. They are so conservative. Also Luc—he can be such a jerk at times."

"Yeah, but that's okay. It's generational, I am sure."

"No, but they've all become so hard. So angry. So militant." Alex seemed to want to drive the point home. "My mother wasn't at all like that in the old days. Joseph has definitely changed her. In any case, it's nice of them to let me stay in their apartment downstairs indefinitely. Although, they really don't use it much at all."

"Ummm."

"Morgan, when you and I both have a little free time I could show you some amazing things around here. Prehistoric caves in the Dordogne, the cathedral at Albi, the chateaux and vineyards of the Médoc, the beaches along the Atlantic—but of course, you have those in California as well. And we are very close to Spain, which opens up another world altogether."

"Thanks, Alex. I would love to see everything." She wanted to add "with you," but held back. It might have been too forward, too soon.

"Having been away for over a year, it will be great for me to rediscover the beauty of this region. We'll just need to plan some trips on and around some weekends," Alex said, putting his brandy inhaler on the table and sliding even closer to Morgan.

"That would be wonderful." Morgan sensed what was coming, but she was feeling really good and wanted to extend the moment for as long as possible, not hurry into anything. Fortunately, she remembered there was an unanswered question she had posed to Alex. "Alex, remember, I asked—you know, in the pool house at the chateau—I saw some old divers' gear. Two sets—what they were?"

"Oh, that ancient stuff!" Alex, seemingly perplexed by Morgan's pursuit of that question at that particular moment, took a large swig of his cognac. "That's Joseph's equipment, as I told you."

"Yes, I remember."

"From a long time ago," Alex chortled and put his glass on the table before continuing. "You know, my stepfather doesn't like this to be known, but he used to work for French intelligence when he was young. He was in a small elite unit of frogmen doing all kinds of weird stuff."

"Like what?" Morgan asked, setting her glass down too, turning toward Alex, who had slid right next to her. But she was no longer listening to his words, no longer wanting an answer to her question, as in her euphoric state, she was deciding that she was ready for whatever came next. Maybe this could be the start of a new relationship. They had the rest of the year ahead of them, and after that, who knew? So, why not? She was ready to fall in love.

Alex seemed to sense this and answered with a kiss, which nevertheless took Morgan by surprise, with its intensity, its passion. She had not had a man other than Michael kiss her for several years now, so the sensation of Alex's tongue playing with hers was new and exciting. As was the roving of his hands over her body.

When they came up for air, she had the presence of mind, though, to say, "Alex, I like you. A lot. But let's just take this slowly, if you don't mind. I don't want to rush things." She picked up her Poire Williams again, to signal that that was it for now.

Maybe it was just the prudish American in her, but she did not want him to think she was easy to get. Or be taken for granted. Her mother had taught her that much.

CHAPTER 10

The following Saturday, the girls woke to a glorious sunny fall day, so Claire called her mother to see if it would be all right if they changed their plans and came down to the chateau after all. She and Morgan had decided the evening before that they would stay in town for the weekend. Despite the recent bombing, the residents of Bordeaux made a point of returning to normalcy as much as possible, so the girls had enthusiastically planned a Saturday morning bridge-to-bridge circuit run along both sides of the Garonne, lunch at Le Petit Commerce, afternoon shopping on Rue Ste. Catherine, and pubbing and clubbing after a bistro dinner at Chez Dupont.

For Sunday, the market and oysters with a good Entre-Deux-Mers on the quay, followed by a leisurely afternoon lounging at home with a little bit of necessary coursework and reading.

But the weather was just too nice, and this could be one of the last occasions to sunbathe by the pool before the fall rains set in, so Claire proposed the idea when she got up in the morning and looked outside, and Morgan acquiesced enthusiastically.

"Of course, darling," Chantal answered, delighted that she would see her daughter. "You know we love it when you come. And Morgan, too, of course. Will you be here for lunch?"

"Yes, Maman. Around one, is that okay?" Claire answered, cupping her hand over the phone as she whispered to Morgan, "That will still give us time for our run and a quick shower." Then putting her cell to her mouth again, "I'll see if Alex wants to come, and we'll text you."

"Sure. But no later than one. Luc and Sandrine came down last night, and oh, you know, General Tolbert will be joining us for lunch."

Claire had forgotten, and that was one of the reasons she had originally suggested to Morgan that they stay in Bordeaux. She told Morgan that she intensely disliked Tolbert, who was a friend of her stepfather from his army days, and whom Luc inexplicably idolized.

But now they were committed, and they would have to put up with the general over lunch.

֍

On the way out, the girls knocked on the door of the downstairs apartment, and a still unshaven Alex opened the door in his boxers and T-shirt.

"Do you want to come to St. Émilion with us? It's beautiful outside, so Morgan and I have decided to go."

"Naw. Maman asked me last night, and I already told her I am not going. The general will be there, and you know how much I like him."

"Yes. Unfortunately, I committed before she reminded me."

"Plus, my buddies have asked me to go to Lacanau to go surfing. Why don't you come?" Alex beamed at Morgan, and becoming more animated, added, "Morgan, as a

California girl, you would wow them on the board, I am sure. Yeah, Claire, why don't you call Chantal back to tell her you're not going?"

Morgan looked at Claire, but her friend quickly said, "No, sorry, brother. It will have to be another time. Maman is counting on us."

֍

In the Twingo to St. Émilion, Claire broached the subject of General Tolbert with Morgan. Her stepfather's friendship with André went back many years, to when they started as young men in the Special Operations Command. Their ways had parted when Joseph's father died in a car accident, and he had to leave the armed forces to take over the chateau and the family business. Tolbert, however, had stayed with it and had risen, first, to be the commander of this elite unit, then to the post of one of the deputy heads of the DGSE, the French foreign intelligence services, eventually being promoted to full general.

"My real father, too, was in the Special Operations Command," Claire added out of the blue, after a few minutes of silence. "He was a good friend of Joseph and the general. In the beginning, that is." And then another pause, which to Morgan, made it seem like she was finding it difficult to discuss all this.

She hesitated but asked anyway. "What happened, Claire? Do you want to talk about it?"

"My mother ran off with Joseph. All of a sudden, fell in love with him. Just like that. Head over heels."

"Wow! How? How old were you at the time?"

"Only four. Alex was six."

And then the dam burst: it seemed that Claire was glad finally to be able to talk about this painful bit of her distant past. "My father was away on some special operation. When he came home, he caught my mother *in flagrante delicto,* in his bed with Joseph."

"God, how terrible for you."

"He told them to get out, and never wanted to see them again. I remember, the day after, I wondered where Maman had gone, and why my father seemed so unhappy and angry. The very next day, though, my mother was back home, but I found it strange that my father would not speak to her. He said goodbye to us and said he would return soon. He was being sent on a secret mission. I never saw him again, and Maman told Alex and me that he had died a hero's death on some operation."

"How? Do you know?"

"No. How would I? It was—and is—all secret stuff. I think it may have had something to do with some big scandal. Money laundering. Arms trading. Angolagate, or something like that. There were so many scandals during the Mitterand years, people disappearing or dying under mysterious circumstances. Murders. Assassinations. Not just my father but even a prime minister. Pierre Bérégovoy. He was a good guy."

"I didn't know that."

"Well, it is all still kept very hush hush. So we just guess. Mostly Alex—he's the one who has tried to find out. Our father must have known something, and was ready to tell after his wife ran off with his colleague and friend and—puff!—just like that, ended up dead. Things like that happen in this country."

"And your mother married Joseph?"

"Yes. Very soon after my father died. She and Joseph got custody of us since my grandparents were deemed too old."

"God, what a story!"

"The wounds have healed. Slowly. Maybe not totally.

Never will. I still do not like my stepfather. And I can't stand the general, who stood by Joseph throughout."

"That explains a lot, though."

"Also, Alex found out he was on that mission with my father. So Tolbert knows what happened. For sure. But he has always refused to tell Alex and me anything about it. Says it's a state secret."

"Terrible."

"Plus, I don't like his politics and the secretive chumminess with Joseph. So there you go. I loathe the man!"

CHAPTER 11

"So this is the lovely California girl you were just telling me about, Joseph," the tall, broad-shouldered man with imposing silver eyebrows and a mop of gray hair said as he entered the room beside the chatelaine. "*Ravissante!*"

"Yes, André," Joseph answered. "Allow me to introduce Morgan Kenworthy. Her parents are good friends of ours. They make excellent wine in California. Morgan, General Tolbert."

The man in the uniform took Morgan's outstretched hand with a solid grip, saying, "Well, if it's as good as yours, Joseph, I am sure it is fine indeed. Very nice to meet you, Morgan. And, my dear Claire, how have you been?"

Although Morgan's first impression of the handsome and congenial older man was favorable, Claire showed her disdain by just uttering, "Good, General. Thank you."

"Shall we go to table?" Chantal asked. "Gaston has everything ready in the dining room. And I'm sure we're all very hungry."

ぐうぐ

"But Aragon just doesn't understand, does he?" Luc

was getting increasingly agitated. "That he simply cannot continue with these ineffective and stupid policies."

Discussion over the sumptuous lunch of pumpkin soup flavored with a dollop of *crème fraîche* and roasted pumpkin seeds, followed by a veal roast with a fig sauce, baby potatoes from the Ile de Ré and a late summer *ratatouille*, accompanied by a vertical *tour de force* of de Carduzac vintages, had turned to politics. For Morgan, it was being immersed in the boiling cauldron of the debate around the de Carduzac table, as it became clear to her that Claire dissented from the views held by the other three—opinions that were vehemently opposed to the government of Frédéric Aragon. As were those of the general, who only intervened occasionally.

"Yes, the country is virtually in a state of revolt against him," Joseph agreed with his son.

"But we must explain to Morgan," Chantal said, looking at the American girl who had not uttered a word since the heated discussion had started.

"Well, my dear—" Joseph was happy to hold forth. "—our esteemed President of the Republic, the Emperor Frédéric, has moved France farther and farther to the left. With the collapse of our uncompetitive economy and mounting joblessness, he has been currying favor among the masses by creating more and more unproductive government jobs. And in the process, he is bankrupting the state."

"But how else could he create employment?" Claire asked.

"France now has, by far, the biggest bureaucracy," Chantal weighed in, ignoring her daughter's question and siding with her husband. "With by far the best benefits, which the unions will not agree to give up. And the smallest private sector of any country in the OECD. Which is dwindling by the day as businesses fold up and entrepreneurs and job creators are taxed to death and leave. We simply cannot pay for it anymore."

"In the meantime, youth unemployment has passed fifty percent. The young of today cannot get jobs in this country. They are out on the streets," Luc said, pouring Morgan and himself more wine, then passing the bottle to his father. "Our companies are uncompetitive because of high costs and taxes. And the government has now enacted a law that makes it even harder for firms to cut expenses by laying off redundant staff."

Just then, Gaston entered the dining room, and, as Chantal complimented him on the main course, cleared the plates away.

"The British were smart. They voted to get out of the European Union. We should at the very least leave the Euro," Claire's mother said once the butler had left the room. "That was a stupid German creation. It has been only good for them and their exports. And hurts everyone else, including us."

"Maman, you know that's not true." Claire was not going to let that one go. "Hasn't it helped the de Carduzac wines sell throughout Europe?"

"But, Claire, our main market is America. And now China," Joseph retorted, dismissing his stepdaughter's argument.

"In any case, it is simply ridiculous. Prices are so much higher with the Euro than they should be." Chantal, exasperated, dabbed her lips with her napkin.

"France is a failed Maoist state." This from Luc.

"I can tell you, our friends in the military are fed up." Joseph took a sip of wine to taste it before continuing. "Aren't they, André? Talking about armed action, this notion of sending French troops to root out Muslim fundamentalists threatening Mali and the Central African Republic and other former French colonies on a piecemeal basis has totally backfired. As has dropping a few bombs on the ISIS strongholds in the Middle East. Either you do it properly, or you don't do anything."

"What do you mean?" Claire asked.

"I think your stepfather is right," the general said. "What this government is currently doing, only irritates our own huge Muslim population, and brings the wrath of al Qaeda, Daesh, and other terrorist groups down on us. Already, several of the jihadist leaders have called on Muslims living in France to take revenge. And there are all those fed up youths who have gone off to join ISIS coming back now, ready to wreak havoc here."

"Nor do we, the mothers of France, want to send our sons and daughters to die uselessly in the desert," Chantal added.

"It is inept foreign adventurism like in the old days of the *Françafrique* policies, just to take the attention of the population away from the real problems in the country. Yes, and adventurism back at home, too. Sure, Aragon has strengthened the armed forces, and he is now using them to clamp down on unrest here," Luc added. "Brother against brother, Frenchman against Frenchmen."

"Well, not exactly," Joseph countered. "It is more Frenchmen against Muslims, as I see it. And rightly so. Isn't it the followers of Islam who are the troublemakers trashing cars and pillaging property in the *banlieues*? They're the ones who attacked the Charlie Hebdo office, that Jewish supermarket, Bataclan and all those cafés and restaurants right here in Paris, resulting in—what is it now—close to two hundred deaths? And now this."

"In Toulouse, Marseilles, Lille—all over the country, for that matter." Chantal heaped fuel on the fire. "They are the rabble-rousers. And need to be dealt with severely. It is unbelievable that we have let so many immigrate here. And the flood still does not stop. Why, we even have several Muslim ministers in the cabinet now! Soon they will take over the entire government. It has really gone too far."

"Hold on, Maman," Claire—indignant that her mother had totally adopted Joseph's views—tried to calm the increasingly volatile dinner argument. "It wasn't just Muslims rioting. They happen to be French citizens. Plus, there are lots of farmers from rural areas and the working class who are very poor, without jobs, unable to feed their children, out there demonstrating."

"In Toulouse, I am certain it was the Muslims who were beaten up. I must say, it was good that the counter-demonstrators taught them a lesson or two before the army stepped in."

"Weren't they from the group that used to call themselves the 'Ouevre Francaise'? Those guys on the fringes of the Front National…or whatever have they transformed themselves into now?" Claire asked. "Are they still causing trouble?"

Morgan could not stand the direction the conversation was taking. She cleared her throat to change the subject. "Claire, would you mind passing the cheese platter, please?"

"Delighted," Claire replied with a smile, happy that the accelerating train had momentarily been derailed. "Luc, why don't you pour Morgan some more wine? And me, too, please. Or are you just hogging it all for yourself?"

"Sure," Luc said, picking up the bottle. "And then we have the Brassault affair. We haven't even talked about that yet. Those were definitely jihadists, who laid the explosives."

"Well, but it was stupid of the government to send that idiot Rostrand and two other leftie ministers to Mérignac to support the unions in their demonstration against those very necessary lay-offs. Pierre LeBrun, the *PDG*—the Chief Executive Officer, Morgan—of Brassault, is a good friend of mine. And I am an investor." Joseph was working himself up again. "Would you believe it? The government's employment program consists of sending the prime minister to speak out in protest on the side of the unions. Couldn't they see that with the shrinking military spending worldwide, Brassault has to cut costs? Otherwise, it will face bankruptcy. Of course, they will no doubt just bail it out with taxpayers' money to save those jobs."

"What pisses me off most, though," Luc continued the tirade, "is that Aragon and his leftist cronies have raised inheritance taxes to seventy five percent. To pay for all these ineffective adventures and policies. So there will be nothing left for us when Joseph and Chantal are gone."

"I wouldn't worry too much. We'll manage," Claire countered. "And I'm sure you will, too, Luc. God, this cheese is awesome."

"Yes. The Comté and the Roquefort are so yummy!" Morgan agreed, showing off the knowledge she had recently acquired at the Jean d'Alos cheese shop.

"We will lose the vineyards and the chateau to the state."

"They have been in the family for four centuries, my son, so we will not let that happen," Joseph said, resolutely sipping the last of his wine. "Come, let's pass *à coté*, and have our coffee and cognac in the salon."

෴

After the copious and well-lubricated lunch, Morgan, Sandrine, and Claire changed, and spent the gorgeous late fall afternoon mostly in their bikini bottoms, working and reading and sunning themselves by the pool. Chantal had excused herself and withdrawn to her room for an afternoon nap, while Joseph, Luc, and the General had retired with their coffees and *mignardises* to the de Carduzac study for a meeting.

It must have been a little after four when Morgan woke from a snooze in the comfortable recliner and realized that perhaps she was getting too much sun. Time to put more clothes on. She looked over and saw that Claire and Sandrine were sound asleep. She decided to let her friends rest. Cutting across the lawn toward the stairs to the terrace, she glanced over and saw that the armchairs were still where Alex had placed them for her the other day.

On the way to her bedroom, which was upstairs at the end of the long corridor, she passed the open door of Joseph's study and was surprised to hear fragments of a heated conversation. Finally in her room, Morgan closed the door, and with her heart beating at high speed, she reviewed the puzzling snippets she had overheard as she sneaked by. She even took a few moments to write them down to try and make sense out of them.

"...successful, from our point of view..." The general's booming voice?

"...the potency of the explosives..." A measured but unfamiliar tone.

"...in any case, set the...garble, garble...up nicely..." Had that been Joseph? Not clear.

"...the president...garble, garble, garble..." No, not Luc. Too high pitched for Joseph.

Were there others in the room? Yes, it was definitely not the voice of one of the three who had been at lunch. Hmm...a hint of a Slavic accent maybe?

"...today, not as good as we..." The general again.

And then she had been no longer in range.

What could they have been talking about?

"...the potency of the explosives..." clearly suggested some bombing.

Could it be the recent one at the Brassault works?

༺༻

Morgan hurriedly slipped a sundress over her head and was already in the corridor, hoping that she might catch a little more of the mysterious conversation on the way back to the garden. She was further intrigued, when—looking out the tall windows of the hall—she noticed that there were three big black cars in front that had not been there earlier when she had descended for lunch.

There were definitely some others in that meeting besides just Joseph, Luc, and the general. And someone with a Slavic accent, she was sure.

But Morgan was disappointed when she passed the study door again. This time, the door was solidly shut, and no sound escaped.

What had they been talking about?

CHAPTER 12

It was after a late Sunday night dinner of salad and cheese back at the apartment that Morgan, sitting cross-legged on her bed, laptop in front of her, had her weekly Skype conversation with her parents—and sister, Carrie, when she was home. Morgan missed her parents and loved catching up on the news about the family and friends and how the harvest was shaping up that year. Sitting there after the call, she mused about how difficult it must be for Claire and Alex who had lost their father after their mother had run off with one of his friends. She could not imagine how they had managed to reconcile themselves to their current home situation. Time must heal a lot of wounds, she told herself. *And how lucky am I, to have such a loving family.*

Since she did not feel like doing any more work, and her laptop was there in front of her, she decided just for fun she would find out more about the Mitterand years, the scandals, and disappearances that Claire had talked about.

What was that prime minister's name? That was probably a good place to start.

As she could only remember that it started with a B, she typed *assassination of French Prime Minister B* into the Google search engine. The first site that came up was Wikipedia talking about a Louis Barthou who had been prime minister for eight months in 1913, and was later one of the victims of an assassination attempt against King Alexander I of Yugoslavia during his state visit to Marseilles in October 1934. *Hmm. Interesting, but definitely not it.*

The second entry was irrelevant. The third, though, which was the English Wikipedia site on Pierre Bérégovoy, prime minister under François Mitterand from 1992 to 1993, seemed to hold more promise. Morgan read it through twice, even though it said nothing out of the ordinary about Bérégovoy's death on May 1, 1993. It did mention a few inconsistencies, but police investigators had quickly concluded that he had taken his own life. The only intriguing question mark Morgan found was in the following comment: *His wife expressed some doubt about whether his death actually was a suicide, mainly because he had not left a suicide note, and that his notepad, which he always kept in his pocket, had disappeared.*

But when Morgan opened the French version of Wikipedia on Pierre Bérégovoy, her heart started to race, as she read the extensive discussion about the possibility that the ex-prime minister may indeed have been assassinated. There was a body of proof that pointed to the death of this humble and correct prime minister as a murder, and that witnesses were hushed up, evidence simply disappeared, and any notion that his death was not self-inflicted totally whitewashed.

As Morgan read the various other sites on Google to do with Bérégovoy's demise, it became clear to her that there were significant discrepancies in the statements and actions of both the ex-prime minister's chauffeur and his bodyguard, which raised questions about the official story. For example, why would the security officer allow the prime minister to drive the car away with his 357 Magnum left in the glove compartment? As another site on Google pointed out, the prime minister was supposed to have two guards with him at all times—even when out on personal business—one within one and a half meters and the other twenty meters away at most, the two in close contact at all times. The officials claimed that one guard stayed behind at the campsite where Bérégovoy had been giving out prizes after some kayak and canoe races, while the other guard—the chauffeur—had an urgent need to go to the bathroom. It was apparently then that Bérégovoy drove away by himself to a secluded spot by the canal in the forest, stopped the car, and taking the 357 Magnum from the glove compartment, shot himself in the temple. Like others before her, Morgan found this version of the story not very credible. If these were professional police guards, their actions themselves spoke of a set-up, she also concluded.

And supposedly Bérégovoy used the Magnum to kill himself, but, if this were the case, at least one side of his cranium would have been blown away, according to ballistics experts. In fact, the very few grainy pictures that were not embargoed showed a relatively small bullet hole on the top of the head. Also, the official version claimed that he shot himself in the temple—the easiest and most likely way to kill oneself with a pistol—whereas the available pictures did not show wounds on either side of the head. No ballistics inquest was ever pursued. In fact, the expert available at the hospital where he was first taken wondered why she was not allowed to perform even simple analyses such as testing for gunpowder residues on the hands.

And why were there two distinct shots heard by witnesses? The official answer was that the prime minister first tested the gun before applying it to his temple. This was refuted by several psychologists as not a very believable scenario, given the likely mindset of a suicide.

In spite of all the official whitewash, Morgan was astounded to read that in 2002, the journal *Le Parisien* brought to light an internal note of the *Renseignements Généraux*, the intelligence services within the French police, detailing an inquest into the death carried out by a Monsieur Hubert Marty-Vayrance, the ex-commissioner of the RG in the Department of Nièvre, where Bérégovoy was both deputy mayor of the capital, Nevers, and the representative to the Assemblée Générale, the French Parliament. The ex-commissioner claimed to have been instructed to open this inquest by the director of the RG, a Monsieur Yves Bertrand—who, however, denied ever having given such direction and indeed the very existence of the report—but did mention a commando that had been charged with the surveillance of the prime minister. In a subsequent film *La double mort de Pierre Bérégovoy* that appeared on France 3, Marty-Vayrance claimed that before his death, several of Bérégovoy's residences were burglarized. Somebody was clearly searching for papers detailing corruption touching the highest ranks of French politics and business that the prime minister supposedly had in his possession.

According to Marty-Vayrance's report, Pierre Bérégovoy was assassinated by a couple of frogmen who appeared out of the canal. This was also the thesis advanced in a book by a local journalist, Eric Raynaud, who, when looking back through the photographs of the day ten years later, saw the deputy mayor, laid out on a wet stretcher, with a hole in the top of his cranium. Raynaud claimed that the frogmen tried to drown the politician, but he got away, and then they finished him off with the bullet in the top of his head. The hypothesis was that the ex-prime minister was on the verge of making revelations to the media about high-level corruption, and may, in fact, have arranged a meeting in the woods along the canal to carry this out.

As Morgan delved further and further into Bérégovoy's death, and who might have wanted him dead, the path became murky but seemed to point to the upper reaches of the political classes in France. Was it Mitterand who gave the thumbs down signal on his ex-prime minister, who, he decided, knew too much of the details of some of the sordid transactions around the president? Or was it one of his activist intelligence lieutenants who took it upon himself to get rid of the dangerous Bérégovoy, who seemingly had lots of information to spill on questionable affairs such as the Péchiney acquisition of Triangle or the sale of frigates to Taiwan or Angolagate or the misappropriation of the Ferraye technology? These must all have been the scandals Claire had referred to.

Or was it the American, Ted Maher, the ex-Green Beret who was later convicted of arson in a 1999 fire that killed Edmond Safra just days after he concluded the sale of Republic National Bank in 1999, and who supposedly met with Bérégovoy an hour before his death? The possible motives and perpetrators, once you started delving into it, seemed to be many…

The information and the extrapolations from her research churned around in Morgan's brain, and she could not fall asleep after she turned her computer off and brushed her teeth. Having just a few weeks earlier come upon the divers' gear at the de Carduzac chateau—which, she remembered, Alex had ascribed to his stepfather's days serving in a unit of frogmen in French intelligence—she found the reference in the French Wikipedia article to two frogmen as the assassins of Bérégovoy particularly disconcerting. Could it have been Joseph de Carduzac's unit that carried out the assassination, she asked herself? In fact—even more disturbing—might he have had something to do with it?

Morgan was so agitated by all these thoughts, that after about an hour of fretting in the dark about whether she should discuss what she had found out with Claire and Alex and how, she got up again and spent the hours till daybreak following up the various other links that had come up on the search engine.

CHAPTER 13

Morgan knew she was running late. But that was always the case, and wasn't it the prerogative of a woman to be tardy? She had agreed to meet John at eight at La Tupina, one of the best traditional Bordelais restaurants in the city, but one that was all the way across town. It was already seven-thirty, and she still had to get dressed and take public transport. At least the tram was usually quick, and it was direct—that is, if there was no malfunction on the line—she told herself as she finished drying her hair, and glanced at her shapely and tanned naked body in the mirror.

Running down the stairs, she reminded herself, *This is going to be nothing more than a date. John seems like such an interesting man, and I can probably find out a lot from him. No need to sleep with the guy, though. Unless, of course, I end up wanting to. Ha!*

Besides, she decided, she really did not want Alex to take her for granted, now that they were seeing each other regularly. She liked him, liked him a lot, but if something serious was going to develop, it was better to let it do so slowly, she was sure of that.

She liked John too, though. And he was American, although that was both a plus and a minus, she told herself.

Morgan breezed in almost half an hour late, as her CIA friend was having his second glass of Pineau des Charentes to accompany the olives and the *saucisson* hors d'oeuvres the white-aproned waiter had put in front of him. He stood up to greet Morgan as she shed her coat and approached him in a low-cut and short silk evening dress.

"Wow, Morgan! You look ravishing. I'm so glad we were finally able to arrange this dinner. I hope your friend Alex doesn't mind?"

So, he knew Alex and she were seeing each other. Perhaps from Jérome, or Claire—whatever, it didn't matter, Morgan told herself. In fact, so much the better.

"I wanted to thank you for asking me out. I do miss talking to people from back home. All this foreign stuff is great—you know, speaking French and all that—but somehow I just find it easier with you. There is no cultural divide to overcome."

"Well then, let's celebrate! Some bubbly?" John asked, waving to the waiter.

"Sure!"

When the waiter brought the two flûtes of Veuve Clicquot brut, Morgan raised her glass, saying, "We need to drink to the success of your investigation. By the way, how is it going?"

"So, so. The French investigators have come up with the names of two brothers of Algerian descent who were working at the plant as the most likely suspects. Suicide bombers, they claim. In fact, they are convinced it was these two who carried out the Brassault bombing."

"Hmm. Is there any evidence?"

"No, not really. And the more I think about it, it seems to me unlikely that these two young men would have been able to mastermind the planting of all those explosives. Not just that EXPLUS I told you about, but now we have found some other more dangerous stuff throughout the plant. Explosive nanocomposites. Some of it still unexploded. This must have involved massive planning."

Just then, the waiter came back to take their order: it was easy, as Morgan just ordered the same as John who had perused the menu earlier. They opted for the *coquilles St. Jacques* and the *maccaronade* the restaurant was famous for as starter and main course. Morgan was impressed by John's choice of wine: a half-bottle of Chateau Haut-Brion 2015 white to accompany the scallops and a Chateau Léoville Las Cases 2003 to follow.

"You were saying. Nano whats?"

"Yes, at Mérignac, the investigators also discovered a powerful explosive material called energetic nanocomposites. Actually, it was Peter, whom you met the other day. It was he who found them."

"Yes?"

"These are also known as thermites. They did not just find traces, but a lot of the stuff was still unexploded. According to Peter, similar material was found in the dust that settled after the World Trade Center tragedy. In fact, he and some other experts believe that it was these materials—probably positioned in strategic places in the Twin Towers by the terrorists before they crashed the planes into them—that actually caused the skyscrapers to collapse."

"Really! I wasn't aware of that."

"That certainly hasn't been the official line. But some of the guys advancing this thesis—including Peter—are pretty reputable explosives experts. And if they are right, it may mean that whoever was responsible for this bombing in Mérignac, wanted to destroy the entire Brassault facility. In a big way. The EXPLUS wouldn't have been enough, but when that was detonated, it would, in turn, have set off the nano stuff. Fortunately, something malfunctioned along the way."

"Or could it have been just made to look like they wanted to destroy the entire facility?" Morgan asked, surprising her CIA companion.

"Hmm. Interesting thought. Why, though? Anyway, this whole direction is just a theory for now, and it certainly broadens the investigation. But those two Algerians couldn't have done it, I am pretty sure of that. At least, not on their own."

"Then who could have planted that nano stuff all over the site?"

"We don't really know, but our working thesis now is that a fairly complex series of nanocomposites might have been engineered into one or more of the components that regularly come from different places in France and elsewhere for assembly at the Mérignac facility. By a single terrorist infiltrator at one component manufacturer, or, for that matter, several at different ones. And Peter thinks that the EXPLUS was meant to be used in turn to detonate the thermites by a worker at the site. A 'sleeper', a terrorist plant. Or it could all have been set off with a wireless control ignition system."

"That sounds like a pretty sophisticated operation."

"Well, yes. At least we think we know how whoever did it, got their hands on the EXPLUS. Peter and I were in on a rather perplexing conversation with one of the EPC employees when we went along with the French investigators to interview them. Also an Algerian. He told us that a French colleague—a Monsieur Bonnard, I think it was—had told him one day after work when he had had too much to drink, about stealing some explosives and selling them on the black market. Can you believe this guy—he asked his Algerian buddy to partner with him since he thought he might have some Arab or African contacts to sell the explosives to? For a part of the profits, of course."

"Pretty shameless. Did you manage to talk to this Bonnard?"

"The trouble is, he is supposedly on leave. We told the French investigators several days ago, and they are supposed to be tracking him. But so far nothing."

"And the Algerian?"

"He, of course, said he refused and has not had any further approaches from Bonnard."

"I guess you need to find this Bonnard guy. He would be a good lead."

"Yes, of course. But enough of this talk. I shouldn't be telling you all this. But you'll keep it to yourself, I know, and I find that sometimes it's good to bounce ideas off a woman colleague or friend whom I can trust."

"Thanks."

"In any case, we should be speaking of more pleasant things. Like the delicious food we are about to eat, which I see is just now coming."

"You are both having the coquilles St. Jacques to start, *n'est-ce pas*?"

"Yes, thank you."

The garçon placed the large bowls with three scallops still sporting their coral shells in front of them and then proceeded to open the half bottle of white wine. "Would you like to taste the Chateau Haut-Brion, monsieur?"

"Thank you, yes." John sniffed the golden liquid and then inhaled a sip with lots of air and rolled it around with his tongue. "Excellent! Thank you."

The waiter smiled, poured some in Morgan's glass, then more into John's, and finally left.

"Hmm. What a treat! Thank you." Morgan hesitated for a moment before continuing. "John, there was one other thing I wanted to tell you about. It is nothing to do with your investigation—it's just something I find weird, and want to get off my chest."

"What is it, Morgan?"

"Well, I was doing some research about the Mitterand Presidency. Just for...you know...out of curiosity. There was this prime minister under Mitterand. Pierre Bérégovoy. Quite a good guy, apparently."

"Yes, I vaguely remember the name."

"He died in mysterious circumstances. Officials claimed it was a suicide, but there are a lot of loose ends and inconsistencies. Weirdly, several credible sources claim it was two frogmen who killed him, just as he was about to spill the beans on some corruption in the government. What has been bothering me, John—and I am so glad I can talk about this with a fellow American—is that the other day, at the de Carduzac chateau, I came upon two sets of divers' suits and tanks in the pool house. They were old, probably sort of from around the time of Bérégovoy's death. And what's more, when I asked Alex about it, he said they belonged to his stepfather and told me that Joseph de Carduzac had been in a special frogmen's unit of the French intelligence services. Now isn't that creepy?"

"My dear," John said, with a little chuckle, "I see what you are getting at, but I am sure it's just a coincidence. What I know of the de Carduzacs is that they are one of the most upstanding families in France, and I highly doubt that Joseph de Carduzac would have anything to do with the secretive assassination of a prime minister. Even a socialist one."

"Thanks, John. That's what I think too." But deep down, she was not persuaded. Even as she said this, Morgan decided she would not tell him of the snippets of conversation she had overheard at the chateau as she passed by Joseph's study. At least, not yet. Perhaps unconvincing by themselves but as just one more thing?

She was definitely starting to feel less comfortable about Joseph de Carduzac.

And did that unease spread to Luc as well?

CHAPTER 14

Another beautiful fall Saturday ripened as Claire and Morgan pulled up on the carefully raked gravel lot in front of the *chais* of the chateau. On cue, Chantal appeared through the door and made her way down the steps, just as the girls slammed the doors of the Twingo shut.

"Nice that you two came down again."

"Oh, it's so lovely here!" Morgan gushed, but the sentiment was genuine. "And you are so kind to have me all the time."

"Well, we love it. Unfortunately, it's just going to be 'us girls' for now, since Joseph and Luc have gone off to a meeting. Sandrine is visiting her sick father, and Alex has decided to meet some friends in Saint Émilion for lunch," Chantal answered. Then, pleased to see the look of disappointment on Morgan's face, she quickly added, smiling. "But he'll come by later for drinks and dinner I think."

"What meeting is that?" Claire asked, slinging her duffel bag over her shoulder.

"Oh, you know, his silly friends. His *Nouveaux Girondins* group."

"Same rooms, Maman?" Claire said, a sultry look appearing on her face.

"Yes, and don't tarry too long. Gaston is ready to serve."

※※※

Over a simple meal of *blanquette de veau* and egg noodles, bottle of de Carduzac 2008, the conversation continued.

"So, Maman, let's explain to Morgan who these Nouveaux Girondins guys are."

"Well, dear, they're just your stepfather's friends, you know that."

"Isn't there some political angle? They may be friends, but it's a bit more than that, I think."

"But darling, friends often talk politics."

"These ones sure do. And nothing but, from what Luc and Joseph deign to tell us. Haven't they adopted some kind of common manifesto? Luc told me that they all swore to do everything they can to save France from the destructive policies of Aragon. Among other 'evils'. Such as immigrants, especially Muslims. Like my friend Rashid, I might add."

"Well, Claire, I don't know, but the whole thing seems fairly innocent to me."

"Not necessarily, if they see themselves as a political movement. And it would seem a neo-fascist one at that."

"They are certainly not that. They have no intention of running for election—"

"Maman, don't be so naïve. Doing everything they can to save France from the destructive policies of Aragon can mean a lot of different things."

"What do you mean?"

"Well, couldn't it also mean, removing him by force, for example?"

Hmm. *Was Claire starting to suspect something?* Maybe she should have a talk with her.

"You're talking nonsense now, Claire." Chantal got up to get the salad bowl and plates from the sideboard.

"I'm not saying that they would necessarily use coercion. But these are dangerous times, Maman. The prime minister and two other ministers were just blown up by some jihadists, so maybe we should be a little careful about the games we play. That's all I'm saying. And somebody better tell Luc and Joseph, before anyone gets hurt."

No, maybe she wasn't. But talking to her might not hurt.

"Don't worry, dear. Your stepfather and Luc are grown men. And besides, there are some pretty illustrious citizens who come to their meetings. The general, for one. You know that he is the operational head of all French intelligence now. And Patrick Joinville. Why, he is the Minister of Veterans in the current cabinet. So don't tell me it's all against Aragon and his government. And then there is Valentin Frantome."

"That's just it, Maman. It doesn't inspire me with confidence."

"Who is Valentin Frantome?" Morgan asked.

"He only comes sometimes. Just another crazy politician. Former mayor of Libourne. Also a member of the Assemblée Nationale. Frantome is sort of the defense critic for the opposition, isn't he, Maman?" Claire poured Morgan and then herself more wine before continuing with a hint of sarcasm. "Definitely not someone on the left, or even the center. A pretty scary guy, all in all. One of Joseph's old friends. And very close to the general."

"Claire, I don't see anything wrong with a group of mature men debating politics and wanting to bring about the right policies in this country. That is all Les Nouveaux Girondins are about. Someone has to care enough, otherwise France will be destroyed."

"There you go, Maman. You should just join them, why don't you?" Claire got up in a huff, and, as she collected the salad plates to take them out to the kitchen, added, "Although they are probably too sexist to welcome a woman among them."

When she didn't come back, Chantal stood up with an "Excuse me," and went after her daughter, leaving Morgan alone at the table. Eventually, Gaston came to offer her dessert and a coffee, which she declined, and saying, "Thank you for the delicious lunch," went up to her room to change into poolside gear.

ღეღ

"We won't wait any longer for Chantal and Claire," Joseph said, opening the bottle of Roederer 2001 with a healthy pop. "They must be having a mother-daughter heart-to-heart. Or just another one of their little tiffs." With a self-satisfied chortle, he poured Morgan a full glass, handing it to her, then his son and stepson, and lastly himself.

"Thank you, Joseph." Morgan had taken to calling both the de Carduzac parents by their first names.

"Here's to your year in France, Morgan. How is it going?"

"Oh, it's awesome. I'm enjoying it so much. And I'm grateful to all of you for being so welcoming and generous."

"Well, we're just so happy you are here. Your parents are such good friends. I hope they come to visit soon."

Morgan saw the momentary lull in the conversation as the opportunity she had been hoping for to ask Joseph a few questions about his past. "What did you do before you took over the estate and got into wine, Joseph, may I ask?"

"Oh, I worked for the government."

"Doesn't everybody in France?" Morgan asked, smiling at her own little joke. "Isn't that what you were saying the other night?"

"Come on, stepdad. Tell her what you were really doing." Alex stopped texting on his iPhone and joined the conversation.

"Well…" Chagrined, Joseph finished his champagne and took the bottle from the bucket to top up the glasses.

"Don't hold back, Joseph. Morgan knows already that you worked for intelligence." Alex picked up his flûte to chug its contents and then held the empty glass out to his stepfather for a refill.

"Does she? How?"

"She found the divers' suits in the pool house the other day. She asked me who they belonged to, and I told her."

"Alex, what did you tell her?"

"That you worked for the intelligence services. In some highly secret unit of frogmen. Doing special missions."

"Morgan, I would appreciate it if you kept this to yourself. Alex—" Joseph said, rather agitatedly.

Just then, Chantal arrived, followed by Claire, whose eyes were red.

Had she been crying? Why?

CHAPTER 15

Morgan was doing research with her laptop on her bed, trying to find out as much as she could about the Angolagate, Elf and other scandals under Mitterand when her mobile rang. She picked it up and saw that it was Alex.

"Morgan, will you be my date for dinner tomorrow?"

"Sure. What do you have in mind?" She was pleasantly surprised with the more than usually formal invitation.

"Well, Luc wants to have a little dinner party. His partner in the catering business, Anne Pernot, who went to school with me, and her fiancé, Serge, who, as it happens is Luc's best friend, are coming to Bordeaux. We all sort of grew up together. Serge, I must admit, is brilliant, and now teaches at L'ÉNA—you know, the École Nationale d'Administration. And she—well, I am sure you will like her. Ahem…even though I did go out with her for a short while. Luc and Anne will be trying out some of the dishes they intend to cater for the president's African get-together in October. It will just be the six of us since Claire and Rashid are going to Cap Ferret for two days."

"Will they want some help? With the shopping? Or cooking?"

"No. No. You've got classes tomorrow, n'est-ce pas? I just need you to be at Luc's to help entertain. And eat.

They said they would be ready around seven, so try and come down by then if you can."

※ ※ ※

On her way out of the flat, Morgan cast an eye in the floor-length mirror and ascertained that she looked stunning in the low-cut but simple red mini-dress she had bought at Zadig & Voltaire the week before, just for such an occasion. She did not want to be shown up by any girl Alex may have gone out with.

In fact, she was right. Alex's mouth was agape for a full fifteen seconds when she entered Luc's apartment before he could utter the words, "My, you look gorgeous tonight, Morgan," and thrust himself forward to grab her by the waist and kiss her fully on the mouth. He seemed to be still in a daze when they disentangled as Morgan, still holding his hand, looked around, and greeted Luc and Sandrine.

"The guests of honor are just taking a shower before dinner. Just so you know, I'm going to let them have my place for the night." Luc said. "Sandrine and I will stay upstairs in Claire's bedroom, Morgan, if that's all right with you, since she's not here."

"Sure." And while Morgan digested this, Luc took down six champagne glasses from the rack and a bottle of Krug 2004 from the fridge.

The dinner was a gastronomic delight—sea bass with caramelized endives and Beluga lentils, a Chateau Carbonnieux white, followed by Morgan's favorite cheeses from Jean d'Alos accompanied by a de Carduzac red, and for dessert, a chocolate hazelnut cake that Anne had created. The company was pleasant. In fact, Morgan quite liked Anne, whom she found charming, intelligent, and genuinely interested in her.

Serge, too, seemed to take to the American girl, and they enthusiastically invited her to come to Paris, with or without Alex.

After coffee and digéstifs, Luc, getting up from the couch, said, "Well, I'm sure you're tired after your trip and all the cooking tonight. Tomorrow we have a lot to discuss. The arrangements for the conference, definitely. But also your wedding. And you will have to tell me if there is anything special you will want your best man to do."

"We're so glad you accepted the role, Luc." Serge, too, got up and helped clear the glasses and demitasse cups from the coffee table.

"Will you come, Morgan? To the wedding that is," Anne asked, glancing up at the American girl as she found her shoes under the couch. "June twenty-fifth? At Serge's parents' chateau, over on the other side of St. Émilion."

"Of course she will, Anne," Alex answered for her, smiling at Morgan. "Send her an invitation. She'll be there with me."

"All right, now I am going to turn the apartment over to you. Sandrine and I will go upstairs for the night." Luc went over to give Anne the usual kisses on the cheek, Serge doing the same to Sandrine.

"Thanks, Luc. As always, you are very generous."

"I will leave the keys in the lock. Have fun, you two."

Luc grabbed Sandrine's hand to go upstairs. At the same time, Alex put his arm around Morgan, led her out onto the landing, and saying, "Good night," to his older stepbrother and his girlfriend, gently led the California girl down the stairs to his parents' suite.

Morgan's heart jumped, as she too, murmured, "Good night," in the direction of the couple just unlocking the door to the apartment upstairs she shared with Claire.

☙☙

Morgan had not been to Joseph's and Chantal's luxurious apartment before, and it took her breath away when Alex switched the lights on, with all the priceless antiques, remarkable paintings, brilliant chandeliers, and Persian carpets. But she did not have much of a chance to look around, as Alex had her in his arms the second after he closed the door and carried her through to the bedroom. Maybe it was the exquisite dinner and all the alcohol, or the fact that Alex had asked her to be his date to meet his former girlfriend and her fiancé, but she did not resist, nor try to temper his passion. She was ready to be swept off her feet.

☙☙

As the morning sun started to creep in through the curtains, still half asleep, Morgan felt the happiness of having Alex's arms reach across the king-sized bed, and pull her naked body into his. He was hard again, and it did not take long for her to become aroused too. She remembered how much she enjoyed making love in the morning, and this was infinitely better than with Mike. Alex brought her quickly to orgasm yet again, followed immediately by his own before their spent bodies separated.

Some quiet time and a few dawn dreams later, Alex kissed her and said, "I promised Luc I would go to Bonnet's to get some croissants for all of us. Afterward, I will go and check on him and the guests upstairs. I'll come and get you when they're all ready for breakfast up there. Just relax until then—it is Saturday, and you should get to enjoy a lie in, *chérie*."

Morgan was glad to be pampered and left alone in the beautiful de Carduzac apartment. After stretching for a few moments between the silk sheets, and trying to make sense of what had happened with Alex the night before, without much success—except that it had been really magnificent, leaving her with a wonderful feeling that still lingered—she got up and went into the marble bathroom. It was like being in a five-star hotel, Morgan reflected as she luxuriated under the hot shower. She vaguely wondered whether Chantal would know it was she who had used her shampoo and body lotion, but when it came right down to it, she didn't care. In fact, she was quite happy to put on the fluffy dressing gown she found hanging on a hook—it seemed clean, no doubt the weekly maid service took care of that and everything else.

Wanting to let her hair air-dry a little, Morgan decided to walk around and look through the apartment. She smiled, remembering the pleasure of the heat of the moment, as she collected the dress and scanty undergarments she had shed on the way to the bedroom the night before, and laid them out on the bed. Then she walked over to the space between the bathroom and the bed where a gallery of photographs graced the wall. Pictures of the five children, together and singly, one of a much younger and gorgeous Chantal, the handsome couple before, and at their marriage. Morgan smiled as she took in a photo of Alex as a toddler, and one of Claire and her brother riding ponies, another of Luc and his two sisters frolicking by the pool. And lower down, the grandchildren, sons, and daughters of Joseph's daughters by his first wife.

Next to the bedroom, another closed door led off the corridor. Curious, she opened it and peeked into what was a small study, probably Joseph's workplace when he was in town. Her attention was drawn by several more photographs, and what looked like a framed certificate over on the far wall.

One black and white picture showed a much younger and very fit looking Joseph—bearing an uncannily close resemblance to Luc—with his arm around a stocky, shorter man of similar age, hair wet and both in divers' suits, in some place with a warm climate. And by their feet, Morgan was astounded to see that each had a rebreather tank just like the ones she had found in the pool house at the chateau.

In the other picture, she recognized former President François Mitterand sitting at his desk in the Élysée Palace, with the same two men standing behind his chair, now fully dressed in suit and tie and with brimming smiles on their faces, each clutching a piece of paper.

The certificate in the simple wooden frame was impressive but simple, and really nothing more than a letter written in black ink on official presidential letterhead. It said: "To Jacques Camurier, for special services rendered to the Republic of France, with my personal gratitude," and it was signed "François Mitterand, President of the Republic."

Who was this Jacques Camurier? It was obvious that one of the men in the pictures was Joseph de Carduzac, and could the piece of paper he was holding in the photo with Mitterand be this very letter? *Hmm.* And then it struck her. *Jacques Camurier. Frogman. The rebreathers. Same initials as Joseph de Carduzac. A coincidence, or could it be him by another name? Some kind of alias?* Morgan asked herself. She'd have to pose the question to Alex, delicately.

Or maybe Claire.

Or Luc. No, not Luc.

Alex was a safer bet.

And then a frightening thought: *could the letter be Mitterand's thank you for Bérégovoy's assassination? Or for some other dirty deed?*

As she was contemplating these questions, Morgan found herself in front of a walnut bookshelf reaching to the ceiling. Lots of titles. The de rigueur *Madame Bovary* and *L'Étranger* along with all the other French classics across the top two shelves. But from the middle of the third shelf down, Morgan was surprised to see staring out at her the Eric Raynaud book, *Un crime d'État?* that she had come across in her research on Pierre Bérégovoy. *God! So maybe...*

There were also several books on diving, a book entitled *L'Affaire Greenpeace dans la presse française*—she couldn't for the life of her imagine Joseph being interested in the environmental protest group—and then one in English, called *Eyes of Fire.*

Intrigued by the title, Morgan went to pull this paperback out, but just then she heard the key in the front door.

She did catch a glimpse of the subtitle—*The Last Voyage of the Rainbow Warrior*—before she quickly slipped the book back into its place.

"Morgan," Alex said, smiling as he stood in the doorway of the study, "what are you doing in here?"

"Oh, just taking a stroll through this beautiful apartment while my hair dries a little." And then quickly, to divert his attention from what she had been up to, and because she wanted to collect her thoughts before confronting him with her questions, Morgan added, "Can I borrow your mother's dressing gown to run upstairs to change?"

"Sure, Morgan, but…"

"See you for breakfast in fifteen." She gave him a peck on the lips and was out the door leaving him to lock up.

CHAPTER 16

After spending the morning in leisurely discussion over breakfast with Alex, Luc, Sandrine, Anne and Serge, mostly about the upcoming Conference of African Heads of State—particularly the menu and how the catering would work—as well as their wedding the following June, Morgan was finally able to have some time alone in her room Saturday afternoon to do some Google-based research on all that she had picked up during the last few days. Jacques Camurier, the *Rainbow Warrior*, *Eyes of Fire* and *L'Affaire Greenpeace*. Not wanting to be disturbed, she turned her mobile off, and eagerly booted up her laptop.

The search engine made it all come together for Morgan.

She very quickly learned that Jacques Camurier was one of a team of secret agents sent by France to disable the aging Greenpeace flagship, *Rainbow Warrior*, in order to prevent it from carrying out its mission of disrupting the nuclear tests planned on Moruroa Atoll in French Polynesia. Camurier and another agent, Alain Tonel, were the pair of divers later fingered as the ones who actually placed the limpet mines that blew two large holes in the ship and killed its Portuguese photographer, Fernando Perreira. The clandestine operation, appropriately codenamed *Opération Satanique,* was carried out during the night of July tenth, 1985, as the *Rainbow Warrior* was berthed in Auckland, New Zealand.

The mission might have remained a secret, had it not been for the bungling of some of the other operatives involved in Satanique. Two French agents, masquerading as a Swiss couple called the Turenges, had rented a white campervan to pick up the frogmen and their Zodiac when they returned to shore several miles from the harbor. The Turenges then dropped Jacques, Alain, and another agent, René, who had piloted the Zodiac for the mission, by another parked van René had rented, and the three sped away, heading south. For the next two weeks, Camurier, Tonel, and René roamed around the South Island, generally staying out of sight, but pretending they were tourists when in contact with locals. They eventually separated, and Jacques and Alain even went skiing for a few days before making their way back to Auckland, from where they left New Zealand on the twenty-sixth of July.

The Turenges—Sophie and (another) Alain—were caught by waiting police when they tried to return their rental vehicle. An Auckland taxi driver, having a drink with friends at the Outboard Boating Club, had seen the crew of the Zodiac unload its contents and climb into the van. Thinking they might be thieves, he alerted the police with the Toyota's license plate. The Turenges were detained as they returned the rented van, and upon further examination, New Zealand police determined that their Swiss passports were laughably fake. In spite of being issued in different years, they had close to consecutive numbers i.e. 3024838 and 3024840, and when asked, the Swiss authorities confirmed them as fakes. The investigation also found that they had been in touch with the crew of the chartered yacht, *Ouvea* from Noumea, which had brought the Zodiac and the explosives into New Zealand.

The Turenges were charged with arson and murder, and as they entered a surprise guilty plea of manslaughter, they were sentenced to ten years in prison. They were later identified as Commander Alain Mafart and Captain Dominique Prieur, high-ranking agents of the Direction Générale de la Sécurité Extérieure, part of France's intelligence services. A clear giveaway was that Captain Prieur made the mistake of calling her husband at a Paris phone number which turned out to be a secret number used by the DGSE.

In all, France had sent three teams plus several solitary operatives—numbering eleven or twelve agents in total—to carry out the task of disabling the *Rainbow Warrior*. Of these, only Mafart and Prieur ever faced justice. New Zealand police never had enough evidence against the crew of the *Ouvea*, and they slipped away back to France. Apparently, the sailors were picked up by the French nuclear submarine *Rubis*, in mid-ocean just north of Norfolk Island, the yacht was scuttled, and the crew taken to Tahiti where the four men boarded a plane for Paris. Three were later identified as DGSE operatives—specially trained combat divers from the secret base at Aspretto in Corsica—which is presumably where also Camurier and Tonel had been stationed—and the fourth, as a willing private citizen accomplice, a doctor chosen for his expertise in diving accidents.

The true identities of Jacques Camurier, thirty-five years old at the time, according to the false passport he used, and Alain Tonel, thirty-three—the two frogmen operatives who actually planted the limpet mines on the hull of the Rainbow Warrior—were never revealed. When they had arrived at Auckland Airport on July seventh—three days before the explosions—they claimed to be vacationing physical education teachers at a girls' school in Papeete, in New Guinea. Nothing else ever came to light about them. This was also true of the agent alias François Regis Verlet who arrived a little later on the same day from Tokyo. He was the one who reconnoitered the *Rainbow Warrior* on the day it was blown up, and probably gave Camurier and Tonel the information they used to place the mines.

Not clear also was the identity of René, the leader of the third team according to DGSE sources. Some press articles identified the commander of this team as Jean-Pierre Dillais, alias Jean-Louis Dormand, but this notion was explicitly refuted by Admiral Pierre Lacoste, who was the head of the DGSE between 1982 and 1985, when he was fired after the sordid affair blew up. Some other sources suggested that René may in fact have been Gérald Royal, the brother of Ségolène Royal, former presidential candidate and ex-partner of President François Hollande, and more recently Minister of Environment and Energy.

So, Jacques Camurier has got to be Joseph de Carduzac, Morgan mused as she got up to go to the bathroom. *The age was certainly right. But then who is this other frogman, Alain Tonel?*

She followed the many different threads on Google, and learned that Opération Satanique had been an international public relations disaster for France. There were numerous significant political consequences over the ensuing years, caused not just by the brazen act of sabotage itself, but at least in part by the French government's continued rejection of responsibility at the highest levels, its refusal to cooperate with the New Zealand investigators, flouting of international arbitration and attempted intimidation of New Zealand. For a supposed ally, this was seen as despicable behavior.

The first response from the French Embassy, when approached, was that "…the French Government does not deal with its opponents in such ways..." and to condemn the bombing as a terrorist act. Once the true identities of Mafart and Prieur were unmasked, though, it was impossible for French officials to continue this charade. They were alerted by Mme. Prieur's lawyers that she may be ready to cooperate with the New Zealand authorities, and since she feared for her life, New Zealand police agreed to move her to a military prison patrolled by armed soldiers. With mounting pressure from the media in France and internationally, on August seventh of 1985, President Mitterand and Prime Minister Fabius named Bernard Tricot, a former Secretary-General of the President of the Republic and a respected administrator and civil servant to head up a commission of inquiry in France. Although the report issued on the twenty-sixth confirmed the identities of five of the agents of the DGSE, it claimed they were on a 'surveillance mission' and absolved the French government of any role in the sinking.

This report was met with condemnation and rejected as a 'whitewash' both in France and in New Zealand. When the French press continued digging and brought to light that in fact there had been a third team of frogmen in New Zealand at the time, and that President Mitterand had personally approved the bombing, Tricot admitted that he may have been lied to by officials. According to the respected journal, *Le Figaro*, the decision to sink the *Rainbow Warrior* was taken at a June meeting at the Élysée Palace that included the Minister of Defense, Charles Hernu, Admiral Pierre Lacoste, the then head of the DGSE, and François de Grossouvre, Mitterand's Conseiller du Président, entrusted with security and all other sensitive matters, and that it was not at all believable that de Grossouvre did not inform the president of the decision. Mitterand ordered Prime Minister Fabius to make personnel changes; this led to the resignation of Hernu, and the dismissal of Lacoste.

Hmm. And didn't de Grossouvre also die later in mysterious circumstances? This was what she fleetingly remembered having discovered in her Google research on Mitterand scandals. She would have to go back and check that out.

Faced with public pressure and the threat that Dominique Prieur would crack, Fabius ordered the newly appointed Minister of Defence, Paul Quiles, to get to the bottom of the sordid affair, and on September twenty-third, the Prime Minister made a public statement admitting that agents of the DGSE, acting on orders, had in fact sunk the *Rainbow Warrior*.

The admission of guilt was at least something, but it only spurred calls for compensation and for those responsible to be brought to justice. Fabius had explicitly exonerated the operatives, who were just following high-level commands as he put it, but promised that those who gave the instructions would be punished.

Meanwhile in New Zealand, Mafart and Prieur were condemned and sentenced to ten years imprisonment. The French government found this outrageous, and, in retaliation, they threatened the imposition of an embargo on New Zealand's exports of butter to the United Kingdom and meat to the European Economic Community if they were not released. This would have been catastrophic for the New Zealand economy, so feelers were put out for international arbitration.

With assistance from United Nations Secretary-General, Javier Pérez de Cuéllar, a deal was reached in June 1986, whereby France agreed to issue an apology, drop its threat of an embargo and pay USD seven million in compensation, while New Zealand agreed to allow Mafart and Prieur to serve a three-year sentence at a

French military base on Hao Atoll. In addition, France agreed to pay USD two million to the family of the murdered photographer, USD six million to Greenpeace and Euro 105,000 to the Noumea Yacht Club for the scuttling of the *Ouvea*. The two governments were also instructed to create a fund to promote friendship between their countries, and France was to finance this with an initial contribution of USD nine million.

France flagrantly violated this accord, allowing Mafart to return to Paris on December 14, 1987, supposedly for medical treatment, and then back to the army where he was promoted to full colonel in 1993. Prieur returned pregnant to France on May 6, 1988—her husband had been sent to the Atoll as head of the security facility—and was also promoted in due course. As a result of France's non-compliance, New Zealand demanded further arbitration, which ensued in April 1990, with instructions for France to pay an additional USD two million into the trust fund.

Thus, in all, this lamentable episode cost the French government a sum of more than USD twenty-six million in hard costs on top of the cost of the operation itself, as well as huge political capital at home and internationally. Nevertheless, France continued nuclear tests in the South Pacific until 1992, when President Mitterand suspended them due to intense international and domestic pressure to comply with French obligations under the Non-Proliferation Treaty and clear indications of severe environmental degradation and health impacts throughout the South Pacific. Tests were resumed though in 1995 under President Chirac, in spite of continuing international protests, which however, finally had their effect in bringing them to an end in February of 1996. France signed the Comprehensive Test Ban Treaty in May 1996.

Morgan's head was spinning with all that she had learned that afternoon. She saw in the corner of her laptop that it was already after seven pm, and knew that she would have to hurry if she was going to be ready to join John for dinner at the Brasserie Bordelaise by eight, a hip restaurant downtown. She would have to mull over the implications of the research as she took her shower and got ready.

It seemed more than likely then that Jacques Camurier was Joseph de Carduzac. A secret agent of France, an expert diver, probably trained and stationed at that base in Corsica, whatever it was. In fact, that photo in the study, was that taken there? And was the other man in the picture the agent who used the alias Alain Tonel? And who was he really then?

So Joseph was one of the divers who blew up the *Rainbow Warrior* in July of 1985. Yes, that would be about right—he could have been thirty-five then. And yes, in the picture, he looked to be in his thirties. And was it Joseph and his partner who also did away with Bérégovoy eight years later? Had they become the hit men for Mitterand and his cronies?

It was when she was brushing her teeth that it came to her: if Camurier was Joseph, then could Tonel be the general?

And that brought her to the present. What about Les Nouveaux Girondins?

༺༻

Putting on her lipstick, Morgan wondered whether she should discuss what she had discovered with Alex. How much of this did he know? Would he tell his stepfather? Definitely not—they were not on good terms, and surely he was smart enough to keep her suspicions from him. He might even be happy to learn all this stuff about Joseph de Carduzac. But it certainly seemed that Joseph was very touchy about his past. And clearly, this must be a very sensitive subject if the truth had been such a well-guarded secret for some thirty or so years.

Claire?

Best not to involve her. She might very well tell her mother, who would then tell her stepfather.

Luc? Certainly not. He went to some of those meetings of Les Nouveaux Girondins.

She needed to talk to someone about it.

Rashid? No, well, that might not be fair to the de Carduzacs, to spill their dirty little secret to someone like Rashid. Particularly not fair to Claire, whose friend he was.

How about John? Yes, John, he would be the best to start with. Even though when she had tried to discuss the suggestion that Joseph may have been one of the frogmen who killed Bérégovoy, he had dismissed it as not possible. In any case, he needed to know, since it could have significance for the investigation.

It would be the best to talk this through with John.

And how perfect: she was just on her way to meet with him.

CHAPTER 17

John was standing at the bustling bar of the Brasserie Bordelaise when Morgan breezed in fifteen minutes late. He was engaged in conversation with two other men, but with his eyes fixed on the entrance, his face lit up when he saw Morgan. He came straight over and gave her a peck, saying, "Morgan, how lovely to see you. Here, let me take your coat."

"Monsieur, your table is ready. This way please."

The waitress led them to a table at the corner in the back, which fortunately was somewhat private. While she brought the menus, John said, "You know, Morgan, I can't tell you enough how happy I am to have met you. And to get to know you a little. Even though it was such a terrible event that brought me here on this investigation."

"I am too, John. It's great."

"Well, when we go back, I hope we can see each other in the good ol' US of A—"

Just then, the waitress arrived with the menus. "Madame, monsieur, can I get you a drink?"

"Morgan, do you care for some bubbly?"

"I'm happy with just wine. I think they have an excellent list here."

"Well, then why don't you choose? Something really nice."

"Red, I think, don't you? This is more of a meat place."

The ordering out of the way, Morgan decided to launch right into what was preoccupying her.

"John, you remember, the last time we went out for dinner, I mentioned that ancient diving equipment I found in the pool house at the de Carduzac chateau?"

"Yes, of course. And you were wondering whether de Carduzac *père* could have been one of the frogmen who killed Mitterand's Prime Minister, no?"

"Yes, that was it. Well, John, you won't believe it, but I think I found some more evidence pointing in that direction. Joseph de Carduzac was definitely up to no good when he was younger."

"Oh? So tell me," John said with a smile.

"For one, in his study in their townhouse—you know, in their apartment on the first floor—there is an old black and white photograph of two frogmen in full diving gear. One of them resembles Luc a lot, so I think he must be Joseph. Then alongside it, there is another picture of the same two men smiling, each holding a piece of paper, with President Mitterand in between them looking out from behind his desk in the Élysée Palace."

"So, that doesn't really—"

"What's more, though, John, next to the pictures, there is a framed letter from Mitterand thanking a Jacques Camurier for performing some special services for the good of France. Jacques Camurier, John, not Joseph de Carduzac."

"Hmm. Could Camurier be the other guy in the picture?"

"No. Just listen. I went and googled this Jacques Camurier. And do you know what I found out? Camurier was the alias of one of two frogmen who planted limpet mines that disabled the *Rainbow Warrior* sometime in

July in 1985. You may have read about the Greenpeace ship that was in New Zealand on its way to protest against French nuclear testing in the South Pacific. French agents blew big holes in it and killed a man in the process. The French government tried to do a big cover-up. And they never released the true identities of the two frogmen who carried out the attack."

"So you think this Camurier is de Carduzac?"

"Yes, I'm certain. The diving stuff I saw in the pool house is the very same as in the photo. And would the letter from President Mitterand thanking Camurier be in Joseph de Carduzac's study if they were not one and the same person? The initials 'J' and 'C' for both? Come on, John. Give me a break, it's so obvious—"

"Well, to be the devil's advocate, that may be a very interesting historical fact. Although I'm sure the de Carduzacs would not be too happy if this all got out. In any case, they would certainly deny everything. Plus, there could be a lot of other repercussions. But it doesn't really advance my investigation any—"

"I am not finished yet, John."

"Okay, well. What else do you have then?"

"The *salmis de pigeon*? For madame?" The waitress was holding hot plates in her hand with a tea towel. "The *filet de boeuf*? Monsieur?"

"Thank you."

"*Je peux?*" She refilled their glasses with the Chateau Lanessan 2007 Morgan had selected.

"So, you were saying, Morgan…"

"Hmm. This is amazing," Morgan said, relishing her first bite, the pigeon cooked to perfection in a red wine sauce. The way only the French knew how to cook it. "Well, there were two men who planted the mines on the Greenpeace boat. The other one, who went by the alias Alain Tonel, according to what I found out on Google, was also never identified. But I think he is still very much around, and a good friend of Joseph de Carduzac. In fact, I believe I have met him at the chateau several times."

"So who is this guy?"

"I think Alain Tonel is General André Tolbert, who was, and maybe still is, very high up in the French intelligence services. At least, according to Claire."

"You've got to be kidding."

"What do you mean?"

"Well, Tolbert is the man appointed by President Aragon to head up the investigation into the Brassault explosions. He's all over them."

"There you go! See, we are getting closer to home."

"Still, it could just be an interesting coincidence that doesn't mean very much."

"I have more to tell."

"You are a fount of information tonight, Morgan."

"Joseph de Carduzac and this General Tolbert are founding members of an organization called Les Nouveaux Girondins. I guess it's more like a loose club, nothing formal really."

"Well?"

"You know who the original Girondins were, do you, John? Besides the Bordeaux football club."

"Weren't they one of the groups who participated in the French Revolution?"

"You're exactly right. They were a faction from this part of France that wanted to overthrow the monarchy, but did not go along with the excesses of Robespierre and others. They ended up being guillotined, swept away by the more rabid masses."

"So what's the relevance?"

"Well, according to what Claire and her mother, Madame de Carduzac, have told me, the stated goal of these latter-day Girondins is to do everything in their power to rid France of Aragon and his destructive policies. Just as the original ones plotted to remove the monarchy."

"I'm starting to see where you are going with this."

Just then the waitress appeared and cleared the plates away. "Dessert?"

"Yes, please. We would like to see the menu."

"Of course, monsieur."

"There is one more thing, John. Perhaps most worrying, although again nothing clear cut," Morgan continued when the waitress left.

"What? But first, let's decide what we will have."

"Hmm. The *fondant de chocolat* is my favorite."

"Okay, we'll split that." And John waved to the waitress, ordering the sweet.

"Well, John, to continue with what I wanted to tell you. One of the times I was at the chateau just a few days ago, after a big lunch with the family and the general, Claire and I went down to the pool to sun ourselves. Later in the afternoon, I went to my room to change, and as I passed the door to Joseph's study, I heard voices. Five or six different men, it must have been. Joseph and Luc were there—yes, he goes to some of these meetings too, Luc does, though I don't understand why—the general and two or three others. One with what I thought was a Slavic accent.

"And at least one of the men who sometimes attend is probably a member of the far right, according to Claire, some former mayor of Libourne. Valentin Frantome, yes, that was it. He is the defense critic for the opposition. Another may be the Minister for Veterans—Patrick Joinville, I think, since Madame de Carduzac said he is a member of the group. Anyway, I heard snippets of conversation that are disturbing if you read between the lines. Here, I wrote them down right after, to try and make some sense out of them."

Morgan handed John a piece of paper on which he read the following:

"...*successful, from our point of view...*" General?

"...*the potency of the explosives...*" A measured but unfamiliar tone.

"...*in any case, set the...garble...up nicely...*" Joseph?

"...*the president...garble...*" Unknown? Slavic accent?

"...*today, not as good as we...*" General.

"Yes..."

"Well, I must say, it doesn't amount to much, this... Hmm. Other than maybe the reference to explosives."

"John, you're the one in intelligence. I am surprised you don't see."

"You tell me then what you read into this, Morgan."

The CIA agent seemed a little chagrined, Morgan thought. But maybe just genuinely perplexed.

"Some more wine?" he asked.

And when she shook her head, John poured what remained in the bottle, less the little at the bottom with the dregs, into his glass, just as the waitress brought the sinful looking melted chocolate dessert.

Morgan relished the first spoonful before she continued. "Okay, here is one possible scenario. The general is saying that the bombing at the Brassault facility was successful from 'their' point of view—that is, the point of view of Les Nouveaux Girondins. Somebody comments on the strength of the explosives: were they too strong or maybe not strong enough? In any case, Joseph comments that this has set something up nicely. What though? That is the niggling question. But then there is a reference to the president. Could that be the 'what'? John, could they—this Les Nouveaux Girondins group—be talking about a plot to assassinate the president of France?"

"Holy Mother of Christ! Morgan, you really are into this conspiracy theory business."

"Why not? In fact, could Claire's friend, Rashid, be right, and you guys are barking totally up the wrong tree with your investigation? Rashid claims that it was a French far right group that carried out the Brassault bombing, making it look like it was some jihadist terrorists. That way, they would be building the case to get rid of an incompetent government they hated and also stoke up venom against Muslims whom they also loathe. And now, to complete the task, they will kill the president. And launch a coup d'état."

"That is very dangerous stuff you're putting out there, Morgan. And I must say, highly unlikely—"

"On the contrary, I think it looks more and more possible."

"Hmm. Come to think of it, it is Tolbert who keeps insisting that it was two Algerians working at the Brassault facility who planted the explosives. Even though I and others do not necessarily see it that way."

"See! I am on the right track."

"And *á propos* the explosives. Remember, I told you about the guy who worked at EPC and claimed to have stolen some EXPLUS? Well, the French investigators finally found him…"

"And?"

"He was dead. An overdose of pills, they claim."

"Hmm. Another suicide. Or might he have been done away with?"

"Morgan, you are one suspicious woman."

"Could someone have killed him to destroy a key link in the supply of explosives? Could it have been Tolbert and gang?"

And glancing at the piece of paper still in front of him, John asked, "So, then Miss Marple, what do you think this last comment by the general means?" He pointed to the last line of the note.

"I think he is commenting to Joseph and the others that secret operatives—or more precisely, hit men—today are not as good as the two of them were in their heyday. Only they know how many successes they chalked up in their time. Including the killing of probably at least one prime minister—now maybe two—and possibly many other people we don't know about."

"So, Morgan, you really do think that Joseph de Carduzac and General Tolbert are murderers?"

"Well, initially they were probably just secret operatives ordered to perform some operations by their higher-ups that may have required the elimination of some people. And at some point, they may have started to take matters into their own hands. Especially the general, I think. It seems to have gone to his head."

"At this point, though, Morgan, this is all just speculation. You have no proof."

"Other than circumstantial evidence, no. You're right."

"Nevertheless, all very interesting. And come to think of it, we have seen these far right groups become more active across Europe. With some support, both financial and operational—our intelligence tells us—from our friend Putin, who is clearly aiming to destabilize western democracies. Sowing a little discord in France could be right up his alley."

"I wasn't even thinking of that, but…could that be why there was a man with a Slavic or Russian accent in the meeting I overheard?"

"Hmm. Hard to tell. It is all a bit of a stretch, though. But certainly very interesting. Let me reflect on it. And maybe do a little digging."

"Good. That was all I wanted. But whatever you do, it better be fast."

"We should not speak about this. To anyone."

"That's for sure. This is all very dangerous stuff."

"We'll talk again. Soon."

"Thanks, John, for listening."

CHAPTER 18

Morgan was still reflecting over what she and John had discussed the evening before, when at seven the next night she started to get ready for her date with Alex. He had asked her to accompany him to the Grand Théatre, the opulent eighteenth century opera house of Bordeaux, for a production of Poulenc's *Dialogues des Carmélites,* his chef d'oeuvre about the French Revolution. Morgan loved opera, and so did he apparently, but even though she didn't care much for Poulenc, she was looking forward to the evening out with Alex—another "formal" date, it promised to be extravagant, with an intimate dinner afterward at Garopapilles, a restaurant on rue de l'Abbé de l'Epée, walking distance from the de Carduzac residence—and it would give her a chance to talk to him too about the many things that had started to niggle at her.

She liked Alex a lot, and it was very clear to her by now that he was not involved in any of this...this sordid business she was uncovering. But he may know about Luc, his stepbrother, and Joseph de Carduzac, his stepfather. What they were up to. Maybe even the general. And he might be able to tell her something about Les Nouveaux Girondins. She needed to find some definitive answers, talk to someone whom she felt she could trust.

While she had hesitated earlier to bring her concerns up with Alex because he was one of the family, she was sure now that he would take her side and not run off to Joseph or Luc to tell them how much she knew or surmised. Or even his mother. That, she had decided, could be very dangerous for her.

❦

The evening progressed delightfully. Now that Alex and she had made love the other night, their relationship had moved to an easier and more natural level. They were eager to catch up on the twelve years that had passed since they had first met as children, and, over a leisurely dinner, Alex asked lots of questions about Morgan's studies and plans for the future.

She kept looking for the right moment to bring up her concerns, but it seemed such a shame to spoil the splendid time they were having.

So it was not until they were comfortably sitting side by side on the couch back at the de Carduzac's apartment—Alex having served himself an ample snifter's worth of his stepfather's Pierre de Segonzac Réserve XO Grande Champagne cognac, which he proposed to share with her—when he started to tell about his year of traveling in the South Pacific—that Morgan saw the right opening to lead into her questions.

"So Alex, was it because you wanted to know more about your stepfather's involvement in the *Rainbow Warrior* affair that you decided to go off to Polynesia? To see what you could find out down there?"

Morgan's question seemed to hit home and was greeted by a few seconds of silence, as Alex took a large swig of the cognac. "How do you know about that? No one, not even the family is supposed to know. I'm not even supposed to be aware of it."

"Come on, Alex. The photographs in the study. The framed letter from Mitterand on the wall. The books on the shelf. The diving gear in the pool house. Putting two and two together. Plus a little bit of research, and presto, there you have it!"

"Jesus, Morgan, you are one smart lady. And very dangerous, it would seem."

"There's more, Alex."

"Here, first have a drink, Morgan. We both may need it before we really get into this stuff." He held the large glass bowl under her nose then handed it to her. Morgan took a large sip, and immediately started coughing, spewing some of the expensive fluid out onto the glass table in front of her.

"You need to aspirate it and then roll it in your mouth. Here, like this." Alex chuckled, as he picked the snifter back up from the table where she had put it down, inhaled a small mouthful of the cognac, turned it around in his mouth with his tongue, and—just as Morgan finally stopped coughing—put his arm around her shoulders and kissed her, releasing some of the liquid—which by now had lost much of its stringency—into her mouth.

"Delicious, isn't it?"

"Yeees," Morgan stuttered after a long moment, still gasping for oxygen, not sure whether she meant the cognac, the kiss, or both.

"Morgan, before I answer any of your questions, I want to tell you something," Alex said, looking straight into her eyes.

"What, Alex?" Morgan had not quite recovered yet.

"I'm falling in love with you."

"Alex—" Morgan could not finish her thought because Alex's lips were on hers again, his cognac infused tongue separating them and titillating her tongue. She did not resist, as his hands roved all over her body.

When they came up for air, Morgan stuck to her resolve, and wiping her lips, tried again. "Okay, Alex. Before we go any further right now, I want to talk about what's going on," she said, still relishing the cognac tasting kiss in her mouth. "First, I will tell you what I think I know. What I have found out, and what I believe is happening. You need to know this, and you need to tell me what you know. And then we should see if there is anything we can do about it." Morgan straightened her mini dress and pulled the thin straps back over her shoulders.

"All right, Morgan. Whatever you want."

"You saw me in your stepfather's study, Alex, looking at the pictures on the wall and the framed letter from President Mitterand thanking a Jacques Camurier for special services rendered to France. It's not hard from there to surmise that this Jacques Camurier—who bears a very strong resemblance to Luc and is in one of the pictures with another man, each of them holding a piece of paper, on either side of Mitterand—is Joseph de Carduzac. The re-breather diving gear in the other picture is exactly what I saw in the pool house at the chateau, I am certain of that. And Google tells me that Camurier was one of two frogmen who placed the limpet mines that destroyed the *Rainbow Warrior* in New Zealand in 1985. The French government did not want Greenpeace to disrupt its nuclear tests in Polynesia, and sent some operatives—including your dear stepfather, it seems—to deal with the environmental activists."

"Morgan, that is amazing. Great detective work!"

"The other man in those pictures, who went by the alias Alain Tonel when he helped Jacques Camurier destroy the *Rainbow Warrior*, is, I am quite sure, your stepfather's close friend, General André Tolbert. The initials again, Alex, are the same in both cases."

"I didn't know that. But of course, it makes total sense."

"What do you know about him? The general, that is."

"Well, he was—maybe still is—my stepfather's best friend. They joined the intelligence services together way back when and carried out many other missions together. My real father, too, was one of that team—but Claire told you all that, you said."

"Well, not really." Morgan had, in fact, tried to get him to talk about his real father earlier, without much success.

"Joseph never said much about their activities, though. And like you, based on the circumstantial evidence I discovered, I suspected my stepfather had something to do with the *Rainbow Warrior* incident. You're right, Morgan, that was one of the reasons I went to the South Pacific. To see what I could find out."

"Did you learn anything there?"

"Not much more than you seem to have uncovered here. Although the general being the other guy in the *Rainbow Warrior* affair is news to me. I guess I just didn't get that far."

"I'm quite positive they were a team."

"But of course, everything Joseph did—the very few times he would talk about it—he claimed he did for the good of France."

"I'm sure..." But she wasn't really.

"In any case, when my stepfather left the service to take over the chateau and the family businesses after his own father died, the general stayed on in intelligence. As you know, he rose very high in both the DGSE and the army, both of which are part of the Ministry of Defense here in France. Tolbert commands a great deal of respect and has a lot of contacts, and more importantly, a lot of debts are owed to him. Right across the political spectrum."

"Hmm."

"Under the previous government, which was a conservative coalition, the general became the Deputy Director of the DGSE. Valentin Frantome, another good friend of my stepfather's and his, was the Minister of Defense then. The general was in effect put in charge by Frantome of all the undercover agencies and activities of France and has been running them with an iron fist. He has continued to talk to Joseph and uses him as a sounding board.

"Well, Alex, I'm sure Tolbert is the other man in those pictures. The other frogman. And that leads me to another point, where you may be able to help."

"What's that?"

"Remember the death of Mitterand's ex-prime minister, Pierre Bérégovoy?"

"Yeah, something vaguely comes to mind."

"It was dismissed as a suicide at the time, but there is some evidence to suggest that in fact he may have been assassinated. By two frogmen! Who appeared out of a canal just outside Nevers where he was waiting for someone, supposedly ready to spill the beans on Mitterand and some of his cronies. Apparently, Mitterand and his gang may have wanted to stop him, so they got rid of him."

"Are you suggesting that Joseph could have been involved?"

"No, Alex. But given everything else, it is a question that crops up, doesn't it? Or maybe just the general. I was hoping you could help find an answer."

"Well, no. I don't know anything about this. But I guess I may be able to do some digging around."

"Good. That will help."

"And that brings us back to my own father. My real father," Alex went on, after thinking for a couple of seconds, "who it was claimed died diving off the coast of Borneo."

This was news to Morgan. "I thought he died on a mission."

"The stories are not very clear. Tolbert will not give me a straight answer, and it's all very shadowy. But it seems the general was there, and he claims that my father and he went diving after an operation and a shark got him. Says the pilot of the boat corroborated this in the investigation. Of course, there is nothing in the files."

"Hmm, that's what Claire said."

"But the question remains: could he have been similarly done away with? Just like Bérégovoy? By members of his unit? My stepfather? The general himself?"

"That terrible thought has occurred to me as well, Alex!"

"Phew. Let's not go there, not just yet. I didn't suspect my stepfather had so much baggage." Alex poured another few ounces of cognac into the large balloon shaped glass. "The *Rainbow Warrior* stuff I was starting to investigate, but the former prime minister—if it is true—boy, that's shocking."

"There is still more, Alex," Morgan said quietly, gently moving Alex's hand holding the inhaler toward her mouth and taking a sip.

"What then?"

"There was a series of other high-level murders here—or certainly deaths under dubious circumstances—during and since Mitterand's presidency. Not necessarily carried out by frogmen, nor in any way could they be connected to your stepfather and the general. Except that I think they may have acted as special servants of the presidency and of France. Even, it would seem, sometimes at their own initiative. It is a murky world out there."

"Holy shit, Morgan, just let up, will you—Enough!"

"And then fast forward to today, Alex."

"What do you mean?"

"We both know Joseph de Carduzac and General Tolbert hate Aragon, his government, and his policies. In fact, it seems from what Claire and your mother told me the other day, the two founded Les Nouveaux Girondins as a forum for like-minded friends to pursue ways to get rid of them."

"That all is true, as far as I know. At least, as a discussion forum."

"And then we have this explosion at the Brassault site. Killing Aragon's prime minister, as well as two other key ministers. On the surface, yes, it all looks like jihadists from North Africa."

"You're…you're not suggesting that my stepfather and the general were behind that…bombing?"

"I don't know, Alex. I'm just raising questions. Could they, at the very least, have facilitated getting the explosives to whoever planted them?"

"God, what a monstrous thought!"

"Well, as it happens, General Tolbert was appointed to head up the Brassault investigation by the president. And John tells me that he has been insisting that it was two Algerian brothers who did it … and is not open to looking into any other theories. Could that be to divert suspicion?"

"Morgan, this is too much. You're freaking me out."

"And when John and Peter went to interview the employees of EPC—the explosives firm that manufactures EXPLUS, which was found at the Brassault site—a worker of Algerian descent told them that one of his French colleagues had approached him to see if he wanted to partner in selling some explosives he was stealing. This colleague has since been found dead. The French investigators say it was suicide. But—and this fits everything I'm finding—could he not have been murdered by someone who wanted to break the link of evidence? After all, the guy could very well have fingered the ones who did the bombing."

"Hmm. Well…"

"I'm not finished, Alex. Even more disturbingly, the other day at the chateau, I overheard a conversation in your stepfather's study—he was there, Luc, the general, and three or maybe more others—that suggested they may be going after the president. Or, at the very least, helping to create enough instability to have an excuse to remove him and take over." And she added, somewhat sarcastically, "But all for the good of the Republic, as you say."

"That's over the top, Morgan. I can't believe it. Joseph? No, and something like that—a coup d'état— would never happen here, in modern day France. You've been reading too much conspiracy stuff lately, Morgan. It simply can't be."

"Even more disturbingly, John also told me that the CIA has some evidence that the Russians are providing support to far right groups across Europe. To destabilize democracies in the West. I am not saying that's what's happening here, but it's something we should have in the back of our minds, don't you think?"

"This is all quite unreal. Here and now in France? A right wing coup d'état? Perhaps even with Russian backing? You must be dreaming in Technicolor, is what I would say."

"Well, we can deny it all we want. I copied down the snippets I overheard. The piece of paper I told you about is up in my room. If you wish, we can go and see."

"Sure. Let's go upstairs. I'd like to get to the bottom of this." Alex finished what was in the glass, picked up the bottle and took both over to the counter.

"Why don't we just stay up there for the night since Claire and Rashid are still away?" Morgan suggested, straightening her dress and finding her shoes. "The apartment is empty. And all my stuff is up there."

"Good idea. I'll just get my toothbrush."

CHAPTER 19

They went up to Claire's flat, but as soon as they closed the door behind them, Alex took Morgan in his arms and kissed her. She responded, and it was not long before they were naked, bodies entwined on Morgan's bed, making love.

It was only, once Morgan had a chance to catch her breath—after first, Alex had brought her to the height of ecstasy with his tongue, and then both of them had reached climax within seconds of each other—that she remembered why they had come up to her room in the first place.

"Alex, that was wonderful," Morgan said, reaching over and kissing him on the lips. "You're amazing."

"You are pretty hot yourself, *mademoiselle*. Especially for an American."

"What would you know, you...you...you dickhead?" She got up on her knees, straddling Alex and playfully giving his member a stroke before she slid off the bed and went over to her desk. "And now I'm going to find that piece of paper we came to look at up here."

After a few moments of rummaging around, Morgan exclaimed loudly, banging on the desktop in frustration. "Shit, Alex, it's not here. I left it in my calendar, folded up at the relevant date, here—the day I overheard the conversation—but it's gone. Someone must have taken it. Shit, shit, shit!"

"Are you sure, Morgan? It's got to be there. Look again. Search all over. Maybe it fell out. Things don't just disappear."

Alex got out of bed and came over to where she was kneeling by the desk, still naked.

"I have looked everywhere. It's not here, Alex."

"Well, who the hell could have taken it? Claire? Or Rashid?" He reached around from behind, cupping her breasts in his hands.

"No, they've been away for some time. Besides, Claire and I never go into each other's rooms."

"Who then?" He kissed her on the back of the neck. "The cleaning woman?"

"Oh, fuck!" Morgan said, disentangling herself from Alex. She hardly ever used that word. "Fuck, fuck, fuck!"

"Whew! What now?"

"Could it have been Luc who found it? When he stayed in the apartment with Sandrine? When he gave his place up to Anne and Serge that night they were here?"

"Hmm. Would he come in here?"

"Alex, it must have been—Oh, no, no, no!" Morgan was on the verge of tears. "That means he knows that I may suspect—"

"What?"

"—what Les Nouveaux Girondins are up to."

"So what was on the piece of paper? Do you remember what you wrote down?"

"Yes, I think so." Morgan opened the top drawer to get a pencil and then started to write on a notepad on top of the desk. "I will try and reconstruct it."

"While you do that, I will pop into the bathroom."

Moments later she had it, and when Alex came back,

she handed him the notepaper, saying, "I think that was it."

He read the following out loud:

"'...successful, from our point of view...' General?

"'...the potency of the explosives...' A measured but unfamiliar tone.

"'...in any case, set the...garble...up nicely...' Joseph?

"'...the president...garble...' Unknown? Slavic accent?

"'...today, not as good as we...' General.'"

"Well?"

"Doesn't make much sense..."

"Come on, Alex! Coming right after the Brassault attack, don't you think the first line might be a reference to it? The general, saying 'successful from our point of view'? Especially when you couple it with the next sentence, where they talk about the potency of the explosives. They were either too strong or not strong enough for their liking."

"Well, maybe. But it could be anything. They could be just talking about a construction site, you know, where explosives were used. You are reading whatever you want into it, Morgan."

"Okay then, humor me a bit. The third and fourth lines could indicate that they have something planned, something to do with the president. Could it be that they plan to bump him off?"

"Hmm. I guess. Shit. No, that is not possible. But again..."

"And in the last line, the general could be saying that today's hit men are not as good as they were. Your dear stepfather and the general, that is. In their heyday."

"Okay, Morgan, so what if what you are saying is true? What do you want me to do about it?"

"Huh." Morgan growled in frustration. "Don't you see what this means, if I'm right?"

"Well, yes…"

"There is a plot against the president. When they will carry it out, I don't know. But there is this big African leaders' conference coming up which Luc and his company are catering. Here in Bordeaux. Could that be the venue they are planning to strike at?"

"Maybe. Gosh, Morgan, you're way ahead of me. Luc. My stepfather…"

"And don't you see? If Luc thinks that I might know, then I am not very safe, am I? I'm afraid he would share it with your stepfather and the general, and then those Nouveaux Girondins or whoever certainly won't want me going around and blabbing to everybody about their plot to blow up the president. Along with countless other French and foreign politicians and innocent bystanders."

"Merde. You're right. We've got to get you away from here. Quickly."

"But first, somehow we have to try to do something to stop this idiocy, don't you think?"

"Well, yes, but what?"

"I've been trying to get in touch with John. He needs to know as soon as possible and move on this. He'll know what to do. But I haven't been able to reach him. He does not answer his phone."

"Yeah, he could certainly help."

"Hmm. Maybe I will call Jérôme in the morning. He should know how to get in touch with John."

"Yes, they're good friends."

"Alex, maybe what you should do is go and see Luc first thing, and without letting on, try to find out what he knows. What Les Nouveaux Girondins are up to. To see whether what we're surmising here is…well, actually real. Do whatever you must to get on the inside. Yes, tell him that you will be one of the waiters at the conference events if he wants."

"That's a good idea…"

"It's important that you disabuse Luc of the idea that we—especially you—suspect anything."

"But, Morgan, we must find somewhere for you to go. Somewhere, where you'll be safe."

"Like where?"

"Hmm. Maybe I can ask one of my friends to hide you."

"It can't be anyone obviously connected to you. They would already know that we're spending time together, but not how much I know or surmise. Nor that I have told you everything. But if I hide at one of your friends' places, it will be pretty clear…"

"I guess you're right."

"Jérome! I'll ask him."

"Call him first thing. As early as you think is reasonable. And I'll track down Luc."

Putting an end to any further discussion of their plight, Alex wrapped his muscular arms around Morgan, lifted her back on the bed, and kissed her deeply. It did not take long for him to get aroused. He gently entered her, and they made love once again before drifting off to sleep.

CHAPTER 20

It was just after seven when Morgan rolled over in bed, and still groggy after the night of intense talk and lovemaking, reached for her phone. She tried John's number again but had no success, so she scrolled down for Jérome's, and pressed the call button.

"Hello, Jérome. Morgan here. I'm sorry to disturb you so early…"

Alex, beside her, propped himself on one elbow, placing his other hand on the inside of the thigh closest to him.

"No, no. I'm up already. Just making my coffee. What is it, Morgan?"

"Jérome, may I come and see you?"

"Sure. Let's meet in my office at the university. Say ten o'clock?"

"No, I mean right now. Can I come over to your place? I can pick up some croissants if you would like—"

"Is everything okay? But yes, of course." Fortunately, even though it was highly unusual for a student of his to call so early and ask to see him at home, the professor seemed to clue in immediately that something extraordinary was behind the request. "My address is…"

Morgan found a pencil and copied it on the back of the note where she had reconstructed the overheard conversation. "Thanks a lot, Jérome. See you soon. Bye."

☙❧

They quickly showered and got dressed. As they were about to go out the door, Alex said, "Morgan, you should take your passport. Just to be sure. Maybe a change of clothes, too."

"Why?"

"I have been thinking, and you're right. It may be best for you to get out of France as quickly as possible."

"You mean it could be that dangerous?"

"Also, it's not clear when you'll be able to return to this apartment safely."

"Yes, I see your point."

"When you come right down to it, if what you say is correct, these guys—my stepfather possibly included, I hate to say it—just killed thirty people. Probably many more earlier. And you have convinced me: they may be getting set to bump off some other world leaders. So, on reflection, I think getting rid of you would not be a big problem for them if they thought you were at any danger to their plans."

"I guess I can't argue with you."

Morgan quickly threw her purse, passport, the return portion of her ticket, a skirt, two T-shirts, some underwear, and a toothbrush into her backpack along with her iPad and a couple of textbooks. She glanced fondly around the apartment, thinking that she might not be back here anytime soon. Once out the door, and just as she was locking up, they heard footsteps coming up the stairs.

"Why, Luc! Up so early?" Alex asked, surprised to see his stepbrother's head appear just above the ornate cast iron banister.

"Yeah. I was coming to get Morgan." Luc threw her a stern glance. "And you too, Alex, if I found you here. But of course, I should have known."

"What, Luc? An invitation for breakfast? How nice. Sorry, but I've got an important class I need to run off to," Morgan lied breezily.

"No. You must come with me to the chateau. Claire is there, and she's not well. She asked to see you. She needs your help."

Under the circumstances, Morgan did not like Luc's tone.

"I'd love to, but I can't, Luc. I have to run right now. Please give her my love." And she tried to slip past the older de Carduzac son, who blocked her way and grabbed her by the arm as she came alongside.

"Luc, for Christ's sake, let her go. She said she needs to go."

"Alex, you don't understand—"

"I said let her go, asshole, or I'll beat the shit out of you," Alex said, nudging Luc off balance, so that he had to grab for the balustrade, allowing Morgan the chance to untangle from his grip and slip away.

"Bye, you guys. Have fun at the chateau." She skipped down the stairs as fast as she could, and just before exiting through the front door, yelled back, "I'll call to see how Claire is doing."

"See you tonight," Alex shouted after her, hoping she would realize that it was meant to put his stepbrother off the track. "Luc, we've got to talk…"

಄಄಄

On the way to the Konatés' place, Morgan dialed Claire's cell phone. She let it ring many times, but there was no answer, so she left a message. She also tried John again, without success. Less than half an hour after leaving Rue Emile Godard, Morgan rang the bell at the building at 23 Rue Lapeyre behind Place de la Victoire. When the front door opened, she quickly bounded up the stairs and was met by Jérome standing in the open doorway, wearing jeans and a polo shirt.

"So, Morgan, tell me what's going on," the professor said, as he ushered her in and took the bag of croissants she proffered, leading the way into the kitchen. "Why the urgency to see me?"

"Well, there's a lot to tell. But first, Jérome, I'm really worried about John. I haven't been able to get in touch with him. It's very important."

"Let me try him." Jérome grabbed his phone from the counter, and scrolling down, dialed the number. "Coffee?" He pressed the speaker button, so Morgan would hear the other end.

"Yes, please. And I'd love one of those croissants. They were still warm when I got them." She realized how hungry she was after all the late night talking and lovemaking.

"Sure. Coming up." The phone rang and rang, making the entire countertop vibrate, but with no answer, as Jérome poured two cups from the pot and served the fluffy pastries on plates.

"See. It's been the same since earlier yesterday. I'm really worried."

"Hmm. John is a busy guy, but he usually calls back…"

"Well, I've left him several messages already."

"I have Peter's number. Maybe I'll ring him."

"Good idea. He might know something."

But the CIA explosives expert was not there either, asking callers to leave a message, assuring them that he would phone them back.

"I can call the American Consul, but Peter's probably a better bet. Maybe let's wait to see what he says."

"Jérome, I just don't know…" She had trouble fighting the tears back.

"So tell me, Morgan. What's going on?"

And Morgan did tell him, everything she knew, everything she had surmised, everything she had told John and Alex. She finished her story by saying, "And just this morning Luc showed up at the apartment, wanting to take me to the chateau. It seemed by force, if necessary—but luckily, Alex was there—on the pretext of seeing Claire, who Luc said is ill and needs me. I wouldn't put it past them to be holding her against her will until this is all over."

"Well, you are safe here, Morgan. You just need to lie low, not go out." Jérome glanced at his watch before continuing. "I will go off to the university. I have meetings set up with a few students, and it's probably best to keep to my program. If for no other reason than to avoid any questions. Let's hope that, in the interim, Peter will call me back, and we can put our heads together with him and John. I'll try to arrange a meet-up for later today if they're available, so we can figure out what to do."

"Thanks, Jérome. I really appreciate it."

"So, just make yourself at home, Morgan, and I'll be back in the evening. Too bad Marie is not here. I know she would love to look after you, but I am sure you'll be fine."

"Yeah, thanks. I'll just get caught up on my work. At the very least, for your seminar, Professor Konaté." She flashed him a smile, as she rummaged around in her bag for her iPad and books.

And Jérome left her alone in the apartment.

CHAPTER 21

Morgan woke to the sound of keys in the door, followed by Jérome's weary "Hi. Anyone home?" greeting just a little after six-thirty. She jumped up from the sofa where she had dozed off, and eagerly answered with a "Hello, Jérome. Any news?"

There was a long silence while the professor put his briefcase down and paused in the hall to rummage through the mail. He finally answered as he came into the living room. "Well, Morgan, Peter called just ten minutes ago. Caught me on my way from the tram. He's up in Paris."

"So? What did he say?"

"I'm afraid the news is not good, Morgan." He went over to where she was standing, took both her hands, and looked into her questioning eyes. "Peter told me that John was found dead. Yesterday. At the Brassault site."

"What? No, no, no. It can't be true." Morgan could not hold back the tears, and crumpled against Jérome, folding herself into his arms. "God, that's horrible!"

"I'm sorry. He was my friend too."

"He was so…so full of life. And so smart."

"Yes…"

"How?"

"Peter was very brief. He was in some meetings and

could not really talk. He said he would call later, or tomorrow if he can." Jérome moved Morgan over to the sofa and gently sat her down.

"Jérome, I just can't—I can't believe it. How did it happen?"

"He said some kind of explosion. At the site. Maybe some remainder explosives from the original bombing. The French investigators are not letting anyone near there. They are claiming now that there may still be explosive material around, left by the terrorists, and that's what caused it. You know, those nanocomposites—"

"No, Jérome. No. I don't believe that at all. A bunch of lies."

"What then?"

"No. They're blaming it on jihadists again. Explosives placed by them. No, it's not true."

"What do you mean, Morgan?"

"Remember, I told John what I had found out, and he said he would do some digging. I think he was killed because he was asking questions that some people did not like. General Tolbert for one, I'm sure—"

"Come on, Morgan, you're upset. So am I." Jérome did not seem to buy her explanation. "Let's have something to drink. What would you like?"

"Do you have some wine? That would be great," she said, remembering too late that Jérome, as a follower of Islam, was a teetotaler.

"Sure. I'll open a bottle. Red?"

༺✶༻

Over a therapeutic *omelette aux fines herbes* and a *salade verte* they prepared jointly, accompanied by a citron pressé for Jérome and the rest of the Chateau Haut Méthée 2009, the prize-winning *petit chateau* Jérome had opened earlier for Morgan, they discussed what they should do. If Morgan was right, there was some urgency, they realized, since the African Heads of State Conference was to take place in two days, with the opening reception the evening before. Tomorrow, at six pm. Jérome, as one of the leading experts on North Africa and Islam in France, had received an invitation to attend the cocktail with Marie and had been asked to be available the following day to give advice to the president and officials as and when required.

When they were washing up, the professor took the card embossed with the presidential seal off the bulletin board by the fridge and showed it to Morgan.

"You know what, Morgan? You should come with me to this reception tomorrow. In Marie's place, since she is still in Africa. No one will know the difference."

Morgan was not sure this was such a good idea. "What would that do? Plus, I don't have anything to wear."

"That's not a problem. You are similar in build to Marie—maybe a little taller—but I am sure we can find you something in her wardrobe that will work. The point is we could then seek out Martin Lemaire, who was recently named deputy secretary general or something like that and is one of the president's key economic advisors. I know him from ÉNA, and I'm sure he will be attending. We can tell him of the threat to the president's life. And that you believe there might be a plot against the government."

"Would he listen? And even if he did, wouldn't he just run straight to the general and his team?"

"I could tell him to stay away from Tolbert and to tell the president directly. He is a good guy, and smart, though a bit full of himself. Yes, that's what we will do. Morgan, a digéstif? Coffee? Or a *tisane*?"

"Well, I guess, at least that would be something." But

she was skeptical. "Do you have any herbal teas, Jérôme?"

"Marie has some Kusmi teas, I think. I'll go look."

"Sure, anything is fine. Maybe it would be a good idea if I brought along this little note tomorrow, with the conversation I overheard." She picked up the piece of paper she had shown Jérôme earlier. "At least that might help us convince your friend that there is some danger to the president."

"Yes, of course." Jérôme was still not sure that Morgan was right about what the exchange she had overheard meant. "Hmm. You know what? I can also try and reach Zaida Bensoussan, another friend from ÉNA. She is now the minister of justice, an excellent lawyer. Born in Algeria, as it happens. A really good lady. Not a Socialist, but a member of the Green Party. Always fights for social justice and environmental protection. No doubt she will still be in Paris tomorrow and not here, but she could still alert the president."

"Do you really think it is safe, Jérôme? For me to go with you?"

"Well, I hope so. I don't think they would try anything against you at the reception. In front of all the guests and those heads of state. And the media. That would raise too many questions. We'll just have to be careful, though. It might even work to our advantage by showing them that you think you're not doing anything out of the ordinary. Set them at ease, thinking that you don't know anything."

"Yeah, I guess you're right."

"And I could just be bringing one of my foreign students—albeit a very pretty one—to the party, since my wife is not here. A very French thing to do, don't you think?" Jérôme chuckled as he brought the teapot with two cups and saucers, a sugar bowl.

"Thanks, Jérôme, for all your help. And for putting me

up. I don't know where else I would go."

"Well, I'm glad I could help out. But it is really I—as a French citizen, although of an immigrant father—who have to thank you. Because you may be helping save democracy in France. And the lives of the president, and many other important people. And prevent us Muslims from getting the blame one more time for terrorism. N'est-ce pas? Sugar?" Jérome poured the tea.

"No thanks, Jérome."

"And also help us avoid massive embarrassment internationally. Plus, a huge scandal."

"Alex thinks I should leave the country as soon as possible."

"Your friend may be right."

"He thinks that I may be next on their list. After John. Jérome, I'm really scared."

"Well, let's see what happens tomorrow," Jérome said, glancing at his watch. "Good Lord, it's late. And I had promised to Skype Marie. Will you excuse me?"

"Sure. Go ahead. I'm tired anyway, so I think I'll hit the sack."

"Do you have everything?"

"Yes, thank you, the accommodations are luxurious." He had shown her the guest quarters earlier, and indeed, they were more than adequate. "Good night, Jérome."

"*Bonne nuit.*" And he kissed her on both cheeks, retiring with his cup of Prince Wladimir Kusmi tea to his little home office where he had his laptop all set up for the Skype call with his wife.

享受

Despite the kindly professor, Morgan felt very alone when she shut the bedroom door behind her. And not just alone, but afraid. What was going to happen to her, if these people—whoever they were—were really after her? Hadn't they already killed John to protect themselves and the pursuit of their crazy cause? John…tears came to her eyes at the thought of the friendly American intelligence officer. And then that EPC employee, Bonnard or whatever his name was. Many more too, before, if indeed they were the perpetrators of the Brassault incident.

How come no one else saw what she saw? Jérome had, yes, finally gone along with it, but she could see that he was still not totally convinced. John, too, had taken some time to come around. Alex, perhaps—maybe he knew his own family and understood. She really yearned to talk to him now, but as she took out her mobile, she decided that to phone or message him would be a mistake. Alex could be with Luc or his stepfather, and a call or SMS from her just then would not be a good idea. She would have to wait for him to get in touch when he could.

Puzzling too, that Claire had not called back. But better not try her now either, in case 'they'—whoever 'they' were—had seized her phone.

Am I becoming paranoid?

Morgan ran a hot bath for herself in the big jacuzzi, hoping that would relax and comfort her. It was once she had been soaking in the hot water for twenty minutes or so—when she finally turned the jets off and was starting to feel that she was sliding into a different level of consciousness—that her mobile started to play her favorite Beatles' tune, "We all live in a yellow submarine." She jumped out of the huge tub, grabbing a towel on the way and ran to get her cell from the bedside table. She was ecstatic when she saw on the screen that it was Alex, and even more so when she heard his deep voice on the other end say, "Hi Morgan. How are you?"

"Okay, I guess. Other than I miss you very much."

Morgan tried to towel herself with her free hand, as a pool of water started to form around her feet. Not quite dry, she slipped under the duvet to keep warm. She almost blurted out how terribly afraid she was, and that John was now dead too, but held back in case somebody was listening.

"Me too. Where are you?"

"You know where." She thought it better not to give out any more useful information. In case someone was eavesdropping. "In a big bed. With nothing on, you might be delighted to know." *Eat your heart out, pervert, whoever is listening in!*

"Good. I love it."

"Did you find out anything?"

"Nothing." He was being tight-lipped too. Maybe someone was indeed tapping their conversation. "Morgan, I'll be working for Luc at the reception for the African Heads of State tomorrow. But after…"

"I will be there too, as someone else's date."

"That's great." Alex's voice showed his surprise and happiness at the news. "Maybe afterward, you'll be mine. So bring your stuff."

What on earth could he be referring to?

Of course, her passport! *He wants to help me get away. No, he just knows I won't be able to go back to Jérome's since they will have seen me with him.* Suddenly, the precariousness of her situation hit her full force. Yes, hopefully, Alex was thinking about how to get her out of this mess.

Once they hung up, now shivering not from cold but from fear, she went through the alternatives she had in front of her. She could, of course, not go to the reception and avoid exposing herself to danger. But even if she just holed up at the Konaté's for a while, they would eventually track her down. And she had to do everything she could to help stop this crazy plot. To prevent the loss of many more lives.

Now Jérome was expecting her to go with him, too. More importantly, she would never forgive herself if she did not try to alert the president and his entourage of the possible plot to kill him. But if she did go to the cocktail party, and she and Jérome tried to tell the president's men of what she thought Les Nouveaux Girondins could be plotting, they—if some of them were there—would no doubt see her. And even if they weren't at the reception, General Tolbert, as the effective head of all the intelligence services, would find out for sure. They would then do everything in their power to discredit, capture, and silence her. Maybe even kill her. And very likely, before the meetings the next day. Yes. Unless Alex and Jérome could somehow help her get away.

But she knew there was no choice. She had to go to the reception. That was what she must do, there was no question.

Now she had to try and sleep. Because tomorrow would be a big day.

CHAPTER 22

The next day was not easy for Morgan since she did not dare leave Jérome's apartment. It was sunny and warm fall weather, and she would have loved to go for a run along the quay, or even out to the de Carduzac chateau to visit the supposedly ailing Claire. But that would have been folly, she told herself. Even calling her friend, despite her promise, was not a good idea. So she had to be content with sitting by an open window and trying to take her mind off the precariousness of her situation, and particularly John's disturbing death, by catching up on the reading for all her courses.

Around four, since Jérome was not back yet, she took her shower, thinking it would be best to start looking through Marie's wardrobe for an appropriate dress if she was going to go to the reception. They had talked about finding one of Marie's dresses for her the evening before with Jérome, but with all the other issues, they had simply not done anything about it.

Morgan had not met Marie, but she did look at the several pictures of her alone and with Jérome on the walls and positioned in prominent places throughout the apartment. Jérome's wife was extremely pretty, with long dark hair, but of slighter build than Morgan. She wondered whether Marie's dresses would fit her or be too small. Especially the shoes might be a problem.

The apartment had been totally redone several years before, so the big walk-in closet off the professorial couple's bedroom was the obvious place to go. Once she found it, still just in her panties after the shower, she started rummaging through the dresses neatly arrayed on hangers. Fortunately, there was a big mirror right in the closet, so the process of selecting what to wear was very efficient.

So it did not take Morgan long to settle on a simple black cocktail dress, strapless and above-knee length. It was perfect, not too flashy, but still showing off her long legs and well-tanned shoulders. Not bad at all, she told herself glancing in the mirror, and then set her mind to the next question. Tights, stockings or nothing? She decided on just skin, since she didn't think it would be appropriate to snoop through Marie's lingerie and stocking drawer, and besides, why cover up one of her best assets? Next, the shoes. This could be the biggest problem, she thought, but once she started to look through Marie's dress shoes neatly lined up on the floor of the closet, she was pleasantly surprised to find the right pair pretty quickly. Black velvet stiletto pumps, again simple, and just a bit small. Nevertheless, she told herself, she would manage to squeeze into them for the couple of hours the reception might last.

Pleased with what she had found, Morgan was just exiting the couple's bedroom dressed to the nines, carrying the shoes, when she heard the lock in the door, and in stepped Jérome.

"Wow. Morgan, don't you look smashing!"

"I was just—"

"No, no. I was hoping you would go ahead and find something of Marie's to wear. I'm running late. Sorry."

"I just need to put my make-up on, and then I'll be ready."

"Good. Give me twenty minutes. I'll order a taxi now."

✺✺✺

On the way to the reception, Jérome reported that he and his friend, the minister of justice, had exchanged calls, but had not talked, and he had finally decided, against his better judgment, and only because of the urgency of the situation, to leave her a message. That he had evidence of a murderous coup d'état against the Aragon government. By what he thought, were right-wing forces. And for her to call him as soon as possible.

Jérome also informed Morgan that Peter had still not called back.

The taxi dropped the good-looking couple in front of the Palais Rohan. The originally planned venue for the reception and all the next day's meetings had been switched from the beautifully restored Bourse on the quays to the stately old palace because of security concerns. The huge hall at the former stock exchange happened to be adjacent to a building with an underground parking facility, which, as Morgan later learned, would have been next to impossible to secure.

At the intricate wrought-iron gates, armed security guards checked the invitation and requested photo IDs. Fortunately, Jérome had thought to bring along his and Marie's university cards with their very blurry pictures, and he pulled these out of his wallet rather nervously. But the guards merely glanced at them—they were distracted by the professor's stunning companion—before letting them through.

Guests were already packed into the large ballroom, and Jérome surmised that the *liste d'invités* must have included not just those involved in the conference, but also supposed experts like himself as well as assorted local and regional dignitaries.

"That means the de Carduzacs could be here as well," Morgan said, giving Jérome a worried look. "Don't you think?"

"Sure, so we better be quick about finding my friend. Stay by my side while I look around for him." Fortunately, Jérome was taller than most of the guests, so he could search the salle above the heads.

As they were moving slowly through the crowd, all of a sudden, there was Alex standing in front of Morgan, handsome in waiter's black tie, a tray in hand with a choice of champagne flûtes or glasses of water or juice.

"Champagne, mademoiselle?"

"But of course. Merci." She flashed him a smile as she whisked a flûte off the tray.

"Monsieur?" Jérome took a glass of orange juice as Alex leaned in closer to them and said in a low voice, "Okay. My stepfather and mother, Luc, the general are all here. Over there somewhere." He pointed with his chin to the other end of the hall. "It is just a matter of time before they see you. Morgan, I will have my eyes on you all the time—and boy, you don't realize what a pleasure that is—and you watch me too. Do what you need to, but when you are ready, or you see my signal that it is time to go, you meet me over there, right away, by that side door." Again, he nodded with his chin. "It's important that we move quickly. Jérome, you should continue to be as visible as possible, mixing with the other guests to try and take the attention away from our get away. Understood?"

"Thanks, Alex." Morgan took a big sip of her champagne, flashing him a grateful smile. In one of the mirrors that covered the wall behind him, she caught sight of Rashid over in the distance making the rounds through the crowd with a tray and some full glasses.

"Morgan, I see my friend." Jérome grabbed her free hand. "Come with me." They made their way through the tangle of bodies, Morgan trying not to spill the glass Alex had managed to fill just before they took off, finally arriving next to two men roughly of Jérome's age, standing and talking near the buffet table.

"Martin, I was hoping to find you here."

"Jérome! What a pleasant surprise. How good to see you." The rather chubby man Jérome had addressed as 'Martin' shook his proffered hand. "It's been a long time. Let me introduce my colleague, Jean Pelletier. Jean is on the political side."

"And this is Morgan Kenworthy, a student of mine from California."

"Very pleased to meet you, Morgan. Hmm. The Golden State is my favorite state in the union, I must say. Almost as good wine and food as we have here in France, wouldn't you agree, Jérome? The women are more beautiful in a very natural sort of way—if I may add, you, my dear Morgan, being by far the best proof of that I have had the pleasure of seeing in a long time. And the weather is much better there. But unfortunately, you do have earthquakes."

What a jerk! Typical French male sexist comment, too, Morgan thought to herself. But she took it in stride and even managed a smile.

"Martin, there is something very important I have to tell you. And there is no time to waste."

"What is it, my friend? You can talk in front of Jean, no problem."

Jérome leaned forward, glanced around and said softly, "We—Morgan, mostly—have uncovered what we think may be a plot, possibly to kill the president of France and the ministers and heads of state attending the conference—"

"*Mon Cher Ami,* we know all about it. Security is onto it, don't you worry," Martin said, smiling as he put his hand condescendingly on Jérome's shoulder. Morgan took a big gulp of her champagne to hide her surprise at what she had just heard, deciding that she definitely did not like this guy. Did they really know? And if so, what exactly, and how?

"Those Muslim terrorists won't get near the conference. That was partly why we moved the venue. My friend, we have checked everything out here at this site. Everything. And on-going security measures are extremely stringent."

Yeah, right, Morgan thought. So stringent that they let me in on Marie's faded university ID card, you asshole. No problem.

"No, Monsieur Lemaire, that's not it. It's not Muslims from Northern Africa or the Middle East. It is local dignitaries, some of the guests here, people even in your government, in the intelligence services we suspect." As she said this, Morgan caught sight of Luc talking to the general and his father and two other men, looking at her and gesticulating in her direction. Searching frantically for Alex, she continued, "Anyway, Professor Konaté will explain. I have to run off. My boyfriend is signaling to me. Bye." Fortunately, she caught sight of Alex over by the side door and started heading that way. As she did so, she overheard the professor's insufferable friend ask, "Who is this *ravissante* American girl? Jérome, I would like you to give me her phone number."

Just then, there was a big commotion by the main entrance to the ballroom as the president and his entourage arrived, bodyguards surveying the crowd, causing everybody to turn in their direction.

The distraction was enough to allow Morgan to join Alex, and the two of them disappeared through the side door.

He gave her a fleeting kiss, and said, "This way, fast. We've got to get out of here before they can stop us. Or follow us for that matter."

"Where are we going?"

"You'll see. My Tante Clothilde's flat. Which is not too far. I have thought about it. It's the best place for you. No one will suspect that you are there."

∽∾∽

"Alex, thanks. Thanks for doing this," Morgan said, as they walked quickly across Place Pey Berland toward the tram tracks that led up Rue Vital Carles. "I don't know what I would do without you. I am so, so afraid. So lost. Especially now that John is dead." She snuggled close as she struggled to hold back the tears.

"What? How—And how did you find out?"

"Jérome tried to call him several times too, and when there was no answer, he phoned some CIA colleague John had introduced us to. Peter, an explosives expert. Chapin, I think his last name was."

"What did this Peter Chapin tell the professor?"

"Not much. Except that the French investigators claimed he was killed by some explosives at the Brassault site. Left there by the jihadists who blew it up. Ha."

"Hmm."

"But I don't believe that. I think he was eliminated because he was asking questions that hit too close to home. By Tolbert and his gang."

"So you think my stepfather and Luc may have been involved?"

"I didn't say that. I don't know what to think anymore." And then she added, "No, maybe not. They are more on the periphery, it seems."

"I don't know. It's all getting too complicated. But we had better get you away somehow. Anyway, here we are for now. My aunt's place."

The building where Chantal's older sister owned an apartment was in fact just a few blocks away from Place Pey Berland, diagonally opposite the bookstore Mollat on Rue Vital Carles, toward the Grand Théatre. As soon as they got to the main entrance, Alex punched four numbers into the keypad, explaining to Morgan, "Fortunately, I recall the code from before I went away. I used to stay here when my parents were spending more time at Rue Emile Godard. The number is fifteen thirty-seven. Remember it in case you go out." They quickly ran up the two flights of stairs, and Alex easily found the key hidden in a niche in the wall just below the lip of the second stair from the top, saying, more to himself than to her, with great satisfaction, *"La voilá, la clef!"*

Alex rang the bell out of courtesy, although he said it was very rare that Tante Clothilde used the flat. Between her beloved property in the Dordogne and visiting her children and grandchildren in Paris, she had very little time or inclination to linger in the provincial capital of Aquitaine. Alex opened the door to a large, pleasant apartment, furnished with antiques, Persian carpets on the parquet floors, chandeliers hanging from the ornate ceiling, lots of paintings on the walls.

"Wow! Are you sure she won't mind?" Morgan asked, as Alex started to open the shutters and a few windows to let in the fading light of dusk and the cool evening air.

"Don't worry, Morgan. I'm by far her favorite nephew—she loved it when I lived here. In fact, back then Tante Clothilde tried to spend as much time in town as possible. You'll like her a lot too, and she, of course, you. You can certainly hole up here until we figure out what to do."

"Thanks. It's a luxurious hiding place, that's for sure," Morgan said, following Alex into the kitchen.

"Yeah. Here, you can help yourself to the wine under here," Alex said, peeking into one of the cupboards below the counter. "It's still left over from when I occupied the place. I don't think you'll find much food in the flat, though, so I hope you're not too hungry. At least until I can bring something back."

Alex led her into one of the bedrooms in the back along a long corridor. "This is the guest room where I stayed. Make yourself at home. I am sure the sheets are clean and there is a towel in the bathroom."

"What about your mother, Alex? Or stepfather? And Luc? What if they come by?" Morgan dropped her purse and kicked Marie's shoes off. They had been hurting her feet since the reception. Too bad she could not shed her fear that easily.

"Don't worry, they never come here. They may even have forgotten that this place exists."

"And what if Tante Clothilde happens to come while I am here? What should I say?" She was not used to being a squatter, invading other peoples' space.

"Again, no worries. I will call her as soon as I can. But right now, much as I'd like to stay, I think I had better get back to the reception before I am missed. I'll come when I can get away without it being noticed." He gave her a deep kiss on the mouth and put his hand on the door handle to open it, but instead of going out, turned around and said, "Chapin, was it? Peter? He could be useful, now that John is no longer with us. You don't have a number for him, by any chance?"

"No. But Jérome does. And so does the American Consul, Charles Townsend. They all exchanged phone numbers when we met."

"Good. That could come in handy."

And Alex was out the door, leaving Morgan all alone again.

CHAPTER 23

Fortunately, Morgan had eaten a few tidbits at the reception, so she wasn't very hungry. But she was certainly ready for a little wine after her hurried and stressful escape from the cocktail party. Alex had offered, so she ferreted around under the counter and pulled out a dusty bottle—of course, it was one of the de Carduzac's, a 2004—then, opening every cupboard up top, every drawer, finally found a corkscrew, a wine glass and even an unopened bag of peanuts, and made her way into the living room. She turned the TV on, finding France 24, and, after slipping out of Marie's uncomfortably tight dress, settled on the couch in just her panties, wrapping the soft alpaca throw blanket on its arm around her shoulders. She hoped that Jérome and Alex would figure out how to get her a change of clothes because she would not be able to go anywhere in Marie's slinky cocktail dress and the tight stilettos. She had had the foresight still at Jérome's to squeeze her passport, credit cards, money and ticket into the evening purse borrowed from Marie, which she had dumped onto the bed in the guest room.

The news channel showed the usual France 24 debate—with the conference in Bordeaux as the main topic this evening, and discussion focusing on to what extent France should continue to play a leading role in Africa and against ISIS in the Middle East. One of the experts did focus on the possible consequences, if that role—especially the military intervention—were, in any way to be interpreted as a continuation of France's colonial past. Among which, one of the more likely ones would be terrorism back home in continental France, he asserted. The speaker also made the point that he hoped the security forces were on top of things in Bordeaux because the Palais Rohan gathering could be a perfect venue for jihadists to strike at France as well as at some of their own largely ineffective and corrupt government officials in Africa.

Morgan found this all very depressing, and even more so, given what she thought she knew, but glad that there was at least some focus on the possibility of an attack at the conference. If it was not going to be the jihadists, then it would seem the right wing elements in France might be the perpetrators of an imminent calamity. She had never felt so alone and afraid. And so dependent. Really, her only remaining lifeline to the outer world was Alex.

What if something happened to him? Alex must stop working as a waiter at the Palais Rohan. Sandrine and Rashid too, for that matter. It was sheer folly. What was Luc thinking, recruiting his stepbrother and friends to work at the event? At least Claire was not there, whether really indisposed or forced to stay at the chateau. Would Luc make sure the others did not work the next day? Which, when she thought about it, would be the likely timing of any move against the assembled leaders. At the meetings themselves, when only government officials were present. Or could he be so callously part of whatever Les Nouveaux Girondins had planned that he didn't care?

Or was this all fantasy, that Luc was involved with an attempt to assassinate the president of France? If it were really the jihadists, the thought came to her, wouldn't they have done it at the reception, kill as many people as they could, for maximum effect?

Not necessarily.

But no, she was not just imagining all this.

Surely, Alex was smart enough to see that something could happen at the conference, now that they had talked it through together.

What about the others?

Just then, her cell's signature Beatles melody penetrated her thoughts through the chatter of the debate, all the way from the guest bedroom. She raced down the corridor, as the phone kept playing the tune. Grabbing it from the bed and hoping it would be Alex, she was all set to punch the green button. But fortunately, she had the wisdom to look at who was calling.

Luc.

Don't answer it, Morgan told herself. Let it go. He is no doubt looking for you. For sure, worried that you disappeared from the reception right after you were seen talking to one of the president's aides with Jérome.

The music stopped and Morgan carried the mobile back to the living room with her. She went to refill her glass and found that her hand would not stop shaking. She was petrified of what might happen. Yes, to the president and the politicians at the conference, to Alex, but most of all to her. With Luc talking to his parents and the general at the reception and gesticulating toward her, she was sure that operatives of the militant French far right were after her at that very moment and certain that they would be connected to the French military and intelligence services. Indeed, they would no doubt have recourse to all the resources they might need to find and silence her. And the easiest way to make sure she didn't divulge what she knew or surmised was simply to get rid of her. Just as they had eliminated John when he started to ask questions that hit too close to home. Probably Pierre Bérégovoy too, and many others.

Yes, it was time to leave. She had to get out of France. But how?

The debate droned on and Morgan clicked the TV off in exasperation, unable to stop thinking about her plight. She took her glass and the still one-third full bottle and made her way back to the guestroom. Parking the wine and glass on the night table with the cell phone, along with the other contents of the evening purse, she went into the adjacent bathroom. She noticed the medicine cabinet above the sink, and hoping to find some old toothpaste she could at least use to brush the bad taste from her mouth, she opened it. When she saw that the cupboard was empty, she decided to try the luxurious *en suite* of the master bedroom. There her eyes scanned a plethora of products, first by the Jacuzzi, then on the windowsill, and lastly, on a little stand by the sink. Quickly glancing through these, she was excited to come upon a bottle of Herbatint hair dye and picking it up to read the fine print, she saw that it was to color gray hair black.

Just what I need, she told herself, *it should work equally well for blonde hair.*

Looking at herself in the big mirror, Morgan momentarily regretted what she would have to do. *Yes, and better still if I cut my hair short, at least shoulder length.* As she searched further, in the second drawer down, she found some scissors and went over to Tante Clothilde's little makeup desk in the corner, which the surrounding mirrors made the ideal place to commence the shearing operation.

Morgan grabbed a few of her long blonde strands and deciding what would be an acceptable, but much shorter length, started cutting away. It took her a good twenty minutes until she was satisfied with her new hairstyle, although, with all the adjustments her makeshift "selfie" cutting job required, it ended up being much shorter than she had originally planned. It would have to do, she told herself.

Reading the instructions on the Herbatint bottle, Morgan saw that her hair needed to be wet for the dye to take—she would go back in the guest bathroom to take a shower. But first, she scoured the large cabinet above the sink for some toothpaste and found a much-squeezed tube in among the deodorant, creams and several containers of different pills. As she grabbed the toothpaste and some lotions, she absent-mindedly read the labels on the medication containers and saw that one of them was a Sanofi box containing Ambien. *Hmm, maybe just what I need for a good night's sleep.* So, stealing one of the little tablets as well, she made her way to her quarters with her loot.

Back in the guest bathroom, Morgan stepped into the spacious shower cubicle and turned the water on full force, letting it run over her hair, face, and body, relishing the stimulation of the hot water droplets. She slipped out of her by now totally wet panties, washing them and tossing them over the shower door into the sink before she soaped and rinsed her body. Feeling a lot better, she stepped out of the stall, dried herself vigorously, leaving her hair wet as per the Herbatint instructions, and carefully spread her panties out on the towel rack to make sure they would dry for tomorrow, whatever it brought. The thought that the flimsy bit of lingerie was the only item of her own clothing she had, again brought home the precariousness of her situation.

Morgan then performed the meticulous job of tinting her hair. It was not perfect, but it would have to do for the purposes of evading the—and here her mind now went blank. *Indeed, whom am I running from? Am I just imagining all this? Have I become totally paranoid, falling prey to conspiracy theory thinking, as John accused me? No, no, there is the general, Joseph de Carduzac, Luc, Les Nouveaux Girondins, and all those evil forces allied with them. The French far right,* she again had to convince herself that this was real, it was happening, *some of the corrupted French intelligence services working with the general. And being egged on by the Russians. Someone is definitely after me, not wanting me to divulge what I have found out. They want to eliminate me like they did John. And Pierre Bérégovoy. And others.*

Yes, the sleeping pill, that's what she needed. Without giving it any further thought, Morgan found the tablet on the edge of the sink where she had placed it and popped it in her mouth, helping it go down with water from the tap. As she did so, she hoped that it would wash away the paranoia, and once in bed, transport her away to the never-never land of sleep.

Back in the bedroom, she closed the blinds and took great delight in stretching out her exhausted body between the clean and crisp sheets. Checking her email and messages on her phone in the dark, she saw that Claire had sent her an SMS saying, "Call me." Morgan was about to press the call button, but thought better of it: what if her friend had been coerced into getting in touch with her so they could trace her? Luc or her father could very well have put Claire up to it. Or taken her phone, and sent the message themselves. Best not to call Claire, or for that matter, anyone. Certainly not Alex, much as she missed and wanted him. He would come back when he could, Morgan told herself.

Fortunately, before Morgan had a chance to reflect too much more on her desperate situation, the Ambien kicked in and she fell sound asleep.

CHAPTER 24

Morgan was still in deep slumber, dreaming of being disguised as an old hag with gray hair and chased naked by a wicked-looking figure who resembled President Mitterand across her favorite beach in California, when she was brought groggily back to the world by a violent shaking of her shoulders and a strong female voice speaking loudly at her in a foreign language. It was only when she opened her eyes, looked around and saw the well-dressed older woman holding a huge kitchen knife at her throat and gruffly addressing her with a stern "Who are you, mademoiselle? What are you doing here?" that she put two and two together.

So this was the famous Tante Clothilde, and Alex had not—for whatever reason—managed to get in touch with her. Under the circumstances "Who are you?" and "What are you doing here?" were reasonable questions from the formidable woman.

Morgan pulled the duvet back over her shoulders—it had fallen off, to her great embarrassment, exposing her naked top half to Chantal's older sister—before starting to explain in French that she was a friend of the family, an American student in France. It was only then that she noticed that the towel she had placed on top of the pillow had turned a splotchy gray with the black dye from her hair, causing her further mortification.

"But, mademoiselle, that does not give you the right to invade my apartment. And to use my bath products. In any case, I am calling the police immediately." And Tante Clothilde put the threatening kitchen knife down on the bed to ferret around in her copious handbag for her cell phone.

"No, please no. Madame, please, not the police. It was Alex—"

The mention of the police on top of her desperate situation brought Morgan to tears, and when Tante Clothilde realized that the naked invader had not picked up the weapon she had so absent-mindedly placed at her feet, and in between sobs was referring to her favorite nephew by his first name, she abandoned the search for the phone and sat down by Morgan at the head of the bed, handing her a tissue from the box on the night table.

"So, mademoiselle, could you please explain to me what has happened?"

Morgan took it as a good sign that Tante Clothilde spoke in a much softer, conciliatory tone.

"Don't worry, Tante Clo."

Morgan's whole being was enveloped by welcome relief as she heard Alex's deep voice take charge from the bedroom doorway.

"I will tell you what's going on."

She extended arms in anticipation, wanting Alex to come and hug her. He did, dropping the bag he was carrying and knocking the knife that was on the edge of the duvet to the floor. "Boy, Alex, am I glad you're here!" Morgan said as they smothered each other with kisses.

It was only when Tante Clothilde made throat-clearing noises that the kissing stopped. And it was as they separated that Morgan realized that her breasts were totally exposed. Mortified, she pulled the cover back up, as Alex said, chuckling. "Don't worry, chérie. My aunt has seen all of us in the buff many times. And you are much more of a feast for the eyes. But what have you done to your hair?"

"I tried to disguise myself a little."

"Well, you certainly managed. You do look different. But still gorgeous, n'est-ce pas, Tante Clo?"

"Mais oui!" Alex's aunt answered emphatically, looking the American girl up and down with a smile, not for the first time as she stood there. *"Elle est ravissante, la petite."*

Alex picked up the rucksack he had dropped on the floor to embrace his girlfriend and handed it to her, saying, "Here, Morgan, I brought you a change of clothes. I hope they're okay. I just gathered up a few items from your room. And I got some food, so when you're ready, come to the kitchen. Meanwhile, I will explain everything to my aunt."

"Thanks, Alex. I love you!"

"And I, you." They kissed again as Tante Clothilde slipped past them discreetly in the direction of the kitchen.

৩৩৩

Alex had set out the *rillettes*, cheeses, and baguette and opened another one of the de Carduzac bottles he had left there more than a year ago, while his aunt whipped up a mixed salad with a vinaigrette dressing. They were already sitting down at the kitchen table when Morgan joined them, showered, hair combed, and comfortable in her own jeans and a sleeveless white blouse, white and blue joggers.

"What time is it?" Morgan asked, realizing that she hadn't eaten for some time.

"It's getting on toward one. Twelve forty-seven, to be exact," Alex said, consulting his watch. "I've just finished telling Tante Clo what you think is happening and how dangerous it has become for you here in France. And that it seems my stepfather and stepbrother are not to be trusted."

"*Oui,* your stepfather—I must admit, I never...how do you say?...have seen eye to eye with him. And that man, the general, you call him—I do not understand how my sister can let him in the house. I hate the man."

"I must say, we all agree, Tante Clo."

"He is a pig, that man. *Un vrai salaud.* In fact," Chantal's sister added in a huff, as she cut herself a large chunk of the Comté, "he once tried to seduce me. Disgusting.

"I did not like him the one time I met him," Morgan concurred.

"Ma pauvre chérie!" Tante Clothilde looked Morgan in the eyes. "How brave you are! And you are doing all this for France." And then she added, after taking a swig of her wine, "Of course, I will help. You can stay as long as you wish. Or we can leave—"

Tante Clothilde was cut short by a deafening blast that shook the whole building, the table, knocking over the glasses and bottle. Alex's aunt gasped, as he and Morgan jumped up and ran to the window.

"Holy shit! It's happened," Alex exclaimed. "They've bombed the Palais Rohan!"

"God! I knew it...."

"I am going over there. You stay here."

"No, I'm coming with you. We need to see if we can do something." A terrible feeling came over Morgan that maybe she should have done more to help avert this tragedy. She had known all along. She had been sure this would happen. But she just couldn't get to the right people to prevent it. Nobody, other than Alex, had taken her seriously. Anyone else, who had considered the truth of what she said, had been removed. Killed.

"You can't go out there, Morgan. It's too dangerous."

"Nobody will be looking at bystanders just now. They will all be focused on the destruction and trying to help any survivors. Besides, I have totally changed how I look. I won't be recognized. I'm going." Morgan was already at the door.

"I doubt that there's anyone left alive at the Hôtel de Ville."

"I wouldn't be so sure. There was, after the World Trade Center bombing."

"Well, okay, we'll just go for a few minutes. But you keep close to me."

"I think I will stay behind and clean up." Tante Clothilde was a lot more cautious than her two younger visitors.

CHAPTER 25

"Morgan, I'll go ahead. You follow maybe ten or fifteen meters behind on the other side of the street. We should not be seen together," Alex said as they ran down the stairs. "And if you see Luc or my stepfather or the general or anyone suspicious, you just turn right around and make your way quickly back to the apartment."

"Okay."

"And if I'm not there in half an hour, you need to ask Tante Clothilde to take you to San Sebastian. In Spain. Just across the border. I already discussed it with her. It's a short hop from there to Madrid, and from there you can fly back to the US."

"But the border crossing—"

"Don't worry, there are no checks. We're all in Schengen. And knowing the French, they will not have notified Interpol or the Spanish yet, so you shouldn't have a problem leaving Spain. If we hurry, that is."

"Thanks, Alex. You've thought of everything." But deep down, Morgan was not reassured. It did not sit well with her to be a fugitive, with Interpol and others looking for her.

Opening the front door to the street, they were overwhelmed by the smoke and dust, the heat and the noise of sizzling flames, the shrillness of sirens and the screams that carried the five or six hundred meters all the way from the Palais Rohan. They turned left on Rue Vital Carles, struggling forward through the haze and coughing from the dearth of oxygen. When they reached Place Pey Berland, they were shocked to see the extent of the destruction: the newly renovated façade of Cathédrale Saint André—that had survived almost a thousand years of turbulent history—had been damaged, while the Hôtel de Ville, the beautiful old Palais Rohan, was a pile of rubble enveloped in flames, with still the occasional loud explosion and crackling, wails and screams emanating from the direction of the conflagration. There was no way anyone who had been inside the conference hall at the Mairie could have survived the explosion. On the square, bodies, limbs, pieces of flesh, and blood were scattered all around in among the debris and broken glass.

The police had arrived and were just putting up a barricade across all the entrances to the Place. Firefighters too, were appearing on the scene, and setting up their equipment to fight the raging blaze. A few ambulances had pulled up and crews of medics were starting to attend to those who were not dead on the square, while some others gingerly approached the entrance of the Cathédrale. The Mairie itself was a burning pyre that was just too hot for anyone to approach.

As they advanced separately in the direction of the barricades, Morgan saw Alex scan the plaza and suddenly stop in his tracks. She followed her boyfriend at the appointed distance as he went over to the police and pointed at what seemed to be a crumpled body in the far corner of the square. Morgan's eyes tracked his gesture, and it was then that she saw through the smoke that the object of Alex's attention was a black man, all bloody and mangled, lying in the middle of the square.

"Oh God, no! Not Jérome. Please, please no!" Morgan muttered to herself.

But then, as Alex passed through the barriers and cut across the square toward what she was sure was the wounded professor, out of the corner of her eye, Morgan caught sight of a group of four men who were also rapidly moving in the direction of the same objective. She saw that they reached the inert body just before Alex, and with a growing sense of horror, noted that it was Luc, Joseph, the general, and another man dressed in a soldier's uniform who surrounded Professor Konaté just as Alex arrived.

When the de Lavallée boy got to the growing assembly surrounding Jérome, he talked briefly to his stepfather and stepbrother, then knelt down by the body. Getting up, he glanced over toward where Morgan was, and with what she thought was a frown and a sweep of his arm, seemed to indicate that she had better get out of there as fast as she could.

Feeling sick to her stomach, and frustrated as there was nothing that she could do to help at the site, Morgan followed Alex's instructions, turned around, and made her way, walking rapidly back to Tante Clothilde's.

გოგო

When she got there, the older woman was glued to the television, watching the France 24 report on the latest incident.

"Alex stayed behind. He saw Luc and Joseph, and wanted to see if he could help with the wounded," Morgan answered when Alex's aunt asked after him. She did not want to tell her that she thought she had seen the general there as well, that their friend the professor was injured, and Alex had really gone over to see what had happened to him.

On screen, the camera was showing Place Pey Berland, where Morgan could now make out soldiers streaming into the square. "The devastation is unbelievable and heart-rending, a scene from Dante's Inferno," the reporter shouted above the din. "We do not know yet how many casualties there are, but for certain, President Aragon, and numerous cabinet members—the Foreign Minister, the Ministers of Defense, of the Interior, of Finance among others we are still trying to determine—as well as six or seven African Heads of State, twelve or thirteen other African ministers and countless French and African government officials who were attending the official luncheon, many staff working at the Mairie, are all presumed dead. Corpses and body parts are strewn all over Place Pey Berland and the vicinity, and you can hear the terrible screams of the wounded behind me. It is still not known if there are any casualties inside the Cathédrale, which, as we can see—" And the camera panned in on the smoldering rubble below the still intact walls. "—in keeping with its almost a thousand years of serving the faithful, remains standing, although it is clear that this holy shrine has sustained some damage. It is hard to fathom who would unleash such horrible destruction and pain on the people of Bordeaux, on France, on the world..."

"Morgan dear, you go and get ready. Alex told me I have to get you away from here. To Spain, and then from there you must go back to the USA. We will leave shortly. Take whatever you have, and we will go down to my car in a few minutes."

"...we are fortunate to have General Tolbert here, who arrived at the site within minutes of the explosion and has taken charge. He is the senior official of the armed forces present and he would like to make a statement to all of France, all Frenchmen. General, please go ahead."

The camera focused on Tolbert, who was surrounded by a group of heavily armed soldiers and a few civilians, among whom Morgan recognized Luc and his father.

"My fellow Frenchmen, my dear co-citizens. Today, a terrible calamity has befallen our country. We and our African allies have been attacked by the most despicable form of terrorism that has taken countless lives of our loved ones and important leaders from us. We will avenge this act of aggression, you can be sure of that. As we believe that much of our government has been annihilated in this devastation, I am declaring martial law in the whole country.

"Until we can assess the extent to which our nation's leadership has been eliminated, we will form a government with the one elected cabinet member who we know for certain is alive, Patrick Joinville, the Minister of Veterans, and Valentin Frantome, former Minister of Defense at its head. I am sure both these distinguished gentlemen are well known to everyone in France. I will ask other surviving cabinet members, *députés,* and officials to get in touch with Monsieur Joinville, Monsieur Frantome, or myself, and to work with us through this difficult time. I am instructing the various branches of the armed forces, the intelligence services, and the police to assist in maintaining order and to enforce a curfew of nine p.m. throughout the country to prevent looting and crime.

"These orders shall be in force until further notice. Moreover, I would also like to assure you that we are immediately starting an investigation into how this calamity could have taken place in our beloved country and who were the criminals behind it. We will search out those responsible no matter where they are and bring them to justice. I will keep you informed of progress over the ensuing days. Thank you, and may God be with France and help guide us through these difficult times."

"Okay, Tante Clothilde, I am ready. I agree, we better move fast, if you don't mind. Things are becoming very scary here."

CHAPTER 26

Tante Clothilde was a very good driver for a lady of sixty-five or so, Morgan remarked to herself, as they headed south on the A63 in her brand new Peugeot 308. Morgan kept looking anxiously at the very few cars that passed them, and back through the rearview mirror, to see if they were being followed, but there were no police, nor any unmarked vehicles that showed interest. The radio was on the news channel, and every half hour there was an update on the main events, by far the most important being the bombing at the Palais Rohan.

The first three reports focused on the increasing number of casualties and a more precise description of the devastation at the site in Bordeaux. Shockingly, by the time of the third update, the total mortality had risen to over one hundred and seventy, with another forty-five or so critically wounded, and it was confirmed that much of the upper echelons of the French government had been wiped out. The reporters surmised that, as with the Brassault incident, the likely perpetrators were jihadists—probably North African, perhaps linked to ISIS or al Qaeda—seeking to retaliate against France for its interventionism and to remove their own client governments.

In between news flashes, as she vaguely listened to discussion on the radio about the wider consequences of the Bordeaux explosion, Morgan used Tante Clothilde's iPhone to check on flights out of San Sebastian. She would take the first flight in the morning to Madrid connecting with the earliest availability for the USA. Morgan saw that these flights were not full, and hesitated whether to hold off buying a ticket until she got to the airport, but decided to go ahead since it would mean fewer questions asked. It took a few anxious moments for her VISA card to be approved, but finally, the confirmation of the reservation came through, and she was even able to check in and select her seats. She also looked at rooms for the night in Hondarribia, the small fishing village just across the border, twenty-two kilometers from San Sebastian, where the airport serving the resort town was situated. On AirBnB, she picked two rooms close to the airport, jotted down the addresses, but did not book either, hoping that if they were not taken and she just went there, the owners would let her have the accommodation.

There was some discussion on the radio about the legality of the declaration of the emergency government by General Tolbert immediately after the devastation, but generally, it was felt appropriate by most pundits that someone had taken charge in the political vacuum when France's president and main cabinet ministers were so brutally assassinated. And who better than someone with proven military and intelligence credentials and connections in these difficult times, when it was not even known from which direction France and its African allies had been attacked. But at least one speaker suggested that the revered Constitutional Court would need to be consulted about the legitimacy of the provisional government declared by General Tolbert.

Just as they approached Bayonne, still a little over half an hour from the Spanish border, Tante Clothilde's phone rang. Alex's aunt asked Morgan to find the mobile in her voluminous purse, and as she pulled it out, she saw that it was Chantal calling. Morgan was suspicious and had the presence of mind to press the speaker button and put the phone on the console in the middle so that Tante Clothilde could talk directly and hands-free to her sister.

"Hello, Chantal, dear. How are you? I am in the car driving, on my way home to Domaine Sonzac..." Tante Clothilde had quickly calculated that her property in the Dordogne was almost as far from Bordeaux as the Spanish border.

"Clo—Clo, something terrible has happened—" It was obvious that Chantal had trouble getting the words out.

"Yes, dear. I know. The conference at the Palais Rohan was bombed. Are Alex and Claire all right? And Joseph and Luc?" It was clear which members of Chantal's little family she favored.

"Clo, it's not that. Clo—Claire—" Chantal said between sobs. "—Claire was found—dead—just a little while ago—"

"No!" Chantal stepped on the brakes, as Morgan could scarcely hold back from crying out. "What? How?"

"Floating in the swimming pool. By Gaston, when he went to clean it of the leaves, as he does every day."

"My dear, how awful! Terrible! Poor, poor girl. What happened, Chantal?"

"Well, I am not sure. Joseph was not at home. Nor Luc. Alex has come and is dealing with it all. And the police came and have been here all day. They say—they say it was suicide." At the mention of Alex, Morgan's despondent heart missed a beat, and she desperately wanted to talk to him. But if someone was with him, best not to reveal that she was sitting there beside Tante Clothilde, she told herself.

"That is hard to believe, don't you think? She was such a bubbly girl. Full of fun and jokes always—"

"I had been so hard on her lately—" Chantal melted into tears again. "—and so had Joseph. He—he hasn't come yet—he has been dealing with the attack at the Mairie. We were such bad parents. I was such a terrible mother."

"Chantal, you mustn't blame yourself."

"Clo, I just want to kill myself. I want to die."

"Chantal, you will do nothing of the kind. Just take a sleeping pill and go to bed. I will drop by Villa Sonzac— I am almost there—pick up a few things, and then I will turn right around and come to see you. Don't do anything stupid. Is Alex there? I want to talk to him, Chantal. Put him on."

"Yes, I will get him. Bye, Clo. I love you."

"I love you too, Chantal. Courage, my dear."

"Tante Clo?" Morgan was delighted to hear Alex's strong voice over the airwaves.

"Alex, my love. I am very, very sorry about what has happened. Terrible. Poor, dear Claire. But you need to take care of your mother now until I get there. Make sure she doesn't do anything stupid. Give her one sleeping pill, but take all the rest and any other medication away. Razors, knives, too. I am almost at home, and will turn right around and come there." She and Morgan hoped he would understand that they were getting very close to the Spanish border.

"Yes, Tante Clo. We need you here, but make sure you do what you need to do. See you soon." And the call was cut off by Alex. Morgan sensed he could not talk.

"God! Claire, poor girl. My friend."

"Yes, one terrible event after another. My poor dear sister! To lose a daughter—"

"Now they've done away with her as well. And she didn't even know all that I know."

"Now, Morgan, you mustn't jump to conclusions."

"But it's so obvious. Claire didn't commit suicide. They eliminated her, just as they struck down John, and that EPC employee. I'm next on their list for sure."

"Morgan, dear, you can't think that way. Not if we manage to get you away. And we are almost there."

There were signs at Hondarribia for the airport, so they knew they were in Spain when the shocking announcement came across the airwaves. "Newsflash! French authorities have taken into custody a suspect who they believe was the leader of the North African terrorist cell that caused the devastation earlier today at the Palais Rohan in Bordeaux, the site for the meeting of the African Heads of State, which killed the president and many other French and foreign government officials. The man, Professor Jérome Konaté—"

"What! No, no, no!" Morgan interrupted.

"—was found on the square outside the venue of the conference, himself wounded in the blast. Konaté has had a distinguished academic career, was teaching at the University of Bordeaux, and acting as an advisor to the French government on African affairs. According to our sources, he confessed to being a 'sleeper' jihadist, and to having masterminded the plot to kill the presidents of France and several African countries, as well as earlier this year, the attack on the Brassault facility in Mérignac where Prime Minister Rostrand and two other ministers were killed."

So that was going to be their tactic! To implicate Jérome—who was a convenient Muslim scapegoat—in this sordid affair. And Rashid was there too, serving. For sure, one of the casualties. Once they go through the list of who was working for Carnot, they will no doubt lump him in with the terrorists.

Then there was she, Morgan. One of those despised Americans. Maybe even dear Claire's "suicide" will be ascribed to remorse at joining Konaté's cell. And God only knows whom else they would drag in.

For sure, though, not Alex. His stepfather and brother would keep him out of the mess. She needed to talk to him desperately.

There was Tante Clothilde's phone. He had just been on it but had not seemed able to talk. What if he was suspect and his cell monitored? Well, she would just have to wait and hope he could get away and use another phone privately. Maybe buy one of those "burner" phones or pre-paid SIM cards. Yes, maybe she should do that too when they got to San Sebastian, and she could give Tante Clothilde the number and hope Alex got in touch with her. Surely he would, to find out whether they made it safely.

They saw signs for the airport and evidence that they were getting to the outskirts of Hondarribia. Tante Clothilde soon turned off the highway and followed her GPS to the address of the more appealing of the two AirBnB sites Morgan had selected. On the way, they stopped at Electricidad Oronoz so that Morgan could purchase a cheap local phone.

"Can I invite you to dinner somewhere, Tante Clothilde?" Morgan asked as they approached the Centro Habitación on Santiago Kalea. "I really would like to reciprocate somehow for your kindness. You have done so much for me."

"That's very nice of you, but I think I had better get back as quickly as possible. I must get to my sister. She needs me. And it wouldn't do to be found missing in action in these difficult times." Alex's aunt had obviously enjoyed her role in this cat and mouse game.

"Well, Tante Clothilde, you have been amazing," Morgan said as the car pulled up in front of the Habitación. "And thank you."

"I'll just wait to make sure everything is all right."

Morgan jumped out of the car and rang the bell. The door was opened by a bearded, dark-haired man of about forty with a huge smile, whom Morgan addressed in her California Spanish, asking if he had a room free. "I did not reserve ahead, but..."

"Of course, *señorita*. No problem." The man looked her over, switching to English after the first sentence. "Delighted to have you with us. Come on in. Do you have any bags?"

"Thanks. No. I'm traveling light. I just have to say goodbye to my aunt." And she gestured toward the car, then ran over to it, and gave Tante Clothilde a double kiss through the open window, asking her to give her love to Alex. With a tear in her eye, and wishing her "Good luck," the older woman pulled away from the curb as Morgan waved to her from the steps of the Habitación. She was on a mission to get back to St. Émilion to console her distraught sister.

Following the bearded Spaniard into his home, Morgan thought to herself that it did seem like she was saying goodbye to her own dear aunt.

CHAPTER 27

Inside the prettily appointed ancient fisherman's house, Morgan was greeted by the bearded man's wife, "*Buenas tardes, señorita. Bienvenida en nuestra habitación.*"

"*Gracias, señora.*"

"Yes, welcome. My name is Roberto, and my wife is Elena."

"And I am Morgan. Morgan Kenworthy. I would like a room just for one night. I am flying to Madrid in the morning."

"Yes, that's good. I will take you to the airport myself after breakfast. It is just five minutes from here. For registration, can I please see your passport?"

Morgan's heart skipped a beat, as she searched around for the document in the outer pocket of Alex's backpack, which now contained all her worldly belongings. This was the first time anyone had asked for her ID…oh yes, since she had managed to pass through security at the Palais Rohan with Marie Konaté's university card.

"You have changed your hair?" Roberto said, smiling as he looked at the picture in the passport and then back at her. She had totally forgotten that she would not look like her passport photo anymore.

"Yes, yes. I was in a play, and this look suited the character better," she quickly mustered a lie, returning Roberto's smile. *God, will this be a problem at the airport tomorrow? And when I leave Spain?*

"Well, you look like a famous actress. A very beautiful one," Roberto complimented her, handing back the document. "Let me show you to your room, Morgan."

"Thank you."

Leading the way up the narrow stairs, the bearded Spaniard asked, "Would you care to dine with us later? Say around ten p.m.? Or should Elena bring up some *jamon iberico, manchego* and *piquinillos* with bread, and a little Rioja for you?"

"I would love to have some of the ham and cheese. And the peppers. I am quite tired, so if you don't mind, I would like to get an early night. Thank you for your kind offer, though."

Roberto took Morgan into the small and sparsely outfitted but comfortable room, gave her the WiFi code, showed her how the TV worked, leaving it on a French news channel, and then left her, closing the door behind himself. As she threw the backpack on the chair in the corner and collapsed on the bed, her ears perked up to hear the reporter giving the latest on the only news item that mattered.

"...investigators have now determined that the actual explosives were taken onto the site by accomplices of the man believed to be the head of the jihadist cell that carried out the terrorist attack. One of the more dangerous members of the cell—Rashid Suleiman, an Algerian-French student of the leader, Professor Konaté of the University of Bordeaux—was actually working for the firm that catered the lunch, and was killed in the explosions. It is suspected that the professor may have recruited other students at the university to turn against France.

Indeed, a female American exchange student in his class is suspected of being a member of the terrorist group. She is still on the loose, and police are seeking her for questioning. We will have further information for you as it is released by the authorities."

So, yes, her guess had been right: they were now implicating poor, innocent Rashid in this heinous affair, as well as her. Feelings of loneliness and fear descended on Morgan, a sense of desperation over her situation, mixed with the grief of the loss of so many of her friends. First John, then Claire, and now Rashid, too. And what about Jérome? What had become of him?

She allowed herself to have a good cry into the down pillow.

༻༄༺

It was only when she heard a gentle knocking on the door and Elena's voice saying, "Señorita, I have brought something for you to eat," that Morgan got up from the bed and found some tissues to wipe the tears away. She opened the door and smiled as she saw the diminutive hostess carrying a huge tray of delicious looking food and a carafe of red wine that she put on the small desk by the TV. "Is everything all right, señorita?" Elena must have seen from her puffed eyes that she had been crying.

"Yes, yes. I am fine. It's just that…I'm missing my boyfriend," Morgan's answer was true, but there was so much more to her unhappiness.

"I am sorry. I know it is very difficult when you are young. Is there anything I can do for you?"

"No, no, thank you. You are too kind, señora. Just a wake-up call at six-thirty please, so I can make my plane. That would be great."

Morgan was glad to be alone when Elena pulled the door shut behind her. She poured herself some of the Rioja and took the tray of food over to the bed, where she made herself comfortable. Looking over at the TV screen, she saw that Zaida Bensoussan, the French Minister of Justice, Jérome's friend from ÉNA, was being interviewed. She turned up the volume.

"...actually, Professor Konaté called me the night before the attack and left a message saying that he had information that there could be some kind of a coup, and warning that the lives of our president, my colleagues, and officials attending the conference in Bordeaux, were in grave danger. When I finally listened to it the next morning, I tried to track him down, without success. Of course, I immediately notified the security services, who told me they had things completely under control."

"Hmm, nevertheless, the terrorist plot seems to have eluded our intelligence officers."

"Well, if that is what it was. It is simply not believable that the professor was the ringleader of a group of jihadists who carried out the bombing, as General Tolbert and others are suggesting. Jérome Konaté was a good friend of mine and a true French patriot, and I have asked my staff to arrange for me to see him in Bordeaux tomorrow in the hospital where I am told he is being held."

"So, Madame Minister, you are saying that General Tolbert's earlier claim is not true? Surely, that is hard to argue, given that he is the deputy director of the DGSE and effectively the top official in charge of French security."

"No comment. His organization, if it knew about the plot—whether from Professor Konaté or some other way—certainly did nothing to prevent it."

"Then, if not a jihadist cell led by this Professor Konaté, may I ask, who were the perpetrators in your opinion?

Again, surely, if anybody, General Tolbert would know—"

"I have no further comment until after I talk to the professor tomorrow. I have told you what I know. Also, as minister of justice, I am asking the Constitutional Court to rule on General Tolbert's declaration of martial law earlier today, and on his self-proclaimed government led by him and his associates. While I recognize that one of these gentlemen, Patrick Joinville, the Minister of Veterans, is a colleague in the current cabinet, I do not believe that General Tolbert and he can unilaterally push aside the elected government, even though many of its members have been killed. Again, I will come back to you and the people of France, once the court has made its ruling. That is all I have to say."

"Thank you, Madame Minister."

Morgan was glad that the justice minister was speaking out against Tolbert, but she feared for Jérome's life. After all, the general and his gang had the wounded professor in custody, and it would be very easy for them to eliminate him and then claim that he died from his injuries. And the more Morgan thought about it, it was very unlikely that they would allow Madame Bensoussan to visit him, because, for sure, he would tell her all he knew. No, unfortunately, Jérome was as good as dead, she concluded and despaired that there was nothing she could do to help him.

She had zoned out from the screen while deep in thought, but was brought back to the reality of the television report when she heard the name of her friend Claire mentioned by the news reporter. "…earlier today, Mademoiselle de Lavallée was found by the butler floating face down in the swimming pool at the family's chateau near St. Émilion. The police have concluded that it was suicide. We do know that she was a student of Professor

Konaté, who is now thought by French intelligence to have been the ringleader of the jihadist cell that committed the atrocity today at the Palais Rohan. The police are looking into whether she was a member of this group, but the fact that she took her own life right after the bombing does arouse some suspicions. We will keep you informed as this story develops."

So, yes, that was it: not only did they get rid of Claire to prevent her from talking, but they had the temerity to slur her reputation by casting her as a member of the fictitious group of terrorists they had dreamt up to cover their tracks. A despicable lot.

The news turned to events elsewhere in France, where alarmingly, the day's earlier bombings—so facilely ascribed to Muslim jihadists—had spurred violence against Middle Eastern and North African communities. Riots in the *banlieues* of Paris, in Marseilles and Toulouse, had resulted in the deaths of thirteen followers of Islam, and gangs of armed members of the youth movement *Génération Identitaire* had burned down a mosque in Lyon, killing another nine. Racially motivated attacks in other small towns and villages throughout the country had also caused a lot of injuries and damage to property.

Increasingly despondent as she listened to this unsettling news, Morgan switched the TV off when the reporter finally turned to the on-going crisis in Syria and Iraq. She poured the wine that remained in the carafe into her glass, and pushed the tray away, thinking that she should check her email before turning in for the night. She grabbed her iPad from the desk, powered it on, found the Habitación's WiFi and typed in the security code. Opening up her Gmail, she was astounded to see a message from—of all people—Claire, along with emails from her mother and sister as well as some California friends. She noted the time on her dead friend's email and saw that it had been written only twenty minutes earlier, so definitely well after Gaston had found her in the pool.

Her heart pounded as she read the note:

Hi, Morgan:
You must remain silent. Otherwise, prepare yourself, for you will be joining me in hell.
Beware the Nouveaux Girondins!
Your former friend,
Claire

Morgan was shaking when she closed the email supposedly from her friend and quickly glanced at the gushy but worried ones from her mom and Carrie. She had not related anything to them about the rollercoaster of a thriller she was now living. Enough time to recount all that once she was back in the United States. But they had seen the news reports of the shocking events in Bordeaux and were obviously worried, asking whether she would like to come home.

They will sure be surprised when I arrive tomorrow!

As she went into the small bathroom, she told herself again that Claire was dead, and it could definitely not have been she who wrote the message.

But who then? The Nouveaux Girondins connection…

Could it be Luc playing games with her? Or more likely some other creep trying to frighten her. General Tolbert perhaps? Surely not: he would be too busy, especially right now.

Well, whoever it was, they were sure succeeding!

Settling into the comfy bed, she focused her mind on examining her own precarious situation. She would certainly be next after Claire, if they could get to her, Morgan thought. But so far, the only reference to her in the media had been in that first speculative report on Jérome and the members of his supposed jihadist cell—the American female student suspected of being corrupted by him and still on the loose. Why had they not yet broadcast pictures of her on the screen? Surely, that would be an obvious way to track her down, and Luc and Joseph would have access to the many photos that Claire had taken on her iPhone, even though they would be of her old blonde, long-haired self. And even more bizarre for Morgan was that they hadn't even identified her publically by name.

Perhaps, was it because Tolbert and gang were suddenly afraid that if they somehow found out about Morgan, the minister of justice and her allies would try to get to her first? After all, she was the only one with any evidence of the plot against the president and the government that Jérome had alerted Madame Bensoussan to. So, the fact that the professor had managed to get in touch with the minister may indeed be a key factor in helping her get away, Morgan mused. The longer her picture and her name were kept out of the media, the better her chances would be to leave, she told herself. Especially, if it could not appear until tomorrow when she exited the European Union at Barajas Airport in Madrid—that would be the crunch. Good old Boubacar, Jérome, or whatever his real name was!

And Alex, he was also in grave danger, she was certain. He knew as much as Claire had known, if not more by now.

But at least he was aware of the threat and would be careful, she tried to convince herself as she finally drifted off to sleep.

ఇఒఎఒ

Morgan woke to a strange ringing sound penetrating

the pitch-black darkness of her room, from somewhere right beside where her head rested on the soft pillow. It took her a few seconds to realize that it was the new Spanish cell phone she had picked up earlier that day and placed on the night table within easy reach.

It could only be Tante Clothilde or Alex, she thought, as she lunged for the vibrating mobile.

"Morgan? Hi," she heard her boyfriend's strong voice at the other end. "Is everything okay?"

"Yes, thanks, Alex. Boy, am I glad you called! And you, are you all right?"

"Yes. So far so good."

"I'm so sorry about Claire. That was terrible news." She struggled to hold back the tears.

"Yeah—"

Morgan sensed over the line that Alex had trouble speaking.

"—my poor sister. My mother took it very badly."

"I'm sure. It's terrible for her."

"Yes. Luckily, Tante Clothilde is taking matters in hand."

"She is great. But do you honestly think it could have been suicide, Alex?"

"No. It was not."

"That's what I think."

"In fact, I am absolutely sure it wasn't. I went to her room soon after I got here, and there was evidence of a scuffle. Also, signs outside of a heavy object being dragged across the grass and the gravel. Clearly, they—whoever did it—got into her room somehow, knocked her out, then hauled her to the pool and dumped her in. Claire's face—which was all I could see of her where she was laid out—also had a bad bruise and a small cut."

"Who do you think did it?"

"It could only have been those frogmen friends of my

stepfather," Alex said with bitter sarcasm in his voice. "The general and his gang."

"God!"

"I'm going to kill them if they're allowed to get away with it."

For a second, Morgan wondered whether she should tell Alex about the weird email. But no need to, she decided. It would just make him that much more anxious. He had enough to worry about.

"Alex, did you hear the interview earlier with the minister of justice?"

"No, I missed it."

"Well, it seems that Jérome—who knew her from ÉNA—managed to warn her that something was going to happen. And she is incensed at General Tolbert's implication that the professor might have been the ringleader of a jihadist plot and the perpetrator of these bombings. And of course, at his crazy assumption of power."

"Well, that's good news at least."

"Alex, you need to get to her somehow. And tell her to get in touch with me once I'm out of Europe. So that I can pass on the information I have about the plot."

"Sure. Good idea."

"The sooner the better."

"Morgan, I also wanted to tell you that I talked to Peter Chapin. You know, the CIA explosives expert. I got his number from the US Consul. I told him that you did not think John's death was an accident. He said he would look into it, as it seemed to click with a lot of other evidence he has unearthed. Chapin is also convinced that the investigation of the Brassault explosion is totally bogus."

"So you see!"

"He's back in the USA now and said if we give him your flight number, he'll meet you when you arrive. He's concerned that Tolbert and his gang will be trying to discredit you to the agency. They are well connected there, I'm sure. Chapin offered to take matters in hand right away."

"That's great, Alex. My flight is…here…here it is. Let me see…American Airlines Flight Ninety-Five, getting into JFK at twelve-forty-five p.m. It'll be great to have someone meet me there."

"You know, Morgan, I would love to, but there are a few things I need to do here. My mother needs me right now—I cannot leave her. And as you say, we need to get in touch with the minister of justice. We have to do what we can to stop this crazy killing. And this…this…coup d'état. Things are totally out of control."

"Yes, of course. Be careful, though. These thugs have killed so many already. I love you, Alex."

"You too, chérie."

"When this is all over—" Morgan stopped mid-sentence, not knowing how to finish the thought.

"Yes. We'll be together, Morgan. Here or over there. But goodnight now. You need to get some sleep. Tomorrow will be a long day."

As she blew him a kiss across the airwaves, she knew Alex was right. She needed to worry about the present. The future would sort itself out.

CHAPTER 28

Elena knocked precisely at six-thirty, and through the graying, early morning darkness of the room, Morgan heard her say at the door, "Señorita, breakfast is ready."

It did not take her long to jump into the shower, get dressed, and pack her very few belongings, and she was down in the kitchen in less than twenty minutes. Fresh squeezed orange juice, a cappuccino and a basket of still-warm home-baked rolls, with jam made by Elena from apricots picked by Roberto in the Habitación's little garden, waited for her on the table. As Morgan tucked into the delicious breakfast, she glanced over at the small TV on the counter where Elena had started to watch the seven a.m. news.

Her attention was tweaked when she heard the announcer say "*Bordeos*," the Spanish name for Bordeaux. She was even more intrigued when the camera showed pictures of her friend Claire, so much so that she asked her hostess, "What are they saying, Elena?"

"Oh, señorita, they talk about a beautiful girl who kill herself in swimming pool at the family chateau. Now they say her brother—no stepbrother—he run the company that make food for the conference where there was that big bombing. They think there is connection."

"How so?"

"I do not know exactly—"

"I think what they are now saying is that the girl killed herself because it was she and her boyfriend who both worked for her brother's company who smuggled the explosives into the room where the meeting was being held." Roberto had been listening to the newscast from over by the coffee maker. "An Algerian student. Rashid something…"

"Unbelievable."

"Yes, very strange, the whole series of bombings in Bordeaux. And now the violence all over France," Roberto continued.

Glancing at the big clock on the wall, Morgan quickly finished the last sip of her coffee, settled up with Roberto, said her goodbyes, and followed him to the little Renault he had brought out of the garage and parked in front of the house.

Less than ten minutes later, Morgan was already going through airport security in San Sebastian, where, after unloading her iPad and coins into a plastic tray, the officer checked her boarding pass and passport. He looked her over several times before he decided it was indeed a woman with a close enough likeness—although clearly an altered appearance—who was trying to board the plane for Madrid, and waved sloppily for her to pass through the detector. Morgan was relieved and went through to look for her gate.

Once she found it, she made her way to the WiFi hotspot, and getting into Gmail on her iPad, immediately saw that the first message was from Claire's address again. God, these creeps were really trying to frighten her! She opened the note with great trepidation, and it read:

Hi, Morgan:
If you open your mouth about what you think you know, you are dead meat, you dumb American whore! As is your asshole of a lover.
Much hate to you,
Les Nouveaux Girondins

These guys sure did not mess around. Of course, they would know about Alex, from Luc or Joseph, and now they were threatening him, too. But Alex and Luc had apparently been so close even before Claire's brother left for the South Pacific and South East Asia—she just—couldn't believe that the de Carduzac son would give his stepbrother away. It must have all been taken out of his hands, though, by Joseph and the general.

She needed to call Alex, Morgan decided, to warn him. So even though the plane was starting to board, she scrolled down for his number on the Spanish burner phone and pressed the green button.

But there was no answer.

God, what if they have taken him into custody as well? Or much worse, done away with him already, like they have with everyone else. Pangs of anxiety overwhelmed Morgan as she boarded the Air Nostrum ATR 72-600 for Madrid.

~~~

She turned the Spanish phone on again right after landing at Madrid-Barajas Airport, as soon as the flight attendant opened the doors of the small turboprop, and saw that there was a message from Alex. Morgan hurried to find a quiet spot inside the terminal, heart pounding extra fast, and pressed the call button once more.

But it was a gruff voice—not Alex's—that greeted her in French.

"Yes?"

"Is—is Alex there?"

"Ha! What's it to you? He may be. But who is this?"

"Can I please talk to him?"

"Is that that Mademoiselle Kenwurzy, the American whore?" So whoever it was, he knew that she would be the one calling Alex.

"Yes, it is Morgan Kenworthy speaking." It made no sense to prevaricate.

"Well, you stupid cunt, how shall I put it?...your boyfriend is somewhat out of commission," the voice answered with a chuckle. "He won't be in shape to fuck you for a while. Maybe you'd like me to stand in for him."

"Can I speak to him, please?" Morgan asked in a bare whisper.

"For that, you dumb American slut, you have to come back to Bordeaux."

"Please, whoever you are, just let me talk to him."

Instead of answering, the man with the gruff voice must have placed the phone near Alex's lips, because all she heard next was a moan. The whimpering of someone in terrible pain.

"Alex…"

"There you go, you whore. That is all your boyfriend will be able to say for a while, you can be sure of that. Certainly, until you come back. And if you squeal to anybody in the meantime, he will never talk again. Nor will you, for that matter."

"Please…"

"Ha, ha. But in any case, don't worry. You will soon be with us, because now we know where you are, you stupid bitch."

It was only then that she realized that they would have

been able to put a trace on the phone as soon as they got the call. And they had her talk long enough to get a good read on her position. Not very smart on her part.

But at least she knew Alex was alive. Although barely, and for how much longer?

꒰꒱꒰꒱

Should I go back to Bordeaux? Otherwise, they might just kill him. But no, Luc would not let that happen. Alex was so adamant that I leave. And if I do go back, they would kill me as well as him. I have to link up with Madame Bensoussan somehow. Alex did talk to Peter Chapin, who will be meeting my flight. The CIA agent will help. He will know what to do. I have got to get to him as fast as possible. That has to be our best chance.

Morgan fought back the tears as she looked at the departure information on the overhead screens and saw that her American Airlines flight left from Terminal 4S and that she would have to take the underground shuttle train to get there. She realized that she did not have much time for the transfer, so she moved rapidly along the corridors to the train. Waiting at the station, Morgan distracted herself by looking up at the TV screen over to the side. She was surprised to see the general being interviewed on a feed from French TV, and although there was no sound, she could make out the Spanish subtitles.

"But General Tolbert, Madame Bensoussan is the minister of justice of the Republic of France," the interviewer was saying.

"Her appointment to that post by former President Aragon was clearly under duress and therefore illegitimate," the general countered cockily. "It was very bad judgment on his part to cater to France's Islamic population to such an extent. It is unconscionable that a foreign-born Muslim female should be the Keeper of the Seals of France …"

"She was legitimately elected to the Assemblée Nationale of France, and duly appointed minister of justice by the president of the Republic …"

"That was a travesty. As I said, just a blatant ploy to keep the huge and growing Muslim population of this country happy. And now, this woman is trying to usurp the power of the presidency…"

The shuttle train came and Morgan had to board, but she was disgusted by what she had heard from the lips of the general. And it was this man who was now in charge of the entire country! Or thought he was. But hopefully, the Constitutional Court would challenge his self-declared rule.

Once at the other end, she made her way to passport control on P-1 and stood in the longish queue for non-EU passports. She kept checking the clock on her cell phone, getting more and more fidgety as she approached the booth of the immigration official at the front of the line, wondering whether it would be as easy to get past him as it had been so far with the various document checks.

The officer took the passport and the boarding pass, checking the names on both, then scanned the passport with the machine in front of him. That task completed, he looked at the picture, then at the name again, the personal details, then back at Morgan. He got up from his chair and said, "One moment, please. You must come with me, señorita."

"Is there a problem?" Morgan asked, suddenly flustered.

"Please follow me."

Morgan did not have much choice, so she made her way along a corridor behind the balding and heavyset immigration officer, who led her to a door marked *No*

Entrar. He knocked then opened the door: the empty room was bare and gray, furnished with a metal table and four chairs.

"Please, señorita, sit down."

"What is the problem, may I ask? I cannot miss my flight. I have someone waiting for me in New York."

"Someone will be with you very shortly. You must wait here."

The official left her alone, taking her passport.

※

Although it seemed like an eternity during which Morgan turned her mobile on several times to check the time—there was no phone reception in the room, she noticed—it couldn't have been more than six or seven minutes before the door opened and three large men dressed in the same gray suit—all with chests bulging, presumably where they carried their weapon in a holster—entered, and positioned their hulking bodies around Morgan.

"*Mademoiselle, est-ce que vous parlez français?*" So these thugs were French. That did not bode well, Morgan thought.

When she answered, "Yes," the biggest of the three, visibly relieved, sat down opposite her. He whipped out a badge and shoved it in front of Morgan's face. "We are with the French police. The Renseignements Généraux. You will come back with us to France. It is a matter of national importance." Morgan had seen on the ID card that the man was indeed with the RG and his name was Captain Denis Marquart. She recalled vaguely that it had been an officer of the RG who had investigated the Bérégovoy death.

"Why, what have I done?" And then Morgan remembered her rights. "I want to see the American Consul. I am an American."

"You will later. But now you are coming with us."

"No. I have someone waiting for me in New York. You cannot just kidnap me."

"Mademoiselle, please do not resist. You are coming with us whether you like it or not."

The man stood up and beckoned to his colleagues, who moved toward Morgan. She saw that she had no choice, so she, too, got up and reluctantly followed the police officers out of the room.

CHAPTER 29

Captain Marquart finally gave Morgan's passport back to her when they were seated in the backseat of the unmarked black Renault Samsung SM7, racing from Orly Airport to the center of Paris.

"You may need this to identify yourself when we get to our destination," he said curtly.

"Where is that?" Morgan asked.

But the taciturn captain did not deign to give her an answer.

It was only when the car pulled into the posh Place Vendôme and stopped in front of the beautiful Hôtel de Bourvallais, and she saw the sign over the entrance that read *Ministère de la Justice* that her heart lifted with hope. So maybe, after all, she had not been kidnapped by allies of the general and his fellow renegades only to be silenced, but rather by French law enforcement agents still loyal to the minister of justice. So that she could recount to the minister what she knew of the recent attacks on the French government and the declaration of martial law by General Tolbert.

But how had they known where to find her? she wondered. It must have been Alex who told Madame Bensoussan where she was and which flights she was taking. Before he was captured by the bad guys. And the police had picked Morgan up before Les Nouveaux Girondins could get to her.

Thank God for Alex! But where was he now? Where was he being held? She would ask the minister to help find him—

The captain ushered her into the late seventeenth-century palace, through security where she unnecessarily flashed her passport, and led her through the big ornate entrance hall and up the *Escalier d'Honneur,* the majestic staircase to the *Salle des Sceaux*—the Hall of the Seals—which served as the waiting room for ministry business. Here, while he jumped the queue and told one of the secretaries what his mission was, Morgan tried to take her mind off what was happening by looking at the replicas of the numerous seals used to formalize the law of the land, as well as the different versions of the French Constitution dating back as far as 1791. Among these, she was pleased to see, was one that was the Girondin Constitutional Project of 1793. Certainly, she remarked to herself, the original Girondins seemed to have been much more respectful of legal process than Les Nouveaux Girondins.

They did not have to wait long before one of the clerks led them back down the staircase to the main floor and through a cavernous but magnificently decorated hall to the massive doors of what he explained was the *Bibliothéque de la Chancellerie*, which now served as the office of the Minister of Justice, who was also the *Garde des Sceaux,* or the Keeper of the Seals.

She knocked on one of the leaves of the door then pushed it open. Morgan, peeking from behind Captain Marquart, saw a diminutive but quite beautiful olive-skinned woman raise her head from the papers strewn across an Empire desk at the far end of the big room.

"*Madame le Ministre,* Captain Marquart and Mademoiselle Kenworthy, the American student," the secretary said, announcing them.

"*Merci,* Madame Jolicoeur. Please have them come in."

The captain stepped aside to let Morgan enter first, and she did so hesitantly, as the minister got up from behind the desk and approached her with a smile. "Welcome, Miss Kenworthy," she said, greeting her fluently in English. "I am so glad you are here. Please sit down," Madame Bensoussan continued, indicating for Morgan to take one of the ornate Louis XV armchairs in front of the desk while she thanked and dismissed the captain.

"I understand, Miss Kenworthy that you have some information that could be of vital importance to the security of the French state. A friend of yours…yes, I have it here," the minister said, as she found a piece of paper among those laid out neatly on her desk. "A Monsieur Alex de Lavallée, called yesterday, claiming that he was an acquaintance of my good friend Professor Konaté, who was injured in the blast at the Palais Rohan in Bordeaux, and who is now accused by our intelligence services of carrying out a terrorist plot. He explained that you had stumbled upon some evidence suggesting that these accusations were false and that the real culprits may not have been Muslim jihadists—and certainly not the professor—but in fact dissatisfied elements on the far right of the political spectrum here in France, led by General Tolbert himself. Who has, in fact, effectively staged a coup against the duly elected French Government. I do not intend to let him get away with this."

"Yes, Madame Minister. But before we go into that, I think my friend, Alex has been taken into custody by General Tolbert's men and is being held I don't know where. His life is in danger. Is there anything you could do to help find him?"

"By all means, I will see to it." The minister picked up the phone and Morgan heard her telling the secretary to ask Marquart to come back. Within seconds, there was a knock on the door. The captain re-entered the library, and Zaida Bensoussan and Morgan explained Alex's situation to him. "We will find him, Madame Minister," was all Captain Marquart said before he left again.

Over the next hour, Morgan related what she had found out, and how, to Madame Bensoussan, who could not help but be indignant at the brazenness of the plot by General Tolbert and his allies. Morgan admitted that she was not quite sure whether Tolbert and his associates had carried out the plot themselves, or whether they had just aided and abetted jihadist terrorists, facilitating and turning a blind eye to their actions. The minister was quite intrigued by the notion that Russia may have been supporting the plotters, although again Morgan could offer no real evidence for this. At the end of it all, Madame Bensoussan said, "Thank you, Miss Kenworthy. What you have told me is monstrous. I congratulate you on uncovering all this. Your actions are heroic, and you are doing France a great service by coming here to recount these details, no doubt at substantial risk to your life." Morgan did not want to remind her that she had been literally kidnapped and brought there by the RG against her will just as she was trying to leave Europe.

"Certainly, what you have told me puts flesh on the already pretty clear case we have in front of the Constitutional Council against Tolbert's assumption of power." And looking over at the priceless eighteenth-century clock on the marble mantel piece, she added, "In fact, I was just on my way to see the president of the council in the Palais Royal. To get the particulars of their ruling, and to announce it jointly with him. Hopefully, that will make it clear to all Frenchmen who the real culprits are in this sorry series of events. And especially to the military and the intelligence services—some of whom seem to have been falling in behind Tolbert—that they are acting against the principles of the French Constitution." And picking up the phone again, she gave instructions to Madame Jolicoeur to order her car and to come into her office.

"Morgan—may I call you that?" the minister of justice asked, but did not wait for an answer before continuing. "Where are you staying in Paris?"

"Well—" Morgan stuttered. "I don't really have—"

"Good. That is what I thought. You will stay with me. Here, in this beautiful palace. The guest rooms are empty, and you deserve to be pampered for a while at the expense of the French state. It will be safer here where I and my security staff can keep an eye on you," Madame Benoussan said as she closed her laptop. "And we will have dinner together after I get back. Unless, of course, you have other plans," she added with a smile.

Just then, Madame Jolicoeur entered, and the minister gave her instructions to take Morgan to the upstairs guestrooms, as she gathered some papers and got ready to depart for her meeting with the President of the Constitutional Council of France.

⁂

Morgan's jaw dropped when the minister's secretary led her into the enormous state guestroom, exquisitely furnished with antiques and decorated with gilt mirrors, luxurious carpets, and priceless paintings. The four-poster bed itself was draped with magnificent textiles, and a cherry wood grandfather clock between the windows ticked away the time. She tested the mattress as soon as the secretary closed the door behind her, having pointed out the bell to ring if she needed anything.

Morgan went over to the French doors on the right of the clock to admire the view of the Place Vendôme, and she smiled as she caught a glimpse of Madame Bensoussan climb into the back seat of her chauffeured car, and drive away to her meeting. For once, she felt safe in the midst of all this luxury. *I am no longer on the run,* she thought. *And moreover, I get to stay in one of the most exquisite palaces in the world!*

Morgan was just about to turn away from the window with thoughts of a steaming soak in the sumptuous en suite all marble private bathroom, when out of the corner of her eye, she saw two unmarked black SUVs come from nowhere and speed after the minister's limousine. At first, thinking this was part of the police cavalcade, she was astounded, when, just as the limo was turning the corner around the square, one of the big Lexuses crashed into the police motorcycle following the minister's car, while the other one pulled ahead of it and, running down the motorbike in front, came abruptly to a stop. Three men got out, armed with machine guns and dressed all in black, with balaclavas covering their faces. Another three similarly attired thugs were already out of the SUV behind and shooting out the rear tires of the minister's limousine. The six men surrounded her car and peppered the windshield and the two front doors with machine gun fire, no doubt killing the driver and whoever was in the front passenger seat. Within moments, they managed to wrench open one of the doors, and reaching in, forced open the back door on the curbside. Horrified, the next thing Morgan registered was a bloody Madame Bensoussan being dragged out of the car, and rapidly moved to the Lexus in front, where she was thrown in the back seat as a thug got in on either side of her, and the SUV sped away.

CHAPTER 30

Shocked and terrified, Morgan knew she had to get away from the Hôtel de Bourvallais as quickly as possible. The feeling of safety she had experienced cocooned in the guest room of the beautiful palace just moments before, had been nothing but an illusion, she realized. Those thugs who took Madame Bensoussan would soon find out that she was here, at the ministry of justice. Probably, some of them were downstairs in the building already looking for her.

Or am I just being paranoid again, she asked herself. *Think, Morgan, think. Think!*

And where to go?

This was Paris, and the only people she knew in the French capital were Anne and Serge, Luc's business partner and both good friends of his. She definitely could not go there, even if she managed to find their address.

John had been living in Paris when he came to Bordeaux for the Brassault investigation, but he was now dead. There was Peter, Peter Chapin his friend. Might he be in Paris? No, he was supposed to meet her at JFK in New York.

But of course, the US Embassy! That was the obvious place for her to go. Even if they didn't believe her story at first, if she kept insisting they talk to Peter, they might come around. The CIA operative would no doubt make his way quickly back to Paris. And—and maybe they would let her stay at the Embassy until then. That was US territory and off limits to Tolbert.

During the few weeks she had spent in Paris early in the summer, Morgan remembered going to the American Embassy just off Place de la Concorde, and that it was actually not that far from Place Vendôme. She would just have to sneak out of the Hôtel de Bourvallais, and try and make it there on foot as unobtrusively as possible. She realized, though, that this would be dangerous because by now Tolbert and his allies would probably know she had changed her appearance. They might even have a picture of her. Plus, she knew she had to hurry because it was almost five p.m., and access at the embassy after that would be difficult, if she remembered correctly.

ଏ⌒ଚ⌒ଚ

At the embassy, Morgan had trouble getting past the security booth since her name was not on the daily access list. It also took a while for her to persuade the doubting official that she was indeed the person in the passport picture. And when, after twenty minutes of arguing, she finally convinced the guard that she needed to see Peter Chapin from the CIA, he deigned to make a call to someone, and then putting down the phone, said, "Mr. Chapin is not here presently."

Morgan was getting exasperated with the guard but tried to hide her mounting anger. "Could I please talk to anyone from the CIA? I have some information relevant to the recent death of John Stanley, one of their agents. He was deputy chief of mission here, so I am sure you know him too."

With this new information, the official promptly made

another call, finally saying to Morgan, "Please, sit over there, miss. Someone will be with you shortly."

This last appeal seemed to have cut through the bureaucracy, as within five minutes, a rather large woman wearing glasses and some pea-green-colored attire that to Morgan looked very much like a sweat suit, finally came over and asked her to follow. The secretary guided her through another security gate then slowly lumbered down a corridor until she reached the door at the end through which she ushered Morgan, asking her as she entered, "Coffee? Tea? Some water, Miss?"

Morgan didn't answer as she tried to register what greeted her in the darkened room. Around a table sat four men, two of them with shirtsleeves rolled up, while a good-looking, dark-haired woman dressed in a charcoal business suit was standing holding an infra-red pointer to highlight aspects of a slide presentation. It was she who greeted her with a smile. "Hello, Morgan. We are so glad to see you. Could Alisha get you something to drink?" And to one of the men: "Sean, would you please turn the lights on?"

"Thank you. Some water would be great, please."

"Morgan—I hope you don't mind me calling you by your first name. I know you are a student in Bordeaux, doing a junior year abroad from the University of California at Berkeley, is that correct?" The woman seemed to be all business, but how did she know who she was? "Let me introduce all of us. We make up the special interagency task force put together to investigate the recent terrorist activity in France that John Stanley was starting to look into. He and I worked very closely together. John's death was a great loss to all of us, and to me personally." That was it: John must have mentioned Morgan's name to this woman.

"To me as well. We had become friends."

"My name is Maureen Corcoran, and I'm the CIA's Chief of Mission here. Around the table, we have Major Steven Jones from the NSA, Paul Talbot, Consul, Political Affairs, Sean Kelly, the Ambassador's Special Assistant for security affairs, seconded from the Agency, and Abdul Hamad, from the Agency's Middle East and North Africa Division. Missing is Peter Chapin, from the CIA's terrorism section and our explosives expert, who I believe was supposed to meet you in New York."

"Yes, it was Peter I was hoping to find here."

"He's meeting your plane at JFK." The CIA Chief glanced at her watch and continued, "In fact, you should be arriving right about now, if I am correct." And then to the blond Special Assistant: "Sean, would you please step outside to call and tell Peter that we have Miss Kenworthy here, and that he should get on the first flight back to Paris?"

"Of course." Sean jumped up and was out the door as Miss Corcoran continued. "Peter told me that a friend of yours, who also claimed to know John, had called him suggesting that you had some important information on the Bordeaux bombings, and that he should meet you at JFK on your arrival to make sure that you got the proper attention. We took this very seriously because John had—and Peter himself also has—doubts about the investigations by the French intelligence services. So, Morgan, we have been hoping to catch up with you, either in the US or here…"

The chief of mission was interrupted by a knock on the door, followed immediately by it being pushed open. It was not Alisha bringing Morgan's water, but a man in uniform, who said, "Excuse me, ma'am, but you should turn the TV on. France Twenty-Four. Or for that matter probably any French station."

"Why? What now?" Miss Corcoran asked, as the Major from the NSA got up and turned on the forty-inch flat screen on the far wall. "Another bombing?"

"No, ma'am. It seems that General Tolbert is about to make an announcement."

He was standing on the steps of the Palais Royal with a tall, thin man the announcer identified as Gilles Montalbert, the President of the Constitutional Council, cowering slightly behind him. Cameras were flashing and representatives of the media scrambled to hold microphones closest to the general's lips.

"My fellow Frenchmen. We now have taken into custody the person we believe is the very top commander in France of the jihadist cell responsible for the recent terrible bombings in our country that have killed many of our elected politicians as well as other innocent citizens. This terrorist leader you will know as Zaida Bensoussan, who was named minister of justice and Keeper of the Seals of France by ex-President Aragon. No doubt under duress, I might add, by direct and indirect pressure from the extensive Muslim population we now have in France. We have reason to believe that Madame Bensoussan is the head of the notorious terrorist group al Mourabitoun in France, reporting directly to Mokhtar Belmokhtar and the al Qaeda leadership. You are no doubt aware that al Mourabitoun, in cooperation with al Qaeda and the Daesh, have vowed to commit acts of terrorism against all French interests not only in France but worldwide, and have, as their ultimate goal, the destabilization of France and Europe and the reestablishment of the ancient Islamic Almovarid empire which included el-Andalus in Spain and a large part of southern Europe as well as much of North Africa. Al Mourabitoun is closely allied to al Qaeda and we believe also has ties to ISIS, and we know that some of these groups have been advancing this strategy of reconquest through massive immigration—both legal and illegal—into these lands combined with infiltration of governments and specific acts of terrorism aimed at weakening institutions and social structures. In order to protect our country and our continent, we cannot sit by passively and let this go on here in France. We must intensify the fight since these international terrorists have declared war on us. It is with this in mind that I have asked the Constitutional Council to endorse the imposition of martial law throughout France until further notice, and the President of the Council, Monsieur Gilles Montalbert, is here with me today to bear witness to the strong support of this distinguished body for our fight. My fellow Frenchmen, through vigilance and unity of purpose, we will win this war. God bless France and our values of *liberté, égalité, fraternité!*"

How hypocritical, Morgan thought to herself. What the general was doing was completely counter to the ethic of freedom, equality, and brotherhood he was claiming to espouse. So this was what the minister of justice's kidnapping was all about! Tolbert wanted to preempt her statement and get rid of his strongest opponent. But how had he managed to cow the Constitutional Council into submission, Morgan wondered.

"Miss Corcoran," Morgan broke the silence that followed the general's statement as Major Jones turned the volume on the TV down. "These are all lies. I believe that General Tolbert and his far-rightist partners were somehow behind the Bordeaux bombings. These acts of terrorism that they have perpetrated, serve the very convenient dual purpose of decimating the elected government of France and staging a coup d'état and putting the blame on France's Muslim community to stoke up hatred against them. I have just come from telling Madame Bensoussan everything I am about to tell you, and I saw her being kidnapped by what I am sure were General Tolbert's forces. I was on the run before that already, and in fact, it was the minister of justice who had me brought back. When I saw her being taken away, I rushed here because I did not know where else I would be safe."

"Bravo! How did you get to the minister of justice?" the political affairs consul asked.

"She had me picked up in Madrid as I was trying to leave Europe. The same friend that called Peter Chapin to tell him to meet me also called her to tell her that she should get in touch with me because I had some information that could be useful. My professor in Bordeaux, Jérome Konaté, had already tried to warn her about what was going on. But he was injured in the bombing, and taken away by the general's forces, I think. He is being accused of leading the team that carried out the bombings and is being held somewhere secret."

"Well, that is very interesting," the station chief said. "Ever since John first started working on this line of investigation—I believe, Morgan, at your insistence—we are more and more of the same opinion as you. That it was not just North African or Middle Eastern jihadists but also the militant far right and rogue elements within the intelligence agencies who facilitated and allowed these acts to be perpetrated. It is, therefore, they who bear much of the responsibility for these deeds of terrorism against the French state. It appears more and more to be the case that they did this with support from Putin's Russia, which has a clear interest in subverting European democracies. But maybe you could take us through your evidence step by step. And if there are any leads coming out of it, we will need to follow them up—"

Just then a knock on the door, and Alisha finally entered with Morgan's water, followed by the tall and handsome, blond Sean Kelly, who just nodded and said, "He's on his way back."

"Maureen, if I may interject," Major Jones interrupted. "Perhaps before anything else, don't you think we should try and find out where they have taken Madame Bensoussan? As the only senior cabinet minister of the elected government still alive and willing to openly stand up to Tolbert, she could be a key figure in reestablishing stability and democracy in France. I think this should be our priority."

"I agree with Steven," Paul Talbot supported his uniformed colleague.

"Hmm. On reflection, I think you are both right," Maureen Corcoran assented. "We must try and track the minister down first. Morgan, do you have anything that could help us?"

"Well, unfortunately, not really. She was taken away in a black unmarked Lexus SUV. There were two vehicles exactly the same, and they knocked down the two police motorcycle escorts. Just as I left the ministry, I saw that one of these officers was being bundled into an ambulance. If he is still alive, he might know more, although I doubt it. The other one was covered with a shroud, so I am sure he was already dead."

"I will have my people check the hospitals," the CIA Station Head said more as a note to herself than to the team around the table.

"Miss Corcoran, if I might add," Morgan continued, "it seems that some elements of the Renseignements Généraux were loyal to the minister. In fact, she had a team led by a Captain Denis Marquart pick me up in Madrid, and when I asked her to help find Alex de Lavallée—the friend who knows Peter Chapin—who is now definitely being held by Tolbert's forces, it was the captain she asked. Perhaps you should get in touch with Captain Marquart."

"Good idea. He could give us some much needed local

assistance and support. We will also try to find your friend. Alex de Lavallée—I have made note of his name." Maureen Corcoran glanced at her watch as she said this, and then added, "But thinking about it, it's getting rather late and if we're going to find these people, we had better get on it while their tracks are still fresh. Plus, Morgan, I see that you are tired. And no wonder, you've been through a lot. If you all agree, I think it would be better for us to meet back here first thing in the morning for the full debriefing. Say at eight? That would have the added benefit that Peter will be with us. And Morgan, don't worry, we will put you up here on the embassy premises. This is US territory and you will be safe here. Sean, would you be kind enough to show Miss Kenworthy her quarters please?"

"But of course, Maureen."

"Thank you." Morgan got up to follow the special assistant to the ambassador out of the conference room, and it was only then that she realized how worn out she really was after the events of the last couple of days. So exhausted in fact, that when Sean Kelly asked her in the corridor if she would like something to eat, all she could say was, "No thanks. I think I will turn in right away if you don't mind."

It did not even matter that the furnishings in the small closet-sized room were extremely sparse, with a narrow cot for a bed and a desk and chair for her to plunk Alex's backpack down. Quite different from the luxurious room at the Hôtel de Bourvallais, but adequate for her purposes.

Time to crash, Morgan's body was telling her. And within moments of stretching out fully clothed on top of the tucked-in sheets and scratchy government-issue blanket, Morgan was sound asleep.

CHAPTER 31

The next morning when Morgan found her way down to the same conference room where they had met the evening before, she was delighted to see that Peter was there, coffee and croissant in hand, standing in the corner talking to Maureen Corcoran.

"Well, well, Morgan," the CIA explosives expert said. "If not New York, then why not Paris? I am so happy that you are here with us. And above all, safe and sound."

"Not as happy as I am."

Morgan's whole being filled with joy when she heard Alex's deep voice resonate from the doorway. Turning around, she saw her boyfriend's muscular form fill the doorframe, hiding most of the pea-green sweat-suited Alisha who must have guided him there.

And then she noticed that his face was hardly recognizable: swollen, bruised, cut—but it was Alex all the same. As he opened his arms, Morgan rushed over to him, oblivious of the assembled bureaucrats, wrapping her arms around him, and lifting her face to receive his kisses.

It did not take long, though, for her tears to start flowing, tears of relief now that she was reunited with her lover and no longer a lonely fugitive.

But also tears for him, since he was visibly in pain.

"Oh, Alex what have they done to you? Who was it? The general?"

"Later, Morgan. I'll tell you later."

"So you are Alex de Lavallée?" The CIA station head took charge. "Very pleased to meet you. What happened?" She went over to Alex, inspecting his wounds.

"It's nothing, ma'am. Just got beaten up a little."

"Well, I'm not so sure it's nothing. We'll get the embassy doctor to look at you. But please grab some breakfast, and then perhaps we could start the meeting by having you tell us how you got here, who captured you and where you were held. It may be very germane to helping us find Minister Bensoussan."

"Yes, that is definitely what we need to focus on now," Paul Talbot agreed.

∽∾∽

Over morning coffee and pastries, Alex—gritting his teeth and not letting go of Morgan's hand for one moment—recounted what had befallen him over the two days since he had last spoken to Morgan when she was still in Spain.

Alex told how he had made that call from the terrace of the chateau with the throwaway phone to inform Morgan that he had proposed to Peter that he should meet her flight. And that right after, he had called the minister of justice, and when no one responded, left a message. At the time, Tante Clothilde was in the salon reading, and Chantal, who was the only other person at Chateau de Carduzac—and who was still on tranquilizers after the death of her daughter—had gone to bed already. On his way to his room, he stopped to check on her.

Alex did not sleep much that night, anxiously wondering whether Morgan would be able to evade General Tolbert's clutches and get out of France and Europe. But the next morning, when he had finally dozed off, he was woken at seven-thirty by the ringing of the burner phone on his night table: it was Madame Bensoussan, herself, on the line. Alex told the minister that Morgan had some evidence suggesting that the general and his far-right allies may have been somehow involved in the bombings and killings, and that certainly, Professor Konaté was not part of any jihadist terror group. He urged her to get in touch with Morgan, and gave the minister her flight information to facilitate this—so that she might be able to catch her before, or between flights. And right after he finished talking to Madame Bensoussan, he tried to call Morgan again, but she did not respond. *She must be checking in, or already on the plane*, he consoled himself.

Sipping his coffee in the kitchen, he heard what he thought were several cars screech to a halt on the graveled drive in front, and when he went over to the window saw that it was a cavalcade of three black SUVs. The general and some men Alex did not recognize got out, and although he suspected that they may have come for him, he knew he would not be able to escape, so he nonchalantly went outside and greeted Tolbert.

"Well, hello, General. I am sorry, but Joseph is not at home. Nor Luc."

"Don't worry. We are not here for them. We have come for you."

"I'm here to help my mother. She needs me right now. You know, she has gone through so much, with the death of my sister—"

"Of course, my friend. We know that. And I will leave two of my men behind to make sure she is all right. But you, Alex, you must come with us now."

"But—"

"Do not resist, my friend," the general said, glancing at the four menacing large men in black who now surrounded the young de Lavallée.

Alex was bundled into the back seat of one of the SUVs with a thug on either side, one of whom Alex thought could have been a replica of the James Bond villain, Jaws, because of his metallic false teeth and oversized square head and body. The general clambered into the rear of the other Lexus RX 350, and the two vehicles sped away, leaving two of the men and the third SUV behind to mind matters at the chateau. As they left the grounds, the Jaws look-alike pulled a black blindfold over Alex's eyes. This heightened Alex's apprehension and he wondered whether he would end up like his sister, Claire, whose corpse was now in the morgue at Libourne, the nearest town to have one.

❧❧❧

The drive was not long—no more than fifteen or at most twenty minutes, so, although he had never been there, Alex guessed they must have been taking him to Chateau Tolbert. He knew they had arrived when the SUV slowed down, stopped, and then proceeded up a hill. Luc and Joseph had talked about the general's magnificent place standing on a natural mound overlooking the whole area, with vineyards covering the slopes.

As Jaws hauled him out of the SUV by the scruff of his neck, he heard the general say, "Take the boy down below, I'll be there in a few minutes." So Tolbert still thought of him as a boy—of course, he had been around already well before Alex's real father had passed away so mysteriously.

With a guard grabbing each elbow, Alex was hustled

along, and he thought they must have been leading him through the wine cellar, judging from familiar odors and echoes. He heard a squeaky door being unlocked and was led down some stairs, along a corridor, then the opening of another metal door and finally he was plunked down roughly onto a hard wooden seat. It took the thugs a few moments to handcuff him to the chair, and it was only after that, that his captors took off his blindfold. They left him alone in the room but did not close the door.

A quarter of an hour passed before the general came in with the Jaws look-alike and another guard. He sat down opposite Alex and said, "So, my boy, tell us where your lover is hiding. We need to talk to her urgently."

"Who do you mean, General?"

"Don't play dumbass with me young man. You know who I am talking about. None other than that stupid American slut who has been staying with the de Carduzacs. Your sister's friend."

"Morgan Kenworthy? I am sorry, General. I can't help you. I have no idea where she is." Alex struggled to keep from letting his anger show.

"Well, my boy," Tolbert continued, "perhaps we can give you a little encouragement." He gave a nod to Jaws who swung Alex's chair around and straddled his legs. "Last chance!" the general shouted. And when Alex did not answer, Jaws gave him a vicious cuff with the back of his hand, then looked over at his boss, who said, "Now, Alex, why don't you be reasonable. You don't want my buddy here to mess up your handsome looks. Your American bimbette of a lover might be less keen on putting out for you if you have a banged up face, you know."

"Fuck you!"

The general gave Jaws another nod, saying, "Surely, you don't want this fine specimen, Jaws here to stand in for you—" as the giant gave Alex another slug, punctuating it with a loud guffaw that echoed in the cavernous cellar. "—once he has turned you into an impotent mass of jelly."

Fortunately, the general's cell phone rang and he answered with a "Joseph! Just a second." He glanced over at Alex, as if to see if he had heard, then muffled the phone against his jacket, before saying, "We'll continue this later," and exited the room talking to Alex's stepfather.

Alex was left alone with Jaws and the other thug, and he sorely wanted some water to rinse the taste of blood from his mouth. He didn't think he had lost any teeth so far, but his lower lip was badly cut and his right cheek was starting to swell up.

Just then, his burner phone rang in the front pocket of his jeans. *Oh God, no! That will be Morgan, for sure.* "Some water please," he begged in an attempt to divert the attention of the guards. But it was a futile request, as Jaws just gave off a raucous laugh, lumbered over, and frisked his crotch. As he did so, he said to Alex, "No wonder you have a gun in your pocket—that will be your slut of a lover." Another cackle, and then to the other guard: "Sam, go and activate the trace." Finding the cell phone, he opened it up and answered in a gruff voice.

"Yes?"

"Is—is Alex there?"

"Ha! What's it to you? He may be. But who is this?"

"Can I please talk to him?"

"Is that that Mademoiselle Kenwurzy, the American whore?"

"Yes, it is Morgan Kenworthy speaking."

"Well, you stupid cunt, how shall I put it?…your boyfriend is somewhat out of commission," Jaws answered with a chuckle. "He won't be in shape to fuck you for a while. Maybe you want me to stand in for him."

"Can I speak to him, please?" Morgan asked in a bare whisper, ignoring the abuse.

"For that, you dumb American slut, you have to come back to Bordeaux."

"Please, whoever you are, just let me talk to him."

Instead of answering, Jaws placed the phone near Alex's lips. Alex moaned in pain and despair.

"Alex—"

"There you go, you whore. That is all your boyfriend will be able to say for a while, you can be sure of that. Certainly, until you come back. And if you squeal to anybody in the meantime, he will never talk again. Nor will you, for that matter."

"Please…"

"Ha, ha. But in any case, don't worry. You will soon be with us, because now we know where you are, you stupid bitch." Jaws hung up, and put the phone on the table in front of Alex, with another loud laugh.

A few minutes passed and the general rushed back into the room, shouting, "Come on, put the boy in one of the cells. Sam, you go tell Fortier to get the helicopter ready. We must fly up to Paris immediately…"

"But, sir, the girl phoned. We traced the call, and she is in Madrid," Jaws said, obviously pleased with himself. "At the airport."

"Good work. I'll call Gomès on the way. He will arrange for her to be picked up."

❧❧❧

Jaws had no trouble in hurrying Alex down the corridor to one of the cells that opened off it. The cubicle was dark and dingy, with a bench and a bucket as the only furnishings. After Jaws shut the door with a "Rot in hell" for a goodbye, for want of anything better to do, Alex sat down and took out his mobile phone—which he had adroitly swept up from the table as the big man had looked away after unlocking his handcuffs—hoping there would be reception down here and wondering whom to call. Morgan would definitely be a bad idea, he decided. Chantal was already extremely upset after Claire's death, on tranquilizers and unreliable. Perhaps Luc? Would he help? Alex tried his stepbrother's number, but to his dismay, there was no answer. He left a message asking him to call back ASAP. And then he thought of phoning Peter Chapin to see if he had met up with Morgan. It should be about time, he told himself. But Peter, too, did not pick up. Exasperated, Alex again left a message.

ಲನಲನ

Frustrated in his prison cell, Alex paced around for a while then lay down on the hard bench. With hands behind his head as a pillow, he may have snoozed for a while. Startled by a stirring in the corner, he noticed a rat or a large mouse scurrying across the floor. He sat up and decided to check his phone and was surprised to see that while he had passed out, he had missed a return call from his stepbrother, who had also sent an SMS asking, "Ver R U?" Alex pressed the green button to return the call, but Luc's phone just rang and rang. So he left him a voicemail saying that he was in what appeared to be an underground jail under the wine cellar at the general's chateau and asking Luc to come get him out.

ಲನಲನ

An hour might have passed again, and he must have dozed off because it was the clanking of the steel door that brought him back to consciousness. This time, Alex was happy to hear his stepbrother's voice in the corridor. "Okay, Sam, you old fool, what the fuck have you done with my brother?"

"He's just down here. And I done nothin' wrong, sir."

"Well, unlock the door then, Sam. Hurry up, man!"

"What took you so long, bro?" Alex asked, greeting his stepbrother with a hug as he stepped into the small cell.

"Come on, Alex. Let's get out of here," Luc said in English, so Sam would not understand. "We gotta move fast before big man Jaws wakes up. I had to bribe Sam and promise he would not get into trouble for bringing me down here."

"I'm ready. Lead the way."

შა

Alex was relieved as he stepped outside and breathed the cool fall night air of St. Émilion. Relieved to be free again, and relieved that his stepbrother was helping him.

"God, what have they done to you?" It was only then that Luc took note of the bruising his stepbrother had sustained while in the general's hands.

"Another little thing to pay that bastard back for." Alex was already in the passenger seat, as Luc revved up the engine.

Just as they were in sight of the de Carduzac chateau and home, Alex's burner phone rang. "Hi, Alex. Where are you?" Peter asked.

"In St. Émilion. And you?"

"Landed in Paris two minutes ago. You better get up here as fast as possible. Morgan is here at our embassy."

"I thought you—How come?"

"We'll explain later. Can you get here by the morning?"

"Sure, if I drive all night."

"Well, start right now. We need you here. See you at eight." Peter hung up, but that was all Alex needed. Morgan was safe, at the US Embassy in Paris.

At Chateau de Carduzac, Luc pulled up beside Alex's car. "Thanks, Luc," Alex hugged his stepbrother on the gravel courtyard.

"No worries, bro."

"I need to get to Paris ASAP. By eight in the morning," Alex said. "I'll leave right after I grab a quick bite and clean up a bit. But you and I need to talk sometime soon. You know, Luc, Claire's death—I don't think it was suicide. I'm pretty sure."

"What are you saying, Alex?"

"Just that. But we'll speak later. There is a lot we need to discuss."

"Definitely. It seems you know something I don't."

"A lot, Luc. And I have quite a few questions for you. We need to talk about everything that has been going on. Compare notes. But not now. I gotta get to Paris."

"Okay, Alex. Don't you worry. I'll take care of Chantal. I'll check on her right now, in fact."

"Thanks." As they went inside, Alex gathered his thoughts and asked, "By the way, Luc, can you find out where Jérome is being held? These buggers must have him in some military prison or some way out secret detention center. We need to get him out if he is still alive."

"I'll see what I can do. Drive safely."

CHAPTER 32

When Alex finished relating his experiences of the past two days, Maureen Corcoran said, "Well, Alex, you're lucky to be alive. And thank God for your stepbrother."

"Yes, without him, I would still be rotting down there in their little cell, or be a stand-in for a punching bag for big man Jaws."

"So you think Luc can help us find where Professor Konaté has been taken? That could be important also because they may be holding Madame Bensoussan in the same place."

"I hope so. At least he can do some ferreting around. But I wouldn't rely only on him. They won't necessarily tell him since it seems he is only on the fringes of all their plans."

"Hmm." the station chief thought for a moment before continuing. "Sean, could you please ask Alisha to track down Captain Marquart of the RG? We need him to come here ASAP. Or at least tell her to have him call in."

"Sure thing, Maureen." Sean sprang to his feet and was out the door.

"In the meantime, could we hear from you, Peter? What are your contacts working on the investigation of the two bombings telling you? What have you learned?"

"Well, Maureen, there is a lot to tell. But the salient point, I guess, is that the direction John was trying to investigate—thanks to Morgan's persistence—seems more and more like it has got to be the right one. The line that this General Tolbert would have the world believe is patently ridiculous. When one reflects on it, there is no way these two bombings attacking the French Government could have been carried out by two random brother jihadists led by a Muslim cabinet minister and a professor partly of North African origins. Who both check out as real French patriots."

"Well, I am glad to hear that. Because the evidence that Morgan has, points in that direction too," the CIA station head agreed. "Doesn't it?"

"My view is that at the very least there must have been connivance by some members of French intelligence," Chapin continued. "And the vehemence with which Tolbert is pushing the notion that Bensoussan and Konaté were the leaders of a cell of terrorists that pulled this off, in fact, points to him as being the real *capo di tutti.*"

"I can add to that," Alex joined in. "My stepfather and the general, who was a friend of his from the DGSE, started some group called Les Nouveaux Girondins, which seems to be made up of former and current members of the intelligence community and the armed forces, as well as some of the more right-wing elements in French politics. Morgan actually overheard snippets of a conversation in a meeting of this group that could be interpreted as the general and my stepfather and a few others discussing what may have been a plot to get rid of President Aragon and his government."

"Yes, it was so difficult to believe what they were talking about, that I wrote it down right after. I have it here." Morgan handed the crumpled piece of notepaper across the table to the CIA station chief. As Maureen

Corcoran looked at the piece of paper, Morgan continued: "Also, I unearthed some evidence—or at least indications—that General Tolbert and Alex's stepfather may have been involved in a number of other...er...how shall I put it?...eliminations of key people in the past. Maybe even some important government officials like former Prime Minister Bérégovoy. And that they carried out the 1985 *Rainbow Warrior* bombing in New Zealand under orders from Mitterand. Joseph de Carduzac and General Tolbert were in a unit of frogmen way back then, and it would seem that it was they who destroyed the ship."

"Morgan, that is pretty serious stuff. It goes back a long way, though—"

"More to the point, and to get back to the present," Peter interrupted the station head, "or at least to more recent times. One of the more puzzling things that has come up at both bombing sites is the presence of nanocomposites. At the Brassault site, we found that they had been engineered into some of the airplane components that were delivered in the normal course of business. At the Palais Rohan, we believe that they may have been part of the plastic trays that the catering company used—and this dovetails perfectly well with what you were saying, Morgan. We have found out that the catering firm, Carnot and Cie., is majority owned by a shell company controlled by Joseph de Carduzac, Alex's stepfather, and is run jointly by Luc de Carduzac, Joseph's son, and a good friend of his in Paris."

"That sounds like a pretty sophisticated operation indeed," the ambassador's special assistant for security affairs observed.

"Phew! That points directly at my stepfather and stepbrother. I will ask Luc to clarify. I doubt that he would have knowingly been party to ordering serving trays that were in effect bombs to blow up the event. And kill people. My stepfather, though, I am less certain about." Alex thought for a moment before continuing, "He may have been coerced by his friend, though."

"Sure. That would be a help, Alex, if you talked to your stepbrother. Of course, I would also like to do so, either with you or separately, if you could arrange it," the CIA station head said, just as there was a knock on the door and Alisha poked her head in before opening the door wider and saying, "Captain Marquart is here."

Maureen Corcoran stood up and went over to welcome the tall French police officer as he came through the door. "Thank you for coming on such short notice, Captain. We need your help."

"And it seems that we may need yours as well," the captain answered, looking around the table to see who else was there. "Ah, Mademoiselle Kenworthy," he added, clearly surprised, "I am so glad to see you are safe. I was worried, because Minister Bensoussan still has not been found, and General Tolbert's forces kidnapped her very soon after I left you in her office."

"Yes. Thank you, Captain. I got away just in time, I think."

"That is one of the things we would like to work with you on, Captain. Finding Madame Bensoussan," the station head interrupted. "In fact—"

"Yes, to find her must be a priority. Minister Bensoussan is the only cabinet member to have spoken out publicly against Tolbert. She is the key to reestablishing democracy in our country. Luckily, when we looked through her desk, we found this list that she must have put together of députés who are close to her, and who we believe she must have thought would be willing to…how do you say?…line up with her against Tolbert. Perhaps you would like to make a copy, Madame Corcoran?"

Marquart took out a page torn from a notepad and handed it to the station chief.

"Thank you, Captain. As I was saying, we may be able to help find her. Alex de Lavallée—but Alex, maybe you can tell the Captain what you know."

"Glad to. To sum up: yesterday, I was taken and held in a cell dug under the wine cellars of General Tolbert's chateau. Near St. Émilion. As you see, I have a few bruises to show for it. I was finally able to contact my stepbrother, Luc, who managed to get me out. I do not think Minister Bensoussan and Professor Konaté—who is also missing—were there, though. I have asked my stepbrother, Luc, to try to find out where Tolbert's gang might have taken the professor—which is likely to be also the same place they are hiding the minister."

"So, we should get in touch with your stepbrother as soon as possible?"

"Yes, but it is a long shot. Depends on whether he is still trusted—he was on the fringes of some of the Nouveaux Girondins activities, although I don't quite know why. Worth a try though."

"Definitely. On another matter of interest," Marquart continued, "you may not have heard yet, but the President of the Constitutional Council, Gilles Montalbert, committed suicide last night. Tragically, he hung himself."

"Terrible," Paul Talbot, the Consul for Political Affairs stood up, shocked. "How? I knew Gilles well. A fascinating man."

"What is more, the other members of the council we have been able to contact are telling us that they were outraged by Montalbert's support of Tolbert, after they had voted almost unanimously the day before that the martial law declared by the general had no legal standing. In fact, several were talking about going to the press."

"This is very interesting. No doubt, Morgan, that result was what Minister Bensoussan was going to announce when she was kidnapped by Tolbert's rogues. They captured her to prevent her from making the statement, and to give them time to pressure Montalbert."

"Fortunately, one of the members of the Constitutional Council—as you may know, it is made up of former presidents and other wise men, most with a bit of legal background—is livid at what has happened and has agreed to take a leadership role in setting matters straight." Captain Marquart had obviously done his homework. "I am talking of former President Fourcade."

"The good thing is that Monsieur Fourcade belongs to the current party in power, although he is from the more conservative end," Paul Talbot weighed in. "Potentially, he could also be part of the solution. In the absence of contact with the minister of justice, our best way forward might be to work with Fourcade. Approach him and get him to work with the names on the list Madame Bensoussan put together. Until we can find her. Hopefully, still alive."

"Hmm. You have something there, Paul," Maureen Corcoran agreed with her colleague. "What do you think, Captain?"

"Yes, I think until we can find Madame Bensoussan, it makes a lot of sense to pursue that approach. Perhaps you, Monsieur Talbot and Madame Corcoran, could come with me to talk to former President Fourcade. And maybe in the meantime, Monsieur de Lavallée and Mademoiselle Kenworthy could go back to Bordeaux to talk to the stepbrother to see if he can help us track down Madame Bensoussan. And the professor."

"Excellent! We have a plan. Alex, does that work for you? Morgan? Maybe, right after the doctor sees you, Alex—I insist, I think he is just outside—you two can take off. Meanwhile, Alisha will organize flights for you."

"I would like to go with them, if that's all right," the CIA explosives expert piped up. "There are a number of loose ends I need to tie up down there to advance the investigation."

"Of course, that makes a lot of sense, Peter. It would also give me comfort to have you with them. Thanks."

CHAPTER 33

Captain Marquart had arranged for an RG car to pick them up at the airport, and Alex insisted that the police drop them off at Rue Emile Godard. He and Morgan would continue their trip in his battered old Citroën, while Peter could call around from there to arrange meetings with his fellow investigators.

Along the way to St. Émilion, right at five p.m., Alex turned the car radio on, wanting to hear the latest news. The first item was introduced as the shocking statement by former President Fourcade that, in fact, the Constitutional Council had decided that General Tolbert's announcement of emergency military rule constituted a coup d'état and that he, as a former head of state, would do everything in his power to return France to a legitimate democratic republic. And that Gilles Montalbert had been forced by Tolbert to say the contrary—probably with the threat of revealing what their investigation had unearthed, that in his spare time the President of the Constitutional Council had been frequenting gay prostitutes. It was presumed that it was this intimidation by Tolbert that led to his tragic suicide. Fourcade called on the military and the police forces in all of France to turn against the usurpers and to arrest the general and his supporters. On charges of treason and perversion of justice. He also spoke out against the wrongful captivity of Minister Bensoussan, demanding her release by those holding her, as well as that of Professor Konaté.

"Isn't that great? Fourcade is a brave man," Morgan said.

"He has nothing to lose and everything to gain. I hope that spells the end for Tolbert and his gang."

"Do you think so?"

"Well, unless he manages to escape the country. And as soon as he hears all this, I am sure that is what he will try to do."

They rode in silence, Alex immersed deep in thought, Morgan dozing off a bit until they pulled up at the steps of Chateau de Carduzac. Chantal immediately broke out in sobs when she saw them—Morgan so reminded her of Claire, she said—but managed to recover and gave them both a hug, before telling Gaston to put on two more places for dinner. She was expecting Luc and Joseph to be back by seven, she told them, and they could all assemble for drinks then.

"They are over at the general's, you know, an important meeting, after all that has happened." Chantal seemed clueless of her husband's nefarious activities.

Alex, glancing at his watch, saw his opportunity and did not hesitate. "Maman, I need to pop out to see a friend, over in St. Émilion. But Morgan has had a long day and will want to freshen up before dinner. I will try to be back as soon as possible but don't wait. With all that has happened, I am sure it will be good if you and she had a talk, and no doubt Luc and Joseph will be glad to see her over a glass of champagne."

"Alex—" Morgan was puzzled, but the look on her friend's face told her not to press any further. He would explain in due course.

☙☙☙

Morgan was on her way down for the promised bubbly, still wondering what Alex might be up to, when passing by the open door to Joseph's study, she heard some mumbling and the frantic opening and closing of drawers. She decided to peek in, only to see the French aristocrat slamming one of the drawers shut, then looking up, straight at her.

"Well, my dear, how lovely to see you," Joseph said, visibly surprised by the presence of the curious American girl. "What are you doing here? I thought you had left for—" He clearly decided in mid-sentence not to finish it. Was it because he knew that Morgan had tried to leave for the USA and did not want to give this away? "And is Alex with you?"

"We came together, but I think he had some urgent errand to attend to. He will be back later, though, he said."

"Hmm. Do you know where he went?"

"No, but maybe Chantal does. To see a friend in St. Émilion was what I think he said."

"Well, let's go down and have that champagne." And with that, Joseph ushered Morgan out of the home office and down to the salon.

☙☙☙

"So much has happened since you came to us, Morgan," Joseph said, pouring the Krug into four of the five chilled flûtes that Gaston had placed on the coffee table. "Here in France—"

"Yes, Claire's untimely death. Since then, things have not been the same for me."

Morgan wanted to remind de Carduzac *père* of the

tragic event for which she thought he might have some responsibility. But she regretted it as soon as she saw the tears well up in Chantal's eyes.

"Sure, I understand. Her suicide was sad for all of us. Tragic. But I rather meant politically."

"Of course. Really a lot. With the two bombings. And an apparent coup d'état…" Morgan looked straight into Joseph's eyes as she said this.

"Well, the minister of justice certainly took an aggressive stance. But she has now been removed—"

"Yes, she was the only one who dared challenge General Tolbert's assumption of power."

"What do you mean?" Joseph's face turned dark and aggressive. "Surely, you are not saying that in these difficult times—"

"The news as we were driving down—the announcement by former President Fourcade that, in fact, the Constitutional Council decided that General Tolbert had acted illegally in assuming power. Fourcade was the one who used the term coup d'état."

"Fourcade—but—but Gilles Montalbert confirmed that they had decided it was all legal. I'm confused. I really don't believe he would have lied. What else did Fourcade say?" Joseph's surprise and alarm at the news told Morgan that he had not heard of these latest developments. So she had the upper hand. For now, at least.

"That was before his suicide. It seems Montalbert took his life out of shame for lying and perverting justice. And because his sordid secret life was about to be revealed. By General Tolbert. A clear case of blackmail."

"What do you mean?"

"He visited gay prostitutes in his spare time."

"Unbelievable! Not Gilles."

"Yes. And Fourcade called on the military and the police to arrest the general and his co-conspirators on charges of treason. And for the release of Madame Bensoussan and Professor Konaté. So you see—"

"Joseph." Chantal had a very concerned look on her face.

"God, this is monstrous. My friend, Alain—" Fear had replaced the aggression in Joseph's face, as he put down his glass, and standing up, whispered more to himself than the others. "I am sorry, but I have to go attend to something. Luc, are you coming?"

Only Morgan noticed that Joseph had used Tolbert's alias from the *Rainbow Warrior* days.

"Why? Where are you going?" Luc answered. "My place is here. I need to talk to Morgan. And to Alex when he returns."

"Your choice." And from the look Joseph gave his son, Morgan could tell that he considered him a traitor.

"Joseph, where are you going?" Chantal asked her second husband. "You just got back!"

But he was already out the door without saying goodbye.

念念念

Morgan was in bed, worrying about Alex when he finally returned.

He kissed her, and to her wondering eyes and the query as to what he had been up to, just answered, "Later," before going straight into the bathroom, shedding his clothes on the way. After his ablutions that included a long shower, still naked, he climbed in beside Morgan, embracing her and holding her close.

"Alex, will you tell me now? Where you disappeared to?" Morgan asked her boyfriend. But instead of answering, he kissed her, and, aroused again, made love to her.

It was only afterward when he jumped out of bed to go to the bathroom, that he said that someday he would tell her, but this was not the time.

CHAPTER 34

Luc was already in the dining room the next morning, reading the *Sud Ouest* over coffee and a croissant, when Alex and Morgan came down.

"Well, good morning, you two. And where did you disappear off to last night, Alex?" the de Carduzac son quizzed his stepbrother. "Morgan was terribly worried about you. Your mother, too."

"Where is she?" Alex posed the question to avoid answering the one asked of him. "Maman. She has been acting very strangely since Claire's death."

"Not down yet. Still sleeping, I guess."

Just then, Gaston came in with fresh coffee and croissants for the two newcomers.

"Did you see the news?" Luc continued after the butler left. "It seems that your instinct was right, Alex, not to trust the general. It's now coming out in the press that he may have been party to these terrible bombings. It was not just the jihadists, as he would have had us all believe. They are saying that he was secretly helping them so that he could remove Aragon and take over power for himself. As a strongman, in a right-wing military coup. A bit hard for me to believe, but who knows?"

"Isn't that what you wanted, Luc?" Morgan asked.

"And tell us honestly, Luc, how much did you really

know?" Alex pressed his stepbrother. "You went to those meetings of Les Nouveaux Girondins. Wasn't that where all this was being planned?"

"Well, I did know that the general and my father were wanting to get rid of Aragon. And you are right, so did I. Along with almost nine out of ten French voters, judging from the polls. I didn't like his policies, and I loathed the man himself. But I was never in on any plot if there was one. Never a part of it. I swear. I wasn't at the meetings where they discussed the bombings if they really had something to do with them. I really had no clue."

"Luc, then at the very least you should have told the authorities what you did know."

"Come on, Alex. As I said, I knew very little. Plus, they would have only relayed the information to the general. And what happened to Claire would probably have happened to me, too."

"Okay, then. To make amends, tell us where they might have taken Madame Bensoussan. And Professor Konaté."

"No need for me to speculate, Alex. Here, read this article. It will tell you that a couple of hours after Fourcade made his statement, a police car pulled up in front of the ministry of justice in Paris and out climbed Madame Bensoussan and Professor Konaté. Both intact, and happy to be alive and free again. Apparently, they had been held in a military prison just outside Paris on the orders of General Tolbert. The commander of the prison took it upon himself to release them when he heard the ex-president's statement. He had been an avid Fourcade supporter."

"Well, that's a relief—"

"Maman! Good morning." Alex saw his mother appear in the doorway. She did not look good—the stressful events of the last few days, the lack of sleep had taken their toll—and seemed very agitated. "Are you all right?"

"Has anybody seen or heard from Joseph? I am really worried," Chantal said, pouring herself a cup of coffee. And then, "I don't want to lose him too, now," as she broke into violent sobs.

"No, not since he left in such a hurry last night," Luc answered his stepmother, as Alex, glancing over at Morgan, went over to hug her. "Maman, are you okay?"

But Chantal just continued weeping on Alex's shoulder.

"When Joseph got up to leave," Luc continued, "I first thought he wanted to get another bottle of champagne. And then on reflection, that he might be going back to the general's—maybe he had forgotten something. Before we came back for drinks, they were having such a long private conversation, just the two of them—all while I was tasting some of the Chateau Tolbert wines with Sam and Jaws. Actually, they make pretty good wine over there."

"I don't know," Alex said, taking a sip of the coffee his mother had poured.

"Well, maybe you two boys could go over to the general's to see if you can find Joseph," Chantal said, wiping her eyes and taking the coffee from Alex's hand. "Perhaps he did go back and decided to sleep over there. But that would be strange—he didn't have his pills, toothbrush, nothing," Chantal worried again. "I'll call the police."

༄༅༄

Morgan and Alex piled into Luc's car for the short drive to the general's. By habit, Luc turned on the radio.

They caught the tail end of an interview with Madame Bensoussan on France Info.

"Yes, six cabinet ministers survived the two bombings, and we will be forming a provisional government with the guidance of former President Fourcade and the Constitutional Council. We will be talking to députés from all the other parties in the Assemblée Nationale to try to form a grand coalition national unity government, which is what we deem appropriate for these difficult times. We need the help of everyone to bring a fractious, troubled France back together and rebuild our great society. And, as you know, according to the Constitution, the President of the Senate, Michel Daubigny, will be the acting President until we organize the next elections."

"Madame Bensoussan, will you be the prime minister in this government?"

"We will leave that to the Assemblée Nationale. One of the first votes will be to elect a prime minister. And then a vote of confidence in the newly formed government."

"What do you see as the priority for the new administration?"

"The restoration of order. Convincing the different ethnic groups in France that they can, and must live together. That only if they are willing to live side by side in harmony, will our society work."

"That seems to be a very tall order, Madame Bensoussan, in these troubled times. Good luck to you and your colleagues."

"Hmm. She seems to have her head screwed on all right," Alex commented, as Luc came to a halt at a stop sign.

"Yes, she is very smart and has a lot of integrity. A great lady," Morgan added.

"Well, it will take a lot more than just some nice words to bring all the ethnic, religious, and ideological groups in France together. For one, you have to have a working and growing economy which everyone feels a part of." Luc was skeptical. "Plus, we will still have the jihadists who are committed to infiltrating our borders and causing trouble."

"Maybe they will be less likely to do so if they see one of their own religion at the head of the government," Morgan expressed a thought that came into her head.

"Not unless Madame Bensoussan is willing to try to turn the whole country into a Muslim fundamentalist state." This from Luc.

"Well, we can be sure that the Tolberts of France will never allow that. Nor will I, for that matter," Alex said. "France is great because it is a truly secular state. And that cannot be allowed to change."

කාකා

They arrived at Chateau Tolbert.

"Hmm. They will be long gone," Alex said, as Luc drove his Peugeot through the gates. "Certainly, by the time the police get here. But it's good that Maman is calling the authorities. It's high time they started looking into Tolbert's activities."

"It seems there is no one around," Luc said as they drove up in front of the chateau. "There are no cars here."

"Yeah. It does seem deserted," Morgan agreed. "You must be right, Alex."

"Well, let's go in and check it out, anyway," Luc said.

"Don't you think we should wait till the police arrive?" Alex asked. "Just to be sure. After all, we would be breaking and entering."

"I guess you're right."

"I'll just call Chantal. To make sure she has them coming."

ひとひ

"So, your father has gone missing?" Sergeant Derain asked Luc. They knew each other from grade school in St. Émilion, where they had been friends before their ways parted.

"Yes, my stepmother is very worried. We think he might have come over to see General Tolbert last night."

"Hmm. No idea where else he would have gone," Alex observed.

"Well, we were coming here anyway, since it seems that the good general may have been mixed up in some nasty business. I don't yet have the warrant for his arrest but I know one is on its way. So I was ready to come."

"Thanks, Olivier. Oh, this is my stepbrother, Alex, and a friend of the family from America, Morgan Kenworthy."

The police sergeant said, "Bonjour," and then beckoned to his colleague. "Okay, Pierre, let's go in. The rest of you, if you want to come with us, keep your hands to yourselves. Just in case. We don't want irrelevant fingerprints all over." He led the way, first through the grand entrance and hallway, then meticulously through every room on the first floor.

On the second floor, as they approached the study, Alex grabbed Morgan's hand and held her back.

"Well, well, well. What do we have here?" Sergeant Derain said to himself as he opened the French doors. Then to the others, "Don't anybody touch anything. Fortin, call for reinforcements. Detectives. Forensics. And a coroner."

Stepping into the room behind Alex, Morgan was aghast when she saw the body spread-eagled in its own dried-up blood, blue and purple, tongue hanging out, eyes bulging. General Tolbert, looking straight at her. Accusatorily, she thought. She felt faint, and Alex had to catch her from falling.

"So, you said that your father came here last night?" Derain, also visibly shocked, asked Luc after a moment of silence.

"I brought him over earlier to meet with the general. But he would not have done this. No way."

"Who else was here then?"

"Just us, I think. I left them alone after a while and went to the cellar to taste the general's wine with two of his aides. My father and I departed together, and we went back home for drinks. But he got up all of a sudden after Morgan told him the latest news from Paris and rushed off, saying he had something urgent to attend to. I cannot tell you for sure where he went. He may have come back here, I don't know."

"Strange. There is no car outside," Morgan observed.

"What did your father drive?" Derain asked.

"A Peugeot, like me. The Focus Three-Oh-Eight. Black."

"License number?"

"SE Fourteen Ninety-Two. Mine is Fourteen Ninety-One."

"I will put out an alert for it."

"I can't believe he would have done this." Luc shook his head.

"Nor I," Alex said. "The general was his best friend."

"Well, we won't jump to any conclusions. We'll open an investigation and wait till the results are back. But I must notify my superiors immediately. And would you mind if we came by your place this afternoon so we could take your statements? Also, speak to your mother?"

"Sure, no problem," Luc answered, looking at Alex, who nodded.

"That'll be fine. But she's not in the best state of mind since my sister just passed away."

"Yes. We know. Very sad. Please accept our sympathies. We will try to be gentle."

"Thank you. See you later then."

CHAPTER 35

When the police cavalcade rolled up at Chateau de Carduzac, Sergeant Derain was accompanied not just by his partner, Pierre Fortin, but also by a pair of detectives, and none other than Captain Marquart of the Renseignements Généraux.

"Captain, what a pleasant surprise to see you!" Alex said as Gaston showed the police team into the salon.

"And for me, to meet this illustrious family I have heard so much about. And to see Mademoiselle Kenworthy again." The police officer bowed toward the American girl.

"I guess you know about General Tolbert," Luc said.

"Yes, he has gotten what he deserved. By whatever means. But it seems also that your father has gone missing, from what Sergeant Derain has said."

"He didn't come back last night. I am worried to death," Chantal said, barely able to hold back the tears.

"We have located his car at the station. Here in St. Émilion," Derain added. "Although no one claims to have seen Joseph de Carduzac there."

"Please. Please. You must find him," Chantal implored.

After the formalities were out of the way, and some of the painstaking ground of the local events over the last twenty-four hours rehashed for Marquart's benefit, the captain said, "So, your father, Luc, may have been the last person to see the general. If he did, in fact, go back to Tolbert's chateau again. Otherwise, Luc, you were together with him earlier. And perhaps his two bodyguards, no? Sergeant, have you sent someone to talk to them yet? And do we have an alert out for Joseph de Carduzac in Bordeaux, and at stations along the way? The airport?"

"Yes, that is all in hand, sir."

"And have you had the analysis of the bullets from the corpse back? The rest of the forensic evidence? Any fingerprints?"

"No, not yet, Captain."

"By the way, did your father have a gun, Luc?"

"Yes. I think he kept a gun in a drawer in the desk in his study upstairs. Didn't he, Alex?"

"Hmm. I think you're right, Luc. I remember he used to take it out and show it to us when we were smaller. Wasn't it some kind of a pistol he held on to when he was decommissioned? He was quite proud of it, actually."

"Could we go up to the study to check if it's still there?"

"Of course." Luc stood up to lead the way.

"Sergeant, why don't you and I just go up with our hosts, and of course, Mademoiselle Kenworthy if she would like to come," Captain Marquart said, adding, "We don't want to trouble you, Madame," as he looked into Chantal's sad eyes.

Upstairs, in the study, Luc led the way to the desk, where he reached under the central drawer to move a latch to unlock the bottom left one. He pulled it open, looked, and stuck his hand in, ferreting around. His face darkened with a puzzled look. "Alex. It's not here. Isn't this where Joseph always kept the gun?" He pulled out a soft gray cloth. "It was always wrapped in this, wasn't it?"

"Yes. That's what I remember. Although the last time he showed me was a long time ago."

"It is not there?" Marquart bent his tall form to look in the drawer himself. "Did anyone else know of the gun's existence? And where Monsieur de Carduzac kept it?"

"No, Captain, I don't think so," Alex answered. "Perhaps, my mother. Maybe Gaston. The butler. And Joseph may have shown it to some of his friends. Do you know, Luc?"

"Not that I know of."

"We'll talk to Madame de Carduzac and the help. Hmm—" Marquart said, continuing to rummage around in the drawer. "—it appears there is a box of ammunition for it." He opened the box and pulled out one of the bullets, saying, "I think these were used in the service some years ago. I recognize them because I used them in my pistol in the very early days. A MAB PA-Fifteen. That was the gun I learned to shoot with. A nice little weapon."

"Yes, I think that was it. Or something like it." Luc wracked his memory.

"Sergeant, call the station to see if the bullet analysis is back yet. We need to know if those bullets were fired by a MAB PA-Fifteen or a similar gun as soon as possible. In the meantime, also have your men who are questioning those aides ask about weapons in their possession. It may not be so difficult to find who murdered General Tolbert, after all."

Aided by the two detectives, Luc and Captain Marquart looked around the library to see if the pistol might have been hidden somewhere else, while Sergeant Derain called his office to ask about the bullet analysis.

Fortunately, the results had just come back. And, indeed, the bullets that killed Tolbert were more than likely to have been fired by a MAB-PA-15. When Marquart heard this, he said, "Well, gentlemen, we may have our man. I'm sorry, Luc, but I think it was probably your father who killed the general."

"Yes, sir, judging from the bullets it does seem like it. Although, it is really difficult for me to believe that he would kill his best friend."

"I can't believe it either," Alex added.

"Perhaps not so difficult if he knew that the general was instrumental in Claire's death." Morgan had been thinking quietly during the discussion about the gun. "The killing of his stepdaughter and knowing what that would do to his wife may have been the final straw that turned Joseph against Tolbert."

"But didn't Mademoiselle de Lavallée commit suicide?" Marquart asked, somewhat surprised.

"I am not so sure, Captain," Alex was the one to answer. "I saw signs of a struggle in my sister's room, and her face was cut and bruised. Also, there was a trail of something heavy being dragged from the back terrace to the swimming pool. A body, perhaps?"

"I must say, sir, I also had doubts that Mademoiselle de Lavallée's death was a suicide," Sergeant Derain added. "But the investigation was taken out of our hands very quickly."

"Well, that puts matters in a different light," Marquart said. "In any case, we need to find Joseph de Carduzac."

೧౫೧

"They will never find Joseph." Alex was caressing Morgan's back as they lay naked in Hélène's bed at the chateau later that night.

"What do you mean, Alex? Why not?"

"And it wasn't my stepfather who killed Tolbert."

"How do you know?"

"Because I did it."

"Alex—" Morgan sat bolt upright, letting the sheet fall away and looking into Alex's eyes.

"After I left you last night, Morgan, I went straight up to Joseph's study, where I knew he kept a loaded pistol locked in one of the drawers of his desk. Just as Marquart said, a MAB PA-Fifteen he had retained after he was decommissioned. He had shown it to Luc and me many times, so I knew exactly where it was. A nice little weapon. I took it, along with a few bullets from the box, and drove over to the general's. Not quite, because I parked a ways away, still at the bottom of the hill, and climbed up through the vineyards, approaching the chateau from the back. Fortunately, from the time I was taken there by Jaws and Sam and rescued by Luc, I more or less knew the lay of the land. And how to avoid the guards. In fact, that was quite easy, because the two were out in front, with the door of the general's SUV open, as if waiting for him to depart. That also told me that I didn't have much time if I was going to get to him."

"Weren't you afraid? After what they had done to you?"

But Alex just plowed on. "I climbed into the chateau through a window that was not locked at the back and searched room by room until finally, I found the man himself. There he was, General Tolbert, in his study, gurgling and laughing to himself like a madman, frantically ripping up papers and shoving them into the open fireplace, where flames consumed them. The scene was Mephistophelean—"

"How scary."

"—I tiptoed as close as I could get, loaded pistol in

hand aimed at his back. When I was just within three meters, he slowly turned around, looked at me with eyes glazed over and emitted a horrific cackle as he dropped the files he was carrying—it was then that I shot him point blank in the chest, saying, 'That was for Claire.'"

"God."

Alex continued. "Tolbert's hands went up to clutch his heart, and he uttered a feeble 'How did—' before he started to stagger, arms reaching toward me. I shot him again, saying, 'And that, General, was for my father.' And as he fell over, I stood over him and pulled the trigger one more time. 'This one, you bastard, is for France,' were the words I whispered, hoping the dying man still heard."

"You killed him? Just like that?"

"Yes, Morgan. Someone had to. And I owed it to my sister and father."

"But—"

"So, let me finish. I stood there a few minutes to make sure that the general was indeed dead, watching the blood seep out from his body amidst his last grotesque convulsions."

"Ugh."

"Just as I was about to leave, sure he was dead, who should come into the study, if not my stepfather. He was very agitated, shouting 'Alain, Alain,'—I guess that's what he called him, still from the *Rainbow Warrior* days—'Have you heard? Terrible news—' But it was when he saw me with the smoking gun and the dead Tolbert lying in a pool of blood on the Persian rug, that he knew the gig was up."

"So, what did you do, Alex? You didn't kill him too?"

"No. I just couldn't. Even though I knew he was bad to the core, led astray by his wicked friend. But he is my stepfather and my mother's husband, after all."

"So?"

"I told him to take the general's waiting car and get the hell out of St. Émilion. And France. And to never come back."

"Then what happened?"

"He looked back at me for a moment with pain in his eyes, and then he ran out. From the window I watched him negotiate with the Jaws lookalike and Sam—I don't know what he told them because suddenly Jaws and he got into the SUV while Sam took his car. They all drove off in a hurry. Once I was sure they were gone, I left by the front door and went around the back of the chateau where, on the way in, I had noticed an ancient, unused well. I wiped Joseph's army pistol well and threw it down into it, hoping it would never be found. Then I made my way back here, Morgan, and you know the rest."

CHAPTER 36

The next evening, back in Bordeaux, Alex and Morgan were downstairs in Luc's flat, finishing an early dinner of *moules marinière* and *frites*, followed by a salad and assorted cheeses, all prepared by Sandrine, when they heard a loud banging with the beautiful big knocker on the front door, followed by the ringing of the bell to the apartment. Luc got up to go over to the buzzer and asked, "Who is it?"

"Captain Marquart. Sorry to disturb so late, but I'd like to have a brief word with you and your brother if he is here. May I come up?"

"By all means, Captain." Luc pressed the buzzer. "Second floor."

The police officer looked exhausted and seemed glad to be able to sink his big frame into the comfortable sofa in the living room, where the group was relaxing with their glasses and the two-thirds full bottle of de Carduzac 2004.

"Captain, may I offer you a glass of our wine? The vintage 2004 was an exceptionally good one for us. You must be officially off duty by now."

"Thank you. I will gladly accept. It has been a stressful day—few days."

"What can we do for you, at this hour?" Alex asked.

"Well, I am trying to wrap up the various loose ends of the investigation into this whole sordid affair. The coup d'état, and the bombings. Luc, I especially wanted to make sure that I could count on you as a witness. Since you would know most of the people who were active in Les Nouveaux Girondins."

"Of course. I will do everything I can to help."

"The other thing I wanted to talk to all of you about is the death of General Tolbert and the disappearance of Joseph de Carduzac. Luc, you told me that your father left the drinks party at your chateau suddenly after…I think you said, Morgan had just said something…"

"Of course, Captain," Morgan interjected. "It was right after I told him about the news that former President Fourcade had announced that General Tolbert should be arrested for treason for leading a coup d'état. Along with his supporters. Joseph had not heard, at that point, and when I told him, he became very agitated and said he had to leave urgently. I think he asked Luc if he would come with him."

"Yes, and I said no. I suspected then that he was probably running back to Tolbert's."

"So he left in a hurry and hasn't been seen since. And the general is dead. Shot with a gun that has gone missing from Joseph de Carduzac's desk. By the way, we have searched high and low and have not found the weapon."

Morgan looked over at Alex, but his eyes did not show any emotion.

"He must still have it with him then," Luc observed. "Or perhaps he chucked it somewhere."

"We still haven't found him either. And, as you pointed out the other day, Morgan, he would very well have a motive to turn on his friend if he thought that General Tolbert might have been behind his stepdaughter Claire's death. Á propos which we have reviewed all the evidence, and we are pretty sure now that she did not commit suicide. She was definitely murdered."

"Who did it, do you think?"

"Not sure. But if Claire did have a suspicion about a coup d'état, Tolbert could well have ordered it. Didn't you say, Morgan, that you thought they were trying to keep your friend at the chateau against her will?"

"Yes," Luc jumped in, "in fact, before the bombing, my father had told me in no uncertain terms to make sure Claire stayed there, and that we must bring Morgan down to see her as soon as possible."

"God, Morgan, just think," Alex interjected. "If you had gone with Luc that morning you might be dead now too."

"I'm sure glad I didn't!"

"Maybe it was those two thugs who worked me over—the Jaws look alike and Sam—who carried out the general's orders," Alex added.

"Very possibly. Since they too, have now gone missing." Captain Marquart pulled out a pen and jotted something in his little notebook. "And probably, also the Montalbert blackmail was perpetrated behind Joseph de Carduzac's back, so he was doubly incensed that Tolbert was going too far. Without involving him. He may even have felt it to be his duty to stop the general—perhaps even the bombings and the coup d'état—since, as you once said, Alex, everything your stepfather did, he claimed he did for France. He was a true patriot."

"Yes, in the end, Joseph had reasons to be livid with the general and to want to stop him," Alex agreed, casting a glance over at Morgan.

"Well, all the evidence points to Joseph de Carduzac, in fact, as being the one who shot General Tolbert," Marquart said. "But under the circumstances, I am sure the government will not want to prosecute him, even in absentia, since he did away with someone who had become an enemy of the state."

"That's good to know," Alex interjected.

"On a related matter, Morgan, you mentioned that you may have overheard someone with a Russian accent at one of their meetings?"

"Yes, Captain. I thought I did. But I am not entirely sure."

"Well, just so you know, we have been looking through Tolbert's documents. And bank accounts. There are some large transfers into his accounts from dubious sources. Ones we know the FSB—the KGB's successor—has used in the past."

"Amazing! That would mean that the Russians were actively supporting the plotters. Didn't the CIA head in Paris say that there was some evidence that they are helping the European far-right movements?"

"Yes. That is correct. So you see, Luc, your father may even be sort of a hero in the end. If he did indeed turn against this coup and kill its leader. Although we would still need to probe how much he himself was involved in the bombings. For example, did he know about the nanocomposites in the serving trays?"

"Hmm…" This from Alex.

"In any case, if he gets in touch with any of you, do let me know. We may offer him some kind of immunity if he tells all."

"Good, Captain."

"Thanks for the wine. I better get off now because I am on the first plane to Paris tomorrow."

"Good night, Captain. Thanks for coming by."

∽∂∽

"For a moment, I was going to tell Marquart what really happened. That it was I who killed Tolbert and banished my stepfather from France." Alex was getting undressed, ready to hop in the shower.

"Why didn't you tell him then? The truth, that is," Morgan asked when Alex stepped out and started to dry himself. "Why did you do it, Alex?"

"Because I am sure that if I hadn't intervened, both my stepfather and Tolbert would have managed to get away and never faced retribution. They were always really slippery with all their aliases. Between that, and their network, they would have escaped for sure. This way, at least one is dead, and the other exiled for life."

Morgan brushed her teeth. "And?" was all she could say.

"Moreover, as good a cop as your friend the captain may be, if he really did want to find out who killed General Tolbert he should have been more thorough."

"What do you mean?"

"Well, for one, he never questioned me."

"So?"

"He never asked me for an alibi, never asked where I was at the time of Tolbert's death. He just assumed I was there at the family drinks all along with you. Once he had Joseph in his mind as the killer, and this seemed to be confirmed by the missing gun, that was it. No need to probe any further."

"And you didn't feel you should tell him?"

"Well, Morgan, if I had revealed the truth, I would have had to face all kinds of questions, and my stepfather would have probably weaseled his way out and gone scot-free. I have absolutely no qualms about what I did. Justice has been duly served, and I have revenged my father and sister. And rid France of a powerful right-wing nut. Just let it rest, Morgan."

"So, my boyfriend is a murderer. And we are going to live a lie?"

"Not so," Alex embraced his naked lover. "You and I know the truth. And it is a just truth. That is all that counts."

A passionate kiss stopped the conversation, as Alex lifted Morgan up in his arms and carried her over to the bed.

CHAPTER 37

Prime Minister Bensoussan looked at the double-faced clock made of yellow brass standing in the middle of the huge oval table around which sat all her ministers. She sat across from Acting President Daubigny—who also saw that the time was ten seventeen on a Wednesday morning—chairing the weekly cabinet meeting with the President of the Republic in the Salon Murat at the Élysée Palace.

Discussion had dragged on about how to handle the anti-austerity demonstrations and strikes in several towns around the country, the burning of public and religious buildings by various factions and the continued killings by jihadist terrorists on the one hand and the inevitable reprisals by the far right. Particularly, the recent threats of various organs of what the government and the media now dubbed the 'Daesh' cutthroats—the various loosely combined factions of al Qaeda, ISIS, al Khorasan and al Mourabitoun were frightening. Their acts were becoming more and more serious after the Charlie Hebdo and Bataclan horrors, with the beheadings of several Frenchmen in Syria, Algeria, and Mali, and most brazenly, a couple just a few days ago right here, in a banlieue of Paris, with threats of more such acts to come. Also, attacks on Jewish-owned stores over the last few weeks, usually by masked Kalashnikov-toting gunmen, with the murder of the owners and any unlucky customers who happened to be there at the time. And on a synagogue in Lyon, with ten lives lost. A Jewish cemetery desecrated by young Muslims or right wing teenagers—still not known for sure. A bomb in a mosque in Marseilles, killing seventeen and injuring many more. The death toll was rising daily and the situation was becoming intolerable.

Madame Bensoussan knew that there was a need for better security and strengthened law and order, but she realized that she had to walk a fine line since that was exactly where the far right wanted her to go. And, in fact, it was not entirely clear how much these internal fires were also being stoked and in fact carried out by neofascist elements, some of which—as they had found out in the context of the sordid "Tolbert affair"—were actively supported by the FSB in Russia, which was bent on destabilizing Western Europe for its own purposes. Hmm, she wouldn't put it past Putin to be supporting several jihadist groups as well to undermine Europe.

Zut, the world had become an extremely complex place!

All of a sudden, just as she was about to make a carefully thought out intervention, there was a tremendous boom and a violent trembling, much as she had once experienced in an earthquake in Egypt many years ago. Some of the spectacular Venetian mirrors around the conference room shattered as ministers jumped up and ran to the cracked windows to see if they could see what was happening. When she came out of her shock moments later, the first thing the prime minister did was to press the button on her cell phone to get her newly appointed chief of security, Captain Marquart, on the line at her offices back at the Hotel Matignon.

"Denis, what was that huge blast we just heard? Do you know?"

"Madame Prime Minister, we heard it here too. We are just trying to find out. We have all the TV's on, and all the lines are busy…Lise, what did he say?"

"What's going on Denis?"

"Madame Prime Minister, a report is just coming in. Let me put you on hold for a second if I may."

"Oh my God! Please—"

Marquart came back on the line. "Madame Bensoussan, there has been an enormous blast at the Louvre. This is monstrous…"

No, no, not again, Zaida thought to herself. *Not so soon after the last horrendous series of explosions.* Not even a month had passed. And now, the heart of Paris. The Louvre. Who was it this time? "Denis, what the hell?"

"Apparently, the Musée du Louvre has been obliterated. There is now just a pile of dust and smoke and an enormous hole where it used to stand. The banks of the Seine there have been blasted away and the river is filling the bomb cavity. I am on my way over."

"Casualties?"

"I don't know. But from the size of the blast and the location, many, I would think."

"Keep me posted, Denis." She fought to keep back the tears.

సొసొ

"*Mesdames et Messieurs*, please sit down. We must maintain order here," the prime minister implored her fellow ministers. "I have just learned that there has been another terrible attack on France. Not just on France, but on civilization. On all of humanity. I am told that the

Musée du Louvre is gone with all its treasures. Obliterated. It is likely that there are many casualties. We don't know how many yet. We also don't know who carried out this horrible deed. But we must act decisively and as one, to contain damage to the nation and minimize casualties."

As if from afar, she heard the various comments of her ministers penetrate her thoughts, uttered in disbelief as they stepped over broken glass to pull back their chairs and sit down again.

"*Impossible!*"

"*Comment? Qu'est-ce qui c'est passé?*"

"Jean," Madame Bensoussan addressed the Minister of Interior, Local Authorities, and Immigration, "Get the police and security forces over there as quickly as possible. Fire-fighting and explosives experts. Close down all roads around the site. Increase security at all exit points from Paris—airports, stations, main arteries, etcetera. Work with Stéfan, Valentin and whoever else. Anne," she continued, turning to her Minister of Labor, Employment and Health, "Ambulances, as many as needed. Prepare all local hospitals to receive the wounded. God, this is horrible!"

"Madame Prime Minister," Valentin Fromont, the Minister of Defense and Veterans Affairs spoke up.

"Yes, Valentin. I was just getting to you. Mobilize the armed forces. This is a red alert. All of our military must be mobilized or on standby. I want them in the streets of Paris, supporting the police. This heinous act constitutes an attack on France. And Stéfan," turning now to the Minister of Foreign and European Affairs. "You know what to do. Notify our friends of what has happened, the actions we are taking, and that we are counting on them to stand by us in our hour of need. Now, Mesdames, Messieurs, the meeting is terminated and I am going over to the bombsite. I expect you all to carry out your duties with courage, efficiency, and speed. Now, let's get on it."

༺༻

As she ran down the Élysée steps to her waiting car, Zaida Bensoussan called Captain Marquart again.

"Denis, where are you?"

"At the Meurice. Beyond here it is total devastation. Everything within a seven or eight hundred-meter radius around the Louvre has been obliterated. Just rubble, dust, and flames. My former colleagues say much of the Palais Royal is gone too. Most of the Jardin des Tuileries is burning. The Pont des Arts no longer exists. Paris has been decimated."

"I am on my way. Will be there in four minutes," she said hoarsely, tears welling in her eyes.

༺༻

"Who would have done this?" the prime minister asked her security chief, who was rapidly becoming a friend. She liked him: his coolness, his analytical mind, his professionalism.

"I doubt this time the far right had anything to do with it. My hunch is that this is the full force of the jihadist retribution. It is no longer just Nimrud and Palmyra—they have brought their fight against civilization to our shores in a major way."

"You may be right, Denis. God help us!"

CHAPTER 38

Morgan was working on her laptop in the library, finishing her term paper for Jérome's class when she saw the breaking news on the sidebar.

"Oh, God! Not another bombing."

With increasing dismay, she quickly read through the brief report that talked about the destruction of the Musée du Louvre and the devastation of much of the most beautiful part of the old Paris she loved: the Palais Royal, the Jardin des Tuileries, the Comédie Française, the Pont des Arts, the Pont Royal and many other timeless monuments and buildings. No count of casualties yet, but expected to be in the thousands. On average, the article postulated, fifteen thousand visitors came to the Louvre each day, so maybe two or three thousand dead there, plus people in all the other buildings and the Jardin des Tuileries, on the adjacent busy streets and the bridges. Could be as many as four or five thousand dead. Many more wounded, damaged, no doubt. Much like the Twin Towers. God, how awful. And then, on top of it, the loss of the priceless art and archeological treasures to add to all the human misery. Unimaginable. A horrendous blow to civilization. To all of humanity.

Who could have done this? Morgan asked herself, as

she saw several university security officers enter by the front door. Their leader announced that the library, indeed the university, would be under lock down, given the heinous bombing in Paris. All students and staff were being asked to go home and stay there until further notice.

Another terrible bombing, loss of life. Three in the space of a little more than three months. One worse than the other. France was becoming a war zone. When she thought about it, this one was not likely to have been the far right. It had been coming, though, with all the demonstrations and strikes and unrest over the last month or so. This was likely to be the jihadists, no doubt taking advantage of a weakened French state. Al Mourabitoun or ISIS or al Qaeda. Perhaps a combination. Maybe even all three, united. Daesh cutthroats, as the media were calling them.

It was clearly time to leave France, Morgan thought, much as she loved it here. The liberté, égalité, fraternité France was known for were rapidly being replaced by lack of freedom, as more and more draconian measures were implemented to counter all the social unrest, by inequality as a select few were able to insulate themselves from the turmoil, and by increasing divisiveness and hatred, as one group blamed the other for its problems and stirred up violence.

Fortunately, this was the last paper she had to hand in, and next week, she and Alex were planning to fly to California for Christmas. They had agreed to live together there, while Morgan finished her studies, and Bill Kenworthy was delighted that the young Frenchman would work with him to help build a company that would own vineyards all over the world. Yes, her term abroad was coming to an end, and it was time for her to return home with the man she loved. She was determined that this latest news would not jeopardize those plans.

But since they had to go via Paris anyway, maybe they would stop over for one night, to see what had happened. Although she was of two minds about this, because one part of her wanted to remember Paris as it had been, untouched by this barbarity. She also knew that these last three months had changed everything. Bordeaux, Paris, France, the world would never be the same again.

☙❧☙

Since they were off vacationing in Guadeloupe, Serge and Anne had lent them their spacious apartment in Montmartre. The newly renovated loft had a wonderful view, with the full spread of the City of Light regaling them from the rare Parisian roof terrace. After dropping their bags, Morgan and Alex made their way down to the Seine to see the damage for themselves.

"Oh, my God! This is unbelievable," was all Morgan could say as she approached the metal fence through which she could see workers with masks still ferreting through the smoking rubble and twisted metal, for corpses and whatever was salvageable. The fence extended as far as she could see in a circle with a radius of about one kilometer around where the Louvre Pyramid had been, and the huge crater was partially filled by water where the Seine had rushed in when its banks were demolished. Tears welled in her eyes—from a combination of the loss she felt and no doubt the acrid fumes from the still smoldering ruins.

They walked a ways around the perimeter, Alex holding Morgan close, solemnly surveying the damage. But it was the same everywhere: much of the beloved Jardin des Tuileries right up almost to where the Bassin Octagonal used to delight visitors, burnt, dug up earth. The Italianate facades of the Rue de Rivoli with their symmetrical colonnades formerly, as far as the eye could see, now abruptly caved in just past the Meurice. The Comédie Française, where she had struggled through several Molière plays in the summer, a pile of stones; the beautiful Palais Royal with its funky internal square and gardens, an unrecognizable part of the huge gaping hole now gashing the heart of Paris, and where the stately Musée du Louvre had once stood, just a brackish pond filled by the brown water of the Seine.

"Let's go." Morgan had seen enough. "I can't stand it."

"Nor I. Beautiful Paris, destroyed."

There was dinner to look forward to, with their CIA friends, Peter Chapin and Maureen Corcoran. No doubt they would be able to help them better understand this devastation.

※※※

They had agreed to meet at Le Dôme du Marais at eight, and Alex and Morgan were the first to arrive. In fact, Alex wondered out loud whether Maureen and Peter would be able to get away, given everything that was happening. The waiter came asking if they would like an *apéritif*. Morgan declined, but Alex decided, with all that had happened, he needed a stiff drink. He ordered a scotch, neat. Just as the waiter brought the whiskey, Morgan's cell phone rang. It was Alysha from the Embassy saying that their two CIA friends would indeed be late, and would have time for only one course, so they should go ahead with the first course.

As a starter, they both ordered the foie gras maison with miso paste—possibly their last chance to have the duck delicacy for a while since they would be leaving

France the next day for California—and were well through it when the two CIA agents arrived.

"Sorry," Maureen started to apologize. "But I'm sure you understand."

"Of course," Morgan answered. "We're just glad you could spare the time. It'll be good to catch up."

Pleasantries and the ordering of main courses out of the way, glasses filled with the Chateau Phélan Ségur 2001 Alex had ordered, it was Maureen who launched into the topic of the day.

"Well, as you see, we have our hands full again. Even more so now, because we don't have the insights from you, Morgan to guide us," she said smiling. "Nor Alex, your help."

"That was just being at the right place at the right time. But here we are totally out of our league," Morgan answered.

"So are we, unfortunately," Peter said, taking a sip of his wine. "And the French, it seems, just as much so."

"Besides, it seems that they are even more the targets of these jihadists now than we Americans are," the CIA Station Head added. "Maybe, because they are geographically closer. To where these guys operate from, that is. And perhaps because the increasing anti-immigrant stance of the new government and the French people is causing even more rage among the already irate Muslim population."

"You think it was al Qaeda? ISIS?" Alex asked.

"Or one of the other allied groups. For all we know, they may all have had a hand in it. The Daesh cutthroats, as you in France now call them."

"So bombing them in Iraq and Syria and North Africa doesn't help?" Morgan asked.

"It will not wipe them out because there are so many now. And they are well interspersed among civilian populations. Plus, they are willing to fight to the death," Peter said.

"And inevitably some will get through. They will manage to kidnap or just shoot infidels as they call them, or get their hands on explosive material to pull off a bombing," Maureen added.

"I actually think that this bombing of the Louvre had been planned for some time," Peter continued. "An attack on the Museum was foiled once by the French police when in the summer of 2014 they intercepted messages between AQIM—al Qaeda in the Maghreb—and an Algerian butcher in the Vaucluse somewhere. He was arrested before he went off for training in North Africa. The targets already then were to be the Louvre and the Eiffel Tower. And after Bataclan too, the authorities closed it, if you remember, fearing it to be the next target."

"So it seems they might have gotten some other terrorist to do it."

"Yes. Now with ISIS weighing in and wanting to damage French interests—as well as al Qaeda, al Khorasan and al Mourabitoun—the jihadist forces have more money and many more soldiers ready to die for the cause," Maureen weighed in.

"And they carried this bombing out at a time when France was reeling from two attacks on its core, unfortunately, aided and abetted by home grown right wing militants it would seem," Alex poured some more wine into Peter's nearly empty glass, and then into his.

"And possibly supported by Russia," Peter said. "Thanks, Alex, that better be it on the wine for me. I still need to go back to work after this."

"This success was huge for these jihadists," Maureen continued. "Carrying out such an operation right in the heart of France. Of beautiful Paris, destroying the center of the capital and a good chunk of Western civilization's heritage. And killing more than six thousand three hundred infidels."

"God! Worse than Nine/Eleven," Morgan observed.

"Yes, you might say."

The waiter brought the next course: the roasted cod for Morgan, the stuffed squid for Maureen, the Iberian pork for Peter and the pan-seared veal for Alex. Alex ordered another bottle of the Phélan Ségur.

They talked about politics, both in France and the US and especially about what a difficult time poor Zaida Bensoussan was having at the helm as prime minister, with France under attack from several different angles. "She has been portrayed as an enemy of the people and is now hated by everyone: non-Muslims because she is dark-skinned and not a Christian, Muslims because she is considered to have sold out and not militant in her support of Islam, the right because she is considered a Communist follower of Islam, the left because she introduced some of the much-needed and very severe austerity and security measures." Maureen summed up the plight of the prime minister. "And, of course, the economy is still in the doldrums. With the devastation of these bombings and all the internecine fighting, GDP is shrinking as opposed to growing, unemployment moving the other way and investment has dried up. Not a pretty picture all around."

It was Alex who brought them back to a comment Peter had made earlier, that the right wing groups helping tear Europe apart had the support of Putin's Russia. "In fact, Captain Marquart mentioned that when they were going through General Tolbert's papers and accounts, they found several substantial transfers from dubious sources. Cyprus banks, dominated by Russian money."

"Yes, there is growing evidence that Putin is using the

European far right nationalist movements as a fifth column to undermine democracy and capitalism, and to work against NATO and American interests," Maureen said. "We don't know to what extent he controls them, but he certainly makes common cause with them. And supports them, we are sure, more than just tacitly."

"Could there also be a link—dare I say it—to the jihadists? I mean the Russians," Morgan asked.

"Hard to say. But not out of the question," Maureen answered. "For example, we know that representatives of the European far right have been visiting Syria and Lebanon since the summer of 2013, initially in support of Assad's regime, and that some members of these extreme right delegations were also 'observers' at the illegitimate referendum in Crimea in March of 2014 and more recently in the Donbas. Led by a Belgian neo-Nazi group, they were basically there to support the breakaway pro-Russian faction. And more recently, Rodina, the Kremlin-backed nationalist party of Russia, hosted 150 members of European rightist movements at a conference in St. Petersburg denouncing the west and expressing support for traditionalist values."

"Yes, one can say that Putin is vehemently anti-jihad within Russia, but when it comes to fomenting trouble elsewhere—whether in Europe or the Middle East or elsewhere—he is quite happy to ally himself with whoever. As long as it works against our interests," Peter added.

"So, what you are saying is that Putin and Russia, the jihadists of the Middle East and North Africa and the European far right movements all have the same goals?" Morgan asked, summing up.

"Their objectives intersect, and that is where they are not against working together. They are all anti-America, anti-NATO, anti-democracy, anti-capitalism and mostly chauvinist and fundamentally religious. Of course, where they don't share the same goals, they will work against each other. So the far right will often express anti-Muslim views, and Putin hounds them in Chechnya. The Muslims that is."

"We have a lot stacked up against us," Morgan mused.

"That's not even talking about China," Peter added with a little laugh.

దంద

"So, Morgan, you will marry me, won't you?" Alex asked, lying in bed after they had made love back at the hotel. "Now that the CIA suspects our little secret."

They had told Maureen and Peter that they were planning to live together in California while Morgan finished her studies, and the CIA station chief had asked pointedly, "Am I to assume that there may be wedding bells ringing in the near future?"

Whereupon Morgan turned beet red, and Alex chuckled.

"You don't mean—Oh, Alex, don't be silly. Of course, I will." She leaned over and kissed him.

"When?"

"Well, once I finish this year, I will have one more year of college left. How about after Christmas next year? That will give us—and my mother—time to prepare. After Carrie's wedding this summer. And for you, my French lover, to see if you can stand working with my very American father."

"Okay, chérie. I guess I can wait for a year. That works for me," Alex said, kissing her back. "Now let's go to sleep because we have a long day ahead of us tomorrow."

"No, I want to make love again." Morgan threw off

the sheet and started kissing Alex's chest and stomach, before moving down lower. She, of course, got her way.

CHAPTER 39

They moved into the apartment in Berkeley the Kenworthys had bought when she started her first year at college, and which had been on short-term rental during Morgan's sojourn abroad. It made a comfortable home for the two of them and was an easy walk to the campus for Morgan. Alex would often spend several days at a time away—either in Santa Barbara working on the vines and brainstorming with Bill, or back in France tasting Maître Martin's latest creation, or else on the road learning from the best winemakers around the world and looking at prospects to buy for the newly formed vineyard holding company he and his future father-in-law were building.

The year passed rapidly, with the major events that summer for them being the weddings of Carrie and Lorne at the Kenworthy home in Santa Barbara in June, and of Anne and Serge back in Paris in July. Of course, Alex and Morgan were at both, and while in Paris, Morgan set up a lunch with Zaida Bensoussan, who related the following sorry tale.

❧❧❧

In the spring, on the morning of Good Friday to be exact, sitting in her car, Zaida wondered why she had been urgently summoned to the Élysée Palace. Since in the Muslim calendar, Easter was not a special feast, she had been looking forward to catching up on the neglected paperwork during these normally slow days. The last few months had been a whirlwind of activity, during which only the most important matters got done. Moreover, she had thought that Michel Daubigny, an avid sailor, would be on the Côte d'Azur where he kept a boat and had a posh villa. But no, he had left a message with her secretary for her to come to the presidential palace as soon as she appeared in her office.

Ushered into the Salon Doré by Mme. Fourcaud, the formidable dowager whom Daubigny had kept on from President Aragon, Zaida was surprised to see Valentin Fromont sitting across from the president. She had included Fromont from the right wing as Minister of Defense in her national unity government—against her better judgment, though, given his rumored role in the Tolbert coup d'état.

So it would just be the three of them.

"Madame Prime Minister," Daubigny addressed her in a very formal tone. Zaida found this ominously unusual since they had started using first names recently. "Please sit down. And thank you for coming on such short notice. Especially during the Easter holidays." He seemed somewhat chagrined—perhaps because he had to forego sailing?

"I am always pleased to come to the Élysée Palace, Mr. President." Zaida took the other Louis XV armchair facing the ornate table that had served also as the previous occupant's desk. "I hope, since the Minister of Defense is here, this is not a national emergency. Bonjour, Valentin."

"No...and yes, Madame Prime Minister," the president—more correctly the acting president, Zaida reminded herself—continued, the stress of the moment audible in his voice. "I must ask you and your government to resign. Effective immediately. You no longer have my confidence, nor seemingly the confidence of the French people."

"Mr. President—" Zaida was completely taken by surprise.

"Hear me out, Madame Prime Minister," Daubigny said forcefully, standing up for effect. "There is open rebellion in the streets. Faction fighting faction, ethnic group killing ethnic group, one religion burning the place of worship of the other. This cannot go on. There is complete lack of security within our borders. No one feels safe. The jihadists and troublemakers have virtual free reign. Many lives have been lost and significant national treasures were destroyed with the bombing of the Louvre. An attempt at the Eiffel Tower or Charles de Gaulle Airport may be next. We have to take control of the situation. We need a strong leader who understands security and has the trust of the armed forces to be in charge at the present time. Someone, who will impose martial law with an iron fist. And I am afraid you are not it, Zaida. You don't have the right background."

"But, Mr. President, didn't France just go through the trauma of getting rid of someone from the armed forces who tried to take control?"

"That's just it, Zaida. I, as acting president, am asking Valentin to form a government in your place. His appointment will be unassailable by the Constitutional Council, or for that matter anyone else. I only hope that he and the colleagues he chooses can restore security and peace in our country."

Zaida saw that there was no room for argument, so after a moment's hesitation, but fuming inside, she said in an icy tone, "Yes, Mr. President. You will have the resignations of all my ministers, including myself and Valentin—" And here she gave a pointed look to her minister of defense. "—on your desk by the close of business today."

So much for liberté, égalité, and fraternité in France. It seemed the far right and prejudice had won after all.

"And congratulations, Valentin." She turned toward the smiling man beside her. "Please let me know how I can be of most help. I will move out of Matignon today. And, Mr. President, thank you for the opportunity to work with you in the service of France, and I am sorry that you no longer have confidence in me and my government." Zaida stood up and added, "Good day, gentlemen," offering her hand for a handshake first to the president and then to her backstabbing former minister of defense.

She turned and walked out resolutely, thinking that at least the meeting had been short.

೧೧೧

Morgan and Alex had dinner that evening with Maureen Corcoran. Peter was back in Langley, with most of the investigative work on the last bombing finished.

After a quick catch up over their entrées on personal and more mundane matters, Maureen agreed to bring them up to speed on events in France over the last few months.

"First, the Louvre bombing. It was as we thought, as you will have read in the papers. The combined forces of al Qaeda, al Mourabitoun and ISIL wreaking vengeance on France for its continued 'aggression' against local populations in Syria, Iraq, and the Maghreb/Sahel region in support of the infidel Americans."

"How was it done, do we know?"

"Powerful bombs. EXPLUS-base again, we think. Several placed strategically in garbage cans around the site. Nanocomposites, to heighten the impact."

"So it must have been them."

"As you know, Zaida Bensoussan was removed within a couple of months of taking over, and Valentin Fromont named prime minister. He has brought a number of right-wing politicians into the still supposedly national unity government. Of course, he left Zaida and her supporters out, though. Security measures across France have tightened up, maybe ten-fold. Curfew every night. Heavily armed police and soldiers roam the streets and are ever present in public places and on all means of transport. With frequent ID checks. Many people picked up randomly for interrogation. Very disturbing, because there is definitely racial profiling going on."

"God, it sounds like fascist rule," Morgan observed.

"Yes. It is martial law. Anyone who speaks out against the Fromont government is hassled and taken in for questioning. Dissent is virtually non-existent, and the public media are now increasingly censored. France has become an authoritarian state."

"What will happen, do you think?" Alex asked.

"Well, that remains to be seen. If there is an election, of course, the right will likely win. Either because people are afraid, or because it will be fixed somehow. Probably both."

"How terrible."

"You should be glad to be away from here."

"What about my stepfather? Did the police ever find him, do you know?" Alex asked.

"Not that I know of. I don't think they really tried very hard in the end. They had more important business to attend to. The authorities are no doubt glad to be rid of yet another issue. Plus, the little that has been written about him makes him out as a folk hero of sorts."

"Well, I would have expected as much," Alex said with a smile.

CHAPTER 40

Morgan and Alex got married in a relatively small but luxurious affair at the Kenworthy home, adjacent to the vineyards, in an open field overlooking the ocean. Luc and Sandrine traveled to Santa Barbara via San Francisco and drove down the coastal route—seeing Carmel, Big Sur and San Simeon—and taking Chantal and Clothilde with them on the car trip, while Hélène and Martine and their families came over just for the wedding. Anne and Serge made the journey too, as did Maureen Corcoran and Peter Chapin, but Morgan was most excited to see Jérome and Marie at the event. The professor brought a special letter of congratulations from Zaida Bensoussan, who was under house arrest with her passport confiscated. She only wished that Claire and Rashid could have been there to see their happiness.

༄༅༄

Alex had planned the honeymoon as a surprise for Morgan. The only clue he gave her that it would be somewhere warm, was a suggestion that she should bring her bikini. It was when they changed in Los Angeles to the overnight Air New Zealand flight 5 for Auckland that she finally found out where they were going, at least on the first leg. Once they had settled into their comfortable first class seats and had been served flûtes of champagne and hors d'oeuvres, Alex told Morgan that he had been really wanting to show her New Zealand and Australia.

"I traveled down there in the Antipodes several months ago and loved it. Yeah, I went to look at some vineyards. To buy. For your father."

"And us, I hope," Morgan added, snuggling closer. "I've never been there, so I'm delighted."

ಲ಼ಲ಼

In Auckland, they transferred to Air New Zealand flight 2650 for the short trip to the Bay of Islands Airport at Kerikeri, much of which took them over the beautiful eastern coast of the North Island. As she walked across the tarmac, hand in hand with Alex, Morgan could not imagine being any happier than she was, discovering these magnificent surroundings with her best friend and lover, who was now her husband. A car with 'The Lodge at Kauri Cliffs' subtly marked on its side was waiting for them, and a twenty-five-minute ride took them to the luxurious resort. They were welcomed with a refreshing tropical drink, which they sipped on the plush sofa as the receptionist sat with them to check them into their Deluxe Suite and gave an introductory explanation of the Lodge's facilities.

They unpacked, with the double doors to the terrace wide open to let in the cooling breeze from the Pacific Ocean, and after a long shower together—which ended up being much more than a shower—they dressed and walked over to the dining room at the main Lodge. They were hungry and enjoyed the three-course lunch made with fresh products from land and sea, Alex choosing one of the excellent New Zealand sauvignon blancs he had come to like to accompany the meal.

The rest of the day was taken up by leisurely walks on the six thousand acre site with its wonderful views of the ocean and then down to the stunning Pink Beach on Waiaua Bay for a late afternoon swim, followed by dinner, some loving and a good night's sleep.

༄༅༄

The next day, after a morning swim followed by a copious and leisurely brunch, Alex arranged a hotel driver to take them for the day to Matauri Bay.

"I have a surprise in store for you, chérie," Alex said, with a smile.

"What?" Morgan asked, curiosity tweaked.

"You'll see."

They walked the kilometer long pristine white stretch of sand, stopping once for a cooling swim in the crystal clear waters of the Pacific. Past the campgrounds at the far end, Alex led the way along a narrow path up the verdant hillock that stuck out into the ocean, punctuating one end of the bay. Up top, he took Morgan's hand again and gently guided her toward a huge semi-circular arch of stones seemingly held up by a massive hexagonal stone pillar with a ship's propeller jutting out from it just below the archway.

"Is this the surprise, Alex? What is it?"

"Yes. Just part of it, though. But can you guess what this is?"

"Hmm. Some kind of a monument, I think. To a ship…"

"You're getting warm."

"The *Rainbow Warrior*?"

"Bingo! You got it. Clever girl," Alex said, giving her a quick kiss, and then looking back toward where they had come. "And I see here comes the other part of the surprise. Right on cue."

Morgan's eyes followed his. "Unbelievable, Alex!" she said, as she immediately recognized the tanned and fit, tall and slim man in polo shirt, shorts, and sandals approaching them. He seemed older than she remembered, but still…

"It can't be. Joseph?"

"Right you are again!"

"Well, well, well! If it isn't my dear stepson and the lovely Miss Kenworthy," Alex's stepfather greeted them. "How nice to see familiar faces from home. Amazing."

"Joseph, you look really good!" Morgan complimented the older man as they hugged and kissed each other's cheeks.

"So do you, my dear. It has been a long time." He looked over at his stepson before continuing, "Alex, I thought I would never see you again. Nor, of course, you, Morgan. But I am delighted, to be sure. We didn't part on such good terms, as I remember, Alex, did we?"

"That's all in the past. And we have a lot to catch up on."

"Indeed. What news of Chantal?"

"She missed you for a while, Joseph, but she got over it. She is even dating someone else now."

"That's just as well. I missed her too, but then you were right. I could not go back. Perhaps I will introduce you later to my new girlfriend. And you will have to tell me about the rest of the family. But first, how did you find me?"

"Well, Jacques—" Alex deliberately emphasized the alias this time. "—it wasn't easy. Morgan figured out that you were one of the two French agents who blew up the

Greenpeace ship, *Rainbow Warrior,* way back when, in 1985, here in New Zealand—"

"How in God's name—"

"—and your ex-friend General Tolbert was the other agent. You used the alias Jacques Camurier, and he, Alain Tonel."

"Amazing!"

"Maybe later she'll divulge her secret. But after she told me, I remembered that when we were little, you often mesmerized us at story time with the Cree legend of the Rainbow Warriors who would save the world from the greed and fighting of its inhabitants and bring about a new era. And all the peoples of all the tribes in the world would create a new order where justice, peace, and freedom reigned, and the earth would be renewed."

"Yes, you're right. It was André and I who carried out that terrible bombing. I have thought about it every day since, regretting what I did. The destruction was a lot greater than I had anticipated, as was the response worldwide. I was truly shocked at what we had done, and full of remorse."

"Well, well. The sinner repents." This from Alex.

"To try and make amends, I started giving donations in support of Greenpeace. Anonymously. And, as I became more familiar with Greenpeace, I looked into the *Rainbow Warrior* story and fell in love with it. I took solace in it, and yes, I remember recounting those legends to you and Luc, and Hélène, Marie, and Claire. That was all part of my therapy. You all loved it so. It's such a wonderful but simple story of hope and good and love. So at odds with the world we have created. And yes, you're right, Alex—that's why I am here—to run away from it all and to do penance."

"I am glad to hear that, Joseph. In fact, finally it was this need for repentance that led you to leave the service, rather than just your father's death and the need to take over the chateau and the family business, was it not?"

"Yes, Alex. I am very sorry...for everything."

But Alex did not stop there. "Wasn't it a few years after the mysterious Bérégovoy death that you left the DGSE? Or was it after de Grossouvre's? You finally got sick and tired of doing all the dirty things you and your buddies were expected to do, n'est-ce pas—"

"How did—But I had nothing to do with those incidents," Joseph, shocked, interrupted Alex.

"So, I assumed when you had nowhere else to go, this would be a good place to look for you. Where the *Rainbow Warrior* has its resting place, and where this proud monument stands. This was your road to Damascus, wasn't it? This is where you now feel at home, don't you Joseph?"

De Carduzac père did not answer. Instead, he took Morgan by the hand, saying, "Come." He led her over to the edge of the hillock and pointed out to near some islands. "There! That's where the ship is resting."

Morgan thought what a beautiful burial place this was. For anyone, not just a ship. Even the *Rainbow Warrior*.

"Tomorrow. Tomorrow, we will go down and see it. The three of us will dive—"

"Yes, Joseph. And that is how I finally found you. The Cousteau Dive Company. In Matauri. Founded just a year and a bit ago. By the expert French diver, Jean Cousteau, relative of the world famous scientist and deep sea diver, Jacques Cousteau—the little white lie is right there on the Cousteau Dive Company website and in its brochure. But who would care here in Matauri? 'JC,' Joseph. That was partly how Morgan figured out that you and Jacques Camurier were one and the same."

"God..."

"In the future, Joseph-Jacques-Jean, you should be more original with your choice of aliases."

"I'd love to dive down and see the boat. I did quite a bit of diving in California. I have kept up my C-card," Morgan said, looking out at the enticing waters of the Bay of Islands.

"Good. So you're not a beginner. Alex isn't either, but I know he hasn't done it for a while."

"Okay, Joseph, we'll go diving together tomorrow," Alex said, glancing at his watch and taking Morgan by the hand. "But now, Morgan and I had better start heading back to Matauri. We have a car coming to take us to the Lodge."

"I say, how posh!"

"Would you like to join us there for dinner, Joseph? There is so much to talk about." Morgan wanted to hear more of what the elder de Carduzac knew.

"Yes, at eight. Bring your girlfriend if you like," Alex added, curious to see who had replaced his mother.

"No, but thanks. I will come alone. I want to hear about back home, and I am sure you still have a lot of questions. You will meet her tomorrow. She is a good diver too."

※※※

They sat close together in the back seat of the hotel limousine, and after a long-awaited kiss, Morgan said, "Amazing, Alex, that you were able to track your stepfather down."

"A lot of lucky guesswork, more than anything else. And following the path of your decoding of how he chose his aliases."

"The Cousteau connection was a stroke of genius, I must say." Morgan kissed him on the cheek.

"Well, once I had that figured out, it was just a matter of timing his appearance."

"How did you get him to come on cue?"

"I just called the number on the Cousteau Dive Company website and told the truth—or part of it—that we are a young French couple coming to New Zealand on our honeymoon. Keen divers, and we wanted to see the *Rainbow Warrior*. I told him to meet us at the monument at three p.m. today."

"And lo and behold, he showed up."

"Thank God. And tonight we'll hear his version of all the events. I can hardly wait."

CHAPTER 41

The rainstorm that had suddenly appeared out of nowhere while they were changing back in the room had come and gone, so the maître d' seated Morgan and Alex at a prime corner table on the verandah, overlooking the golf course and beyond it, the vast Pacific Ocean.

"Oh, look, Alex! Look at that amazing double rainbow," Morgan remarked as she took in the breathtaking view. The colors arched across the still dark sky in the southwest.

"It must signal a new beginning," Alex answered. "Didn't one appear when you first arrived at the chateau, chérie? I remember on the terrace, with Joseph, Chantal, Luc, and Claire. That was when it all started. It seems so long ago now."

"Yes. That was when you first left me breathless."

The sommelier came, and Alex ordered a bottle of the Hawkesbridge Marlborough Méthode Traditionnelle 2011 New Zealand sparkling wine, one he had heard good things about. As he was tasting it, his stepfather appeared beside the waiter.

"I see you know your New Zealand wines as well," Joseph said as he pulled out a chair. "Hello, Morgan." He bowed down to give her a peck on the cheek. "You don't know how much pleasure it gives me to see the two of you. It's been so long. And see what I arranged for you again?" He gestured toward the sky and the sea.

So he too, remembered, the other double rainbow.

After the waiter filled all the glasses and the pleasantries were out of the way, Alex took up their conversation where they had left off. "So, Joseph, you were saying earlier that you were not one of those frogmen who may have killed Bérégovoy. And that you were not involved in the assassination of de Grossouvre, or any of the others who met their deaths mysteriously during Mitterand's presidency. Or since, for that matter."

"Why do you think that Bérégovoy was killed by divers? I thought it was a suicide."

"That is bogus. There is a lot of evidence cited online that Morgan unearthed suggesting it was more than likely to have been murder. By two frogmen. That's why we thought it was the special unit you were in, carrying out orders from on high to remove someone who was about to divulge damaging information."

"Well—at the risk of giving away French state secrets—yes, in fact, Morgan is right. It was our unit. But not me. After the *Rainbow Warrior* debacle, I did not want to participate in any further killing. No more strikes at the supposed enemies of France. Or its political elite. I was asked, but refused, at some cost to my career."

"So then, who?"

"I don't need to answer that."

"Okay, Joseph. Then what about Brassault and Palais Rohan? And my father? And Claire?"

"Hold on, Alex. I know I have a lot of explaining to do. But don't accuse me of everything. And let's take it one at a time."

Just then the waiter arrived to take their orders. Alex and Morgan ordered the scallops to start and the rack of lamb to follow, Joseph, a tuna carpaccio and the filet mignon. The wines the two French experts agreed on were the Villa Maria Cellar Selection Hawke's Bay Viognier 2018 to accompany the starters, and with the mains, a La Collina Syrah 2009, also from the famous Hawke's Bay wine producing area.

"Excellent choices," the waiter said as he divided the remainder of the sparkling wine among the three glasses.

"So?" Alex prompted Joseph.

"As I said, the *Rainbow Warrior* incident changed me. At first, I was moved to an administrative job—I think the higher ups hoped that my squeamishness was only temporary and I would change my mind. Probably André and other friends interceded on my behalf. But then, as you indicated, a few years later I was forced out. They no longer wanted a wimp like me around in the unit. My father's untimely death gave me the face-saving opportunity of saying I would quit because I had to take over the running of the chateau."

"So then, Joseph, who was it who assassinated Bérégovoy?" Morgan asked again point blank. "You must agree, you owe it to us to tell—"

After a moment's hesitation while he drained the last few drops of his wine, Joseph said in a bare whisper, "All right then. I guess it doesn't matter anymore. And it will be good to get it off my chest. It was Alain—André. And François. They were the ones."

"And who, pray tell, is François? Alex continued the interrogation.

"François Regis Verlet. The agent from our group who carried out the last minute reconnaissance of the *Rainbow Warrior,* and gave us a drawing so that we would know where to place the limpet mines. After I 'withdrew,' he replaced me as André's usual partner."

"Verlet?"

"That's his alias." Joseph looked out to sea, before adding, almost as an afterthought, "His real name is Valentin Frantome."

"The prime minister?" Morgan asked, stunned.

"Yes. One and the same."

"Of course! The switched initials."

"Holy shit! If this ever comes out…" Alex thought of the consequences.

"That is why I am happy to have a low-key life here, you will no doubt understand. And so glad that you forced me to leave France, Alex."

Just then the starters came, and the sommelier brought the Viognier for Alex to taste.

"A truly great wine, just as I expected."

"Excellent. Miss, some white?"

They tucked into their meal, and it was only after several bites amidst "Oohs" and "Aahs" that the conversation resumed.

"What of my father, Joseph? You ran off with my mother, and then soon after, he died mysteriously. Did you have anything to do with that? You can't imagine the hurt you caused Claire and me."

"Alex, I am truly sorry for what I did, the pain you and your sister suffered. The only excuse I have is…well, our youth. Our love for each other. When our affair started, your father was away on an extended mission. Several weeks. My wife, Dominique, had just left me, and the members of the unit and their partners were all invited to dinner by Valentin and his wife. Chantal was a very beautiful woman and there had always been a mutual attraction. Perhaps she was already having trouble in her marriage with your father, or so she told me later. Anyway, we were both without partners at the dinner, and I drove your mother home. She invited me in, things progressed, and I ended up staying the night. After that, we just couldn't stop seeing each other. She was a wonderful lover, your mother—"

"Spare us the details, Joseph."

"—your father found out. In fact, when he came back from the assignment he caught us in bed together in *flagrante delicto*. He chased us out of your home, and never wanted to see us again, shouting that he would expose me, and all the things that I had done. Including the *Rainbow Warrior,* which he knew about in great detail, since he had organized all the logistics. Although I was no longer doing missions, I was concerned and told André, who was still my best friend, and Valentin, who by now had become the boss. They told me not to worry; they would take care of it."

"So it was they—"

"The next day Chantal got a call from your father telling her that, despite her odious behavior, she would need to look after you and Claire because he was being sent on another operation. Frantome had ordered Tolbert and your father to go to Singapore to dive for the *Calypso,* Jacques Cousteau's research ship that had been accidentally rammed by a barge and sunk. To ascertain whether there had been any foul play."

"So that's where Jean Cousteau came from."

"Your father never came back from the mission. When he returned, Tolbert made a statement, saying that after the operation they decided to take the weekend to dive at Sipadan Island off the coast of Borneo. One of the most beautiful dives in the world, by the way. Your father, who Tolbert claimed, was down on the dive longer than he, fell prey to a tiger shark—Tolbert said he could see the attack from the diving boat—and did not survive."

"I suspect the shark was none other than Tolbert," Alex snorted sarcastically.

"You may be right, Alex, I don't know. Although during the investigation that Frantome carried out, the owner of the hired diving boat apparently confirmed Tolbert's story. In any case, I am truly sorry for my role in this. And although he was my friend, deep down, I feel some satisfaction that you have had your revenge on the general."

The wait staff came to clear the plates, the sommelier to pour the rest of the white wine.

"What about Claire?" Morgan asked when it was just the three of them again.

"Yeah, Joseph. You may as well confess all your sins."

"I truly had nothing to do with—"

"Come on, Joseph, you insisted she stay at the chateau. You even sent Luc to fetch Morgan. You and Tolbert were afraid the girls knew too much."

"That was earlier, you will remember. I was not at the chateau when Claire died. I have no knowledge of what happened. Did she not drown herself in the pool? That was what the police said."

"No, Joseph. Somebody knocked her out in her room, dragged her body across the lawn, and threw it in the pool."

"God. How awful."

"Who was it? Tolbert's thugs, on an order from him?"

"No idea, Alex."

"And my kidnapping? By then, Tolbert was desperate to find out what Morgan knew."

"Again, Alex, you must believe me. I knew nothing of it."

"Come on, Joseph. That is hard to believe. You cannot deny everything."

"But truly—"

"That gets us to the bombings. The Brassault and Palais Rohan explosions. And the Tolbert coup d'état right after. Surely, you were in on those, Joseph. After all, you were one of the founding members of Les Nouveaux Girondins!"

"Yes, that is correct. I did set up Les Nouveaux Girondins with André. But it was André's idea. He suggested the name too. And in retrospect, I guess right from the start the group must have served as a cover for what he and Frantome were plotting. Don't you see? I was used by them. I was a convenient tool since I was no longer part of the military intelligence complex. And with my chateau and wine business, totally legitimate. I may have been naïve, maybe even stupid, but I was not involved in any plot or criminal activities. Besides, those were terrorist attacks."

"Maybe. But, Joseph, you must have seen what Tolbert and Frantome and their gang were up to"

"All the planning, all the operations were done outside the group, sometimes immediately before or after the meetings, behind my back. They did not trust me but kept me feeling that I was in the loop superficially since I was of use to them. After a while, I grew paranoid, because I knew they were up to something terrible."

"What about the meeting at the chateau where I think the general said something was successful and you said whatever it was set matters up nicely and another person referred to the president and then someone else made an undecipherable remark about the potency of the explosives?" Morgan asked. "This was right after the Brassault bombing and before the assault on the African heads of state meeting. I overheard your conversation as I passed by the open door to your study at the chateau."

"As I said, I may have suspected that something major was going on. But I had to let on that I was with them, supportive of whatever they were doing. Otherwise, they would have done away with me. They were already unhappy with my reasons for leaving the service and had given up on me. However, again, as I said, I was useful to them. I had to keep up this charade, if for no other reason than to save my neck. I was very afraid."

"The trays, though, the special trays you ordered for the Palais Rohan events. You must have known about them?" Alex continued to press.

"What about them? I vaguely remember Luc wanting to order some serving trays because Carnot and company did not have enough."

"Well, Joseph, the trays you bought had explosives built into them. They were made partly from highly destructive nanocomposites."

"God Almighty!"

"You didn't know?"

"No. We took the general's recommendation to order from a certain firm. I don't remember the name anymore. Luc was pleased because they gave him a special deal."

"Well, there you go. So it was the general and his friends. But apparently, not you, Joseph. Although it is hard to believe you were totally innocent."

"Please, you must believe me. I had no knowledge."

"You said you suspected something. You could have gone to the police, no?"

"The general controlled the police. You know that. They would have killed me."

"Okay, enough of this. Let's talk about tomorrow and the dive we have to look forward to," Morgan said, just in time as the main course arrived, with the sommelier bringing the Shiraz and the appropriate big-bowled wine glasses.

༺༻

They said goodbye to Joseph at the front entrance and

since there was still some light, decided to go for a short walk around the premises. Over to the cliff side, from where they would have a beautiful view of the ocean and the islands.

"Do you believe what Joseph was telling us?" Morgan asked. "That he knew nothing of the assassinations and bombings?"

"I'm not sure. But it's quite possible that, at first, he was in it for the good of France but then got disillusioned, and only played along. He could have been just very afraid—after all, he saw what happened to Bérégovoy and others who knew too much and were no longer trusted. And with time, the mind always revises history."

"His remorse. Do you think it is genuine?"

"Yes. I think he is truly sorry for everything. Except for running off with my mother. I don't think he regrets that, even if he is remorseful about the pain he caused. He really loved her."

"Do you forgive him?"

"No. Never will. Let him burn in hell. He can do penance for the rest of his life. For whatever his sins were."

CHAPTER 42

After an early breakfast, Alex and Morgan were driven over to the white sandy beach of Matauri Bay in one of the hotel's cars and dropped in front of the little dive hut with the hand painted wooden sign *Cousteau Dive Company* nailed over the open doorway. As they entered, a pretty, dark complexioned woman with flowing long black hair and a great body in a white bikini looked up to greet them.

"Hi there," the woman said, "you must be Jean's stepson and his girlfriend. Alex and Morgan, is it?" She must have been in her early forties, Morgan reckoned, and very fit, judging from her well-toned muscles. The Kiwi woman's comment reminded her that they had not yet told Joseph that they were married.

"Yes, we're here for the dive. The *Rainbow Warrior*."

"My name is Maia. I am Jean's friend—"

"So you have met," they heard Joseph—or Jean, as he was evidently known in New Zealand—say from the door. "Maia will fit you out with all the gear—you will definitely need a wetsuit, even though it's summer here. I'll finish getting the boat ready, and we'll see you outside."

As she selected and put on the basic diving equipment, Morgan wondered whether Maia knew that her Jean was one of the two men who had blown up the Greenpeace ship they were going to see. Probably not, on reflection. Joseph must have completely buried his secret to be able to live his new life.

❧❧❧

It was a short ride of less than ten minutes in the Cousteau Dive inflatable boat to the surface buoy that marked the wreck. On the way out, Maia recounted the tale of the end of the *Rainbow Warrior*.

"I am sure you know that the boat was callously sunk by the French on the night of July tenth, 1985. They did not want it to disrupt their nuclear testing in French Polynesia. Two of their secret agents positioned limpet mines along the starboard side that blew two huge holes in the hull where water rushed in, sinking the ship, and drowning the Portuguese photographer, Fernando Perreira." Morgan glanced back at Joseph, but he was dispassionately looking straight ahead with his hand on the tiller. "The ship was eventually refloated and brought here, where it was scuttled on December the second, 1987, to function as a dive wreck and artificial reef for marine life. Just as in its two previous lives, first as a fishing vessel, and then as the Greenpeace protest ship, it has provided good service to the underwater world."

When they got close to the buoy, Joseph stopped the engine and threw out the anchor. Maia went on to tell them that the marker was connected by a long chain to a large concrete block located just a few meters from the stern of the *Rainbow Warrior*, making it easy to find the ship once they got down there, and at the end of the dive, the buoy up top, marking the inflatable. The seabed was twenty-six meters below the surface here, and the ship's superstructure rose to within fifteen meters of the surface, so Morgan reckoned it would be a fairly deep dive. About an hour total, Maia concluded.

After last minute instructions to stay together and follow Jean's lead below at the boat, they strapped on their tanks, pulled on their flippers and masks. Maia was first in the water, and once Morgan and Alex jumped in after her, she led the way, rappelling down the heavy tethering chain. She stopped in the middle of nowhere, and Morgan thought they might be level with the top of the wreck. Visibility was poor, so she could not see the ship, as Joseph finally reached them, and leaving the security of the chain, led the way through the dimly illuminated green void.

It was not long before the hull of the wreck loomed eerily just ahead. Tilting slightly to starboard, it lay quite deep in the sand, over the years having settled to its current position. Some scrap bits of its superstructure dotted the sand all around, separated from the main body by the action of waves and current.

Joseph led them to the area underneath the sticking up stern and pointed to the propeller shaft that protruded from the bottom of the keel. Morgan remembered that the actual propeller was up on the hill, an integral part of the monument. They started to head up the starboard side, and Joseph stopped at a large aperture, measuring about two and a half by one and a half meters. From the torn metal defining it, it was obviously made by one of the two blasts that sank the ship. As he tried to imitate an explosion with his arms and body, Morgan wished that she could see his eyes inside the mask, or better still, read what was going on in his head.

They headed up toward the rear deck and swam forward along the starboard side, past cabins and doors, following the passageway toward the bow. All along, the railing and the surfaces of the hull were studded with a kaleidoscope of sponges, anemones, and corals. Moving ahead, Joseph signaled them to descend one by one through a large hatch to the lower deck. Morgan swam through the eerie half-light all the way to the bottom of the hold. All alone, she came upon another breach in the hull of the boat sitting deep in the sand. This was smaller than the one Joseph had shown them earlier and presumably made by the first mine blast. She wondered which hole was the work of Joseph, and which the general's, finally concluding that the bigger one must have been Alex's stepfather's.

Back up on the deck, Maia showed Morgan the access to the engine room behind the bridge. The engines were no longer down there, although a few rusting ladders and bits of other equipment could still be seen. She exited through the opening in the deck where presumably the funnel had been, and was relieved to rejoin the others.

As they made their way back down along the wreck, Morgan was amazed at the abundance of marine life. The sunken ship had become home to a complex ecosystem. The sunlit port side was overgrown by many different species of seaweed, with leatherjackets and goatfish swimming through the forests of green and black, while moray eels, scorpion fish, and crayfish hid in their own little nooks. Other exotic species, such as snapper, mackerel, demoiselle, and big-eyed fish swam in and out of the various orifices of the living wreck. The colors were magnificent, so that Morgan observed to herself that in its afterlife, the ship certainly still lived up to the first part of its name, if no longer the second.

As they reassembled at the anchor chain and did the requisite safety check before going up, Morgan was glad to have had this chance to witness the underwater wreck of the *Rainbow Warrior*. Strangely, down here in the lonely beauty of the sunken ship that had become part of the marine ecosystem, she felt a peace and contentedness she hadn't felt before. Maybe it was seeing down here in the deep that nature does have an inexorable ability to adapt and survive, indeed thrive, if left to its own. But she also sensed the fragility of it all, the immense power of mankind to destroy and kill. And she felt hope, that despite all the evil man commits against man and nature, that there was enough good in the world to overcome the bad. Why, just look at someone like Joseph, she thought, who after carrying out a despicable act against peaceful environmentalists to safeguard France's nuclear program, had renounced it all and was devoting the rest of his life to making amends. There was cause for hope.

⁂

Joseph was already unsuited and ready to start the engine when Alex helped a tired Morgan back into the inflatable dinghy. Maia handed towels around, as Alex and Morgan pulled their wetsuits off. It was a beautiful, warm late morning, and Joseph pointed the bow in the direction of the Papatara Bay anchorage on nearby Motukawanui Island for a picnic lunch on a deserted beach.

"That was fantastic," Alex yelled above the motor.

"Yeah. I love going down, although these days I leave it to Maia to lead most of the diving groups. But I had to show you and Morgan myself."

"Thank you, Jo—Jean," Morgan said, glancing quickly at Maia to see if she had noted her slip of the tongue.

"You know what is the best part of it all for me?" Joseph asked. "Well, as the Cree Indian legend puts it, *'When man has destroyed the world through his greed, the Warriors of the Rainbow will arise to save it again.'* And that is really what we are seeing in action down there, the *Rainbow Warrior* housing a healthy, living marine ecosystem."

"Yeah."

"And you know what I have learned from this, and through all the ordeals of my life, Alex and Morgan?"

"What?" Morgan asked.

"That in the end, we all have a responsibility to be Warriors of the Rainbow. That even as our greed destroys the world of both man and nature, we all have to work at creating the new order of love and harmony. And we all have to be Warriors to cleanse the world that we have sullied. Every one of us. It is our sacred duty. Which makes life worth living in the end, don't you agree?"

The End

Author's Note

This was a fun book to write, partly because it allowed me to capture some of the wonderful aspects of living in Bordeaux, which is where most of the book was written. The city and the region are beautiful and have a lot to offer, with a heavy emphasis on the culture of food and wine, which I hope comes through in the novel.

The University of California still has an exchange program with L'Université de Bordeaux. My wife, Marcia, had the privilege of being a student who availed herself of a similar system that existed with the University of Colorado several years ago. Many of our friends in Bordeaux were the ones she made back then.

For the novel, I did substantial research on the sinking of the *Rainbow Warrior*.

(see for example:

http://www.seafriends.org.nz/issues/res/rw_mike_andrews.htm,
and
http://www.greenpeace.org/usa/en/campaigns/ships/the-rainbow-warrior/20th-anniversary/the-terrorist-plot/ and
http://www.tahiti-pacifique.com/Articles.divers/17107.html)

and the other murky scandals during the Mitterand era. Wikipedia is a good initial source, and the 2005 book by David Robie, *Eyes of Fire: the Last Voyage of the Rainbow Warrior,* is definitely worth a read.

The true identities of Jacques Camurier and Alain Tonel, the divers who placed the limpet mines on the hull of the Greenpeace boat, were never revealed in the aftermath of the *Rainbow Warrior* affair, and everything that I posit in the book is fiction. This includes some of the other nefarious affairs mentioned in the book, many of which nevertheless did take place (e.g. the deaths of Pierre Bérégovoy and others under questionable circumstances.

See for example http://ferraye.blogspot.fr/2009/05/pierre-beregovoy-execute-explications.html).

There are indeed some claims that Bérégovoy was killed by two divers traced to French intelligence.

Explosives were really found in Mali after the Serval intervention.

(See http://news.yahoo.com/hidden-explosives-found-mali-city-131214544.html).

Nitram-5 is made by EPC, the French explosives manufacturer, which also makes the newer and more powerful explosive EXPLUS. The question of nanocomposites and their potential role in bringing down the Twin Towers is a very controversial one, and certainly not the official line. This is addressed in http://www.globalresearch.ca/active-thermitic-material-discovered-in-dust-from-the-9-11-world-trade-center-catastrophe/13049 among others.

The French far right movements have been gaining strength since the jihadist bombings in Paris. However, in today's world it may be a stretch to suggest that French intelligence would have been infiltrated by them. Nevertheless, the active support for the French far right party, the Front National, by Russia financially and otherwise is well documented (see for example http://dailysignal.com/2015/12/09/france-just-had-a-political-earthquake-and-it-looks-good-for-the-kremlin/).

Other than the obviously historical ones, the characters and the story are entirely creations of my fancy, and any resemblance to reality is coincidental.

ACKNOWLEDGMENTS

I would like to express my gratitude to Lauri Wellington, the Acquisitions Editor at Black Opal Books, for agreeing to publish this book and for putting together a superb team to make it happen. To Faith C. for the painstaking and very helpful editing, to Jack Jackson, who designed the attractive cover, and to all the others who contributed to the birth of *The Rainbow Warrior*.

I also want to single out my wonderful wife, Marcia, whose earlier years as an exchange student in Bordeaux served as a model for Morgan and who took us back there to live and enjoy *la vie bordelaise* for five years.

About the Author

Born in Budapest, Geza Tatrallyay escaped with his family in 1956 during the Hungarian Revolution, immigrating to Canada. He graduated with a BA from Harvard in 1972 and as a Rhodes Scholar from Ontario, obtained a BA/MA from Oxford in 1974. He completed his studies with a MSc from London School of Economics in 1975. He represented Canada in epée fencing in 1976 at the Montreal Olympic Games. His professional experience has included stints in government, international finance and environmental entrepreneurship. He is a citizen of Canada and Hungary, and currently divides his time between Barnard, Vermont, and San Francisco.

Tatrallyay's international crime thriller, *Twisted Reasons,* the first book in the Twisted trilogy, was published by Deux Voiliers Publishing in December 2104, with the second book in the series, *Twisted Traffick,* brought out by Black Opal Books in October 2017 and the third book, *Twisted Fates,* in June 2018. Earlier, Tatrallyay self-published *Arctic Meltdown,* an e-thriller, but an updated and revised second edition of this will be published by Black Opal Books during 2019.

For the Children, Tatrallyay's memoir about his family's escape from Hungary in 1956 was published by Editions

Dedicaces in May 2015, and a second memoir, *The Expo Affair,* the story of three Czechoslovak girls who approached him at the world's fair in Osaka, Japan in 1970, was published in April 2016 under Guernica Editions' MiroLand imprint. A third memoir, *The Fencers,* the story of a Romanian-Hungarian fencer Tatrallyay helped defect to Canada at the Montreal 1976 Olympic Games, will be published by Deux Voiliers Publishing during 2019.

A collection of Tatrallyay's poems, *Cello's Tears,* was published in April 2015, by PRA Publishing and another volume of poetry, *Sighs and Murmurs,* was brought out by the same publisher in April 2017. Tatrallyay's third collection of poems, *Extinction*, is slated for publication by PRA Publishing in April 2019.

The Rainbow Vintner was conceived while Tatrallyay lived in Bordeaux and traveled throughout France. All of his books are available through his website at http://www.gezatatrallyay.com or on Amazon, Barnes & Noble, or directly from the publishers, or they can be ordered through most bookstores if they do not carry them.

Made in the USA
Columbia, SC
16 March 2019